THE MARKS OF BIRTH

Farrar, Straus and Giroux

New York

THE MARKS OF BIRTH

Pablo Medina

LIBRARY OF CONGRESS CATALOGING-IN-PUBLICATION DATA
Medina, Pablo.
The marks of birth / Pablo Medina.
p.   cm.
1. Caribbean Americans—New York (N.Y.)—Fiction. 2. Immigrants—
New York (N.Y.)—Fiction. 3. Family—New York (N.Y.)—Fiction.
I. Title.
PS3563.E24M37   1994
813'.54—dc20   93-33609   CIP

ACKNOWLEDGMENTS

Versions of "Inner Light," "Expiation," and "Spider's Bite" first appeared in *Cuban American Writers: Los Atrevidos, Folio,* and *Iguana Dreams,* respectively.

I gratefully acknowledge the National Endowment for the Arts for its financial support during part of the writing of this novel.

My thanks to Meg Adkins, Serge and Deborah Cartaya, and Marta Sánchez Lowery for their support and encouragement. My special thanks to John Glusman, my editor, and Elaine Markson, my agent, for their intelligent readings and suggestions.

For Juana María Unanue
and
Etelvina Brito

PART

ONE

INNER LIGHT

*T*he boy was born sickly and too pale for a creature of those latitudes, but only Felicia the grandmother dared think that from such parents so sorry a future was conceived. The rest of the family blinded itself and celebrated the occasion with great glee. The waiting room of the maternity ward soon filled with well-wishers; bottles were opened and toasts made to the firstborn; flowers were sent to the hospital in such profusion that they filled the room and spilled into the hallway. Some of the nurses, susceptible to floral allergies, took several days of sick leave; eventually a directive from the hospital administration forbade the delivery of any more bouquets to the ward—already a few bees had been seen around the nurses' station, and after three days, the wilting flowers saturated this place of hope with the stench one normally associates with funeral parlors.

And all this for a child who weighed four pounds, half of which was head and ears, and whose skin was so thin and colorless that the outlines of several organs were visible in his sunken stomach. The uncle, after a bottle's worth of toasts in the waiting room, bent over the crib and loudly proclaimed the vigorous appearance of the liver. The parents ignored the comment, but the grandmother, sitting in a corner still mourning the event, glared at him with such intensity that her younger son went immediately back for another round with yet another group of visitors.

The baptism took place a week later at the Church of Santo Tomás, a gloomy and cavernous temple chosen by the grandmother. In spite of her attempts to force the situation into what she believed to be its proper tone, the christening was a great success. Two hundred fifty-three people from all over the city and beyond signed the guest book, and the priest, an old Spaniard who no longer believed in God or the angels or anything supernatural, was happy that, for the first time in the thirty-five years he had been assigned to the parish, the place was half filled.

The pride the parents felt on this most hopeful of occasions added to their handsomeness a certain gleam that forestalled the gloom and put the grandmother's tragic sense to the test. The father was dressed in a white linen suit that contrasted sharply with his jet black hair, greased and combed straight back in the style of the times. His confident posture, particularly on this Sunday of 1949, made him appear much taller than he actually was. The fine lines of his face, his aquiline nose, his dark eyes and easy smile complemented each other so gracefully that his few detractors equated them—rather than intelligence and a focused aggressiveness—with his continuing success in the business world.

The mother, still pale and delicate from the long labor a week before, was nevertheless the most beautiful woman there. She wore a cream-colored muslin dress with a white collar. A small cultured-pearl necklace that matched her earrings hung around her neck, and her only other piece of jewelry was a gold filigreed wristlet that had belonged to her grandmother. Her auburn hair was tied in a bun at the back and over it she wore a white lace mantilla. She was the picture of reserve, but in her eyes burned a lively sensuousness. Her skin was white and smooth, and at the edge of her lips a small birthmark punctuated her cheeks with a touch of the Orient. No submission to the husband was evident in her demeanor, and she stood as tall and proud as he.

The grandmother had hoped that the grandchild would inherit the beauty of at least one of the parents. But this was not to be. Even wrapped in the fine Holland sheets presented to him by maternal cousins, the boy looked a freak, more rodent than human.

It was the grandmother Felicia herself who had casually dropped the name so pleasing to both parents they adopted it over the preplanned Jean-Jacques (after the mother's father). It had come to her in the middle of the night after considering the paradox of the situation: Antón, she thought, as in antonym, Antón García-Turner. The name suited the boy's nature perfectly, and there would be no objection as to its connections to the family. Her own brother was named Antonio, a good man with a good heart whose weakness for gambling and women most people accepted good-naturedly.

But Antonio had not come to the ceremony as he had promised. He was most likely involved in another of his escapades, or was mulling over a poker hand at the Yacht Club. His absence unsettled Felicia, for Antonio had a biting wit and he was always ready to ease her tension with a joke or two. He was not above remarking on this little aardvark of a nephew of his. Felicia thought of reprimanding him the next day, but she quickly put that idea to rest. It would do no good. Her brother was implacably indifferent to guilt, and as the boy was only half named after Antonio, Felicia's admonishments would have little weight behind them.

The party following the baptism lasted until midnight, and the grandmother would have thought it an imposition on the part of the guests to have stayed so long were it not for the opportunity it gave her to appreciate the family's strength and the depths to which its branches had spread in all levels of society. Besides the relatives who had come from all corners of the country, there were a great many friends and acquaintances who had been drawn there not to pay social dues or to impress any of them—the García-Turners were not important or powerful enough in any significant sense. They had come because through the years the family had opened its doors to them, and provided a warmth and understanding they did not experience among their own kind. Once the grandmother had flattered herself in this manner—she was, after all, the unofficial head of the family and had no small part in setting the tone and direction of its existence on this earth—she relaxed, forgot about her monster grandson, and allowed herself to enjoy the company, and even to dance a few numbers with the retired general who had courted her many years ago, when neither of them yet knew of the sudden twists and disappointments of fate that no amount of preparation could forestall.

The relief was short-lived, however. The very next morning

she walked over to her son's house for breakfast, as was her custom, and found out the cost of the affair.

"I am glad everyone had a good time," Rosa, her daughter-in-law, said to her husband, whose eyes belied an excess of drink.

"That's the least they could have done, considering the thousand dollars I spent," said Fernando, gulping down the last of his *café con leche*.

In spite of the sun warming the room through the French doors that opened onto the back porch, Felicia shivered as if a Nordic wind had just blown through her veins. She held her breath and clamped her jaw shut to keep from lashing out at the two of them. A brutally unkind thought tried to formulate itself in her mind, but she pushed it away.

Normally Felicia stayed until well after Fernando left for the office, but today she excused herself without finishing the buttered bun before her, and when Rosa rose from her place and asked if she felt ill, Felicia waved her off and mumbled something about having been up late the night before. It was a beautiful day outside, one of those clear, breezy tropical mornings that convince people of the goodness of God, but Felicia did not linger as she sometimes did by the rosebushes she had planted under the bedroom window five years ago, when her son and his wife bought the house next door to hers. Nor did she stop in the kitchen to set the day's chores with the maid; instead, she went to her bedroom, closed the door behind her—a sure sign to everyone who knew her—and sat in the rocking chair that had been in the family since the Ten Years' War. Lighting a cigarette, she rocked away.

She remembered the sugar-mill town she grew up in, and her father, who always brought home surprises for her and her two brothers, sometimes candy, sometimes small toys which he hid in his suit pockets so that the children had to search to find them; and she recalled how one day the three of them searched him all over and there were no gifts and they were about to walk away when her father led them to the back yard. In the middle, next to the water pump, there was a cardboard box with holes poked in the top. Felicia's father asked her, as the oldest, to open the box, and as she did so she heard chirping inside. The others gathered around and found two yellow ducklings and one black one. "The black one is for Antonio," their father called out, and they laughed and picked up their ducks. Antonio was the first to give his a name—Tino—after one of the boys who helped out in the kitchen. Tino was the only bird that grew to adulthood. But one day one of the maids sent to gather eggs found it dead beside a can of rat poison behind the chicken coop. Antonio suffered terribly. For days he sat on his bed and wept inconsolably. Neither his parents' concern nor the dozen ducklings friends and neighbors presented to him helped. Felicia always blamed her brother's dark habits on this one incident.

She also remembered her wedding day and the births of her children and that night when she got a call from Ruperto, her younger brother, who told her Luis was dead of a heart attack. Later, she found out he had died in the arms of another woman, and although she had long ago stopped caring for him, she had cried for a week, such were her anger and embarrassment. Her husband was a good-for-nothing cheat, but he had no right to die like that, bringing shame on her and the children.

One month to the day after her husband's death, the woman he had been with had come to her demanding a piece of the inheritance. Felicia sat like a sphinx watching her. The girl was not a prostitute; her face was too soft for that, and she sat too primly on the edge of the sofa, avoiding Felicia's eyes and speaking to the floor. She had an unfinished, clumsy look about her. Just an office clerk, Felicia thought. She claimed to have been Luis's mistress for six years, during which time he had provided her with a monthly stipend. Felicia stopped her at that point, asked her to leave and never to set foot in her house again. The girl threatened to take the matter to court, but the older woman disarmed her with one of her icy stares, so that the girl flinched, and in one motion flew out the door, her feet barely touching the ground.

Felicia laughed to herself, the rocking chair still moving back and forth at the same rhythm, the rhythm of the past that made her life now seem a peaceful and comfortable perch from which she could, with some measure of certainty, look into the future. If that girl had known that Luis had left only debts and that she and the children would have to struggle as hard as any puffy-faced clerk, she would have stayed home and saved her bus fare.

Within a year of her husband's death, Felicia found herself working next to girls like Luis's lover, but she was oceans away from them. They, younger than she for the most part, slaved not just to keep from drowning in the despair of poverty, but with the hope that those fantasies they had heard on radio soap operas and read about in paperback romances were, in fact, realizable: innocent girl of humble origins and obscure racial mixture marries scion of renowned family and is assumed bodily into the Elysian fields of beach clubs and servants and teacups. For these girls there was only the hope that they would be asked out by the men of success. As they grew older and their features faded and sagged with fatigue, their fantasies drooped as well. The smart ones went back to their barrios and married one of their own, had children, let their novels gather dust in the closet; the foolish ones held on to their dreams until they were nightmares, each double entendre from the men of the offices, each hotel room pushing them closer to the time when they would no longer be looked at, spoken to, asked out. Their lives then became an endless series of days doing gray-dull work and nights spent hovering around aging parents.

Felicia enjoyed romances as much as anyone, but she did not go to work for fantasies. She knew the men she worked for as well as she knew her brothers and as intimately as she had known her husband. She had not worked out of the home a day in her life, but now that she had to, she put illusions aside, held her head high, and earned enough money to keep her children well dressed and properly fed. When the Depression came and she lost her office job, she took two others, as a lottery agent during the week and as a piecework seamstress Saturdays and Sundays. Her sons had become professionals and would marry well.

Felicia fought her mind's attempts to drift to the present by quickening her rocking and by pulling out of her pocket the handkerchief that helped her weather bouts of anxiety. Her habit of twisting it into knots was one she had acquired so many years ago that her sons and all who knew her took it for granted. She started by twisting one corner tight as she could, folding it over the loose cloth, twisting that, and continuing in this manner until the piece of cloth was one perfectly round ball, at which point she would undo the thing and start over. She never looked down, and her hands worked independently of her thoughts.

Midway through her third ball, she heard the familiar greeting *Vaca vieja* in the peculiar voice of Antonio and saw his large frame filling the doorway, a tired half-smile on his face, which angled downward to meet her gaze. At over six feet he was a giant in a country where anyone five and a half feet in height was considered tall. Once he had been handsome, but now he was overweight and his large belly made him waddle comically when he walked.

At once Felicia's anxieties ebbed, and the room grew light and airy. She rose to greet him, but he was already sitting on the straight-backed chair in the corner by the window, lighting one of the oval cigarettes he liked.

"Caridad," she called out to the maid. "Bring don Antonio some coffee."

She turned her rocker to the left to face her brother and sat down. They talked of small things for a while, her rocking a gentle sort now, her feet never leaving the floor. The maid came in with the coffee and a glass of water.

Antonio took a sip. "It is the baby that bothers you," he said.

Felicia stopped rocking and looked away. She said she did not want to talk about it, but meant otherwise. After a moment of silence, she asked her brother if he had seen him.

"Just now. A strange-looking child. Put together by a committee without a blueprint."

"I had all the best plans. With his looks little can be done," she admitted.

"Felicia, since when have you bothered with appearances?"

"Appearances help."

"The boy will do fine."

"Playing prophet, are you?"

"He was sitting up and reading Plato when I left," Antonio said, throwing his head back and laughing silently so that his belly quivered and his shoulders shook.

Felicia turned her face abruptly and blew smoke toward the armoire.

"All right. I didn't come here to feed your self-pity but your stomach. Get dressed and I'll take you to lunch. I'll be back soon."

There was refusal in her eyes, but before she had a chance to say no, Antonio was out the door on his way to God-knows-what appointment.

Her brother's method of transacting business—in brief spurts between food, cards, women, and liquor—had kept him from being a wealthy man, but he lived comfortably enough. I have all I need, he would say to his sister when she questioned his unorthodox style. But you could have twice as many clients as you have now, she would insist. Yes, and I would hate them all, and every time I came to visit you, I would hate you, too, for keeping me from getting more. Money is an abstraction, and like all abstractions it bores me. Now, if I had Bedouins for clients and they paid me three camels each for my troubles, I might feel differently. Camels I can feed and ride and milk. A thousand of them would make me a very wealthy man in certain quarters. Money, hah. Little pieces of paper fools collect. But you could take Julia on a tour, Felicia would say just for the sake of arguing. Julia is happy at home and so am I. This is the most wonderful city in the world. Paris is for arrogant fools; London is cold and clammy; Rome is where the Pope shits. No, thank you.

The truth was, Antonio could have had not twice but three times as many clients. He was a brilliant lawyer in the courtroom, and he had the ears and pockets of every judge in the city. It was not discipline or dedication that made him excel when he wanted but the regular satisfaction of his vices. I know who I am, he would finally say to his sister, and by now you know, too.

In an hour and a half he was back, dragging her out the door and into his new car. Hot as it was inside Antonio's Buick at midday, Felicia was nonetheless comforted by the rich smell of plush leather and by the chrome-lined panel like a wide metal smile and the intriguing dials that measured the mysteries of speed. Felicia was of that generation for whom automobiles were still harbingers of the future, metaphors of hope, products of ingenuity and work, and so in no subtle way manifestations of the achievements of her class. Let there be mobility and the middle class invented the car. The Buick glided away from the curb, gathered speed, and slowed down at the corner. Then brother and sister turned to the west and disappeared down the simmering avenue.

The long ride out to the open-air restaurant facing the sea further enlivened Felicia's spirits. The splash of the waves on the beach combined with Antonio's political gossip to make the present an impregnable fortress neither past nor future could breach. Several times during the lunch a veil of sadness tried to cover her eyes and bring back the grayness which had enveloped her the last week, but she easily fought it back. Even the clinking of glasses at neighboring tables was enough to wake her.

Antonio smiled often as he spoke of the President unabashedly filling his pockets with state money and conspiring to have himself reelected for a fifth term.

"Corruption," Antonio said at one point, "is the only governing system that has worked in our country."

"Not so loud," said his sister. "People will hear you."

Antonio raised his volume. "There hasn't been an honest president in our history who has lasted his full term. But the corrupt have, and more. Look at the sauce on your fish. It is delicious, isn't it?"

"Yes, quite."

"It makes palatable an otherwise bland meat. The sauce transforms the reality of the fish, even though you and I know that without the sauce, seafood is healthy and good for you."

"I don't follow."

"The red snapper's face, who does it look like?"

Felicia didn't need to answer. It was a common fact that the President looked like a fish.

"Corruption is the sauce that makes people stomach him. And in the end everyone benefits."

"Antonio, how can you say that?"

"Because it is true. So long as there is enough sauce left over for the other politicians to swim in, the President stays in power, the money flows freely, people have jobs, and we can sleep soundly at night. The rest is ideological crap. Eat your fish and enjoy the sauce."

Felicia was home by late afternoon. Lying down in her bed to recover from the fresh air and sumptuous food, she fell asleep. She had a dream in which an angel appeared whose wings were made of scales instead of feathers. The angel beat its wings furiously in an attempt to fly away, but all he did was create a storm of dust that blocked out all light and made her choke. When at last he ascended into a sky that looked like an ocean with blue waves crashing against cloud rocks, she saw at her feet a small fish, beautiful and wet. She picked up the creature and realized that it had feathers on its body and dark hair on its head. It spoke some unintelligible words laced with numbers and metamorphosed into a being the likes of which she had never before seen. It gleamed with the colors of the rainbow and purred softly like a cat and made her disregard all time, so that when she told herself that she'd been sleeping too long, the fish-bird-angel-rainbow-kitten laughed, and she laughed with it so hard she ascended to the ocean-sky, where the angel had gone, propelled by little farts that smelled sweet as roses and which, a voice at her ear told her, were the words of God. The divine winds awoke her, and fearing that the dream was blasphemous, she

recited ten Our Fathers and ten Hail Marys. The dream nevertheless stayed with her.

It was seven-thirty in the evening and the room was heavy
with shadows. She sat up and thought again of the creature she
had held in her hand. Then she noticed some movement in the
corner by the window: a large cockroach moving slowly across
the floor, parallel to the wall. She picked up her slipper and
stalked the insect, which had by now stopped moving, its antennae
flicking nervously about. Felicia bent over and swatted at it, but
due to poor aim or an extremely resilient carapace, the roach
survived the impact and rushed over her foot and under the bed.
She jumped when she felt the barbed legs scratch her toes, but
she controlled her panic. She knelt to inspect the area under the
bed. It did not take her long to find it, an inch-and-a-half brown
coconut roach by an empty gift box. This time she slipped her
hand into the shoe and, instead of hitting, slowly stepped on the
roach until she had trapped the hard oblong form under the
rubber sole. She pressed on it as hard as she could and heard a
crack. She would have pitied the insect, innocent and helpless as
it was, were it not for the revulsion that filled her mouth with
a strange metallic taste. She turned her face and lifted her slipper-
encased hand. As she stood, her head cleared and the dream
returned, dimmer and less vivid than before. She decided at that
point that she would call Marina.

Marina came that night at Felicia's insistence, although she
would have preferred waiting until the following day. She had
just spent the afternoon with one of her wealthy clients in an
attempt to communicate with her dead husband. And all to no
avail, Marina explained to her friend over the phone. Either the
man's spirit was already in hell and no invocation could call him
from that place, or he didn't much care for the wife to begin

with. Given the wife's behavior, the seer believed the latter to be the case. At least she had made enough money for the week on that one consultation. And the lady had insisted on trying again the following week.

The seer appeared at Felicia's door still wearing her working costume: an unbelted black caftan that covered, but did not hide, her rotundity, and turned her breasts into mere foothills to the enormous upswell of her belly. My roundness, she would say time and again, reflects the fullness of the earth and the spheres of existence. On her forearms jingled dozens of gold bracelets. Her hands were small and delicate as a nun's, but she let her fingernails grow to impressive length and painted them a deep wine color. The features of her face, which was deeply lined and covered with layers of makeup, all seemed to fade into the twin maelstroms of dark green eyeshadow, anterooms to her mesmerizing lazuline eyes. Over the dome of her skull, her wavy hair, dyed red, flamed as if her mind were on fire. Few would have dared question the abilities of such a spectacular figure, and fewer still her fees.

Marina never charged her friend. They had known each other since childhood, and Felicia had always shown an unusual interest in her friend's special gift. This gift, or power, as it was referred to by people less aware of it, first became apparent during Marina's thirteenth year, when, after listening to her father and his friends discuss European politics, she accurately predicted, six months before it happened, the start of the First World War.

Soon after, word spread around the neighborhood and people began coming to the house with all manner of questions to which they wanted answers. *What will happen if I visit my mother in Arica next week? Will I get pregnant this year? Who is going to be the next Pope? When will the world come to an end?* The girl's mother, a shrewd woman, saw a perfect opportunity for making money, and within the week she was charging one dollar per question posed to the prodigy. Curiously, the imposition of the fee increased the number of clients significantly, even though Marina was correct at best 30 percent of the time. The low percentage bothered the mother, for it would only be a matter of time before the disaffected customers spread the word and seriously undermined the business. Had she used common sense, or consulted experts in the field, she would have realized that the gift had to be nurtured through study and meditation, and that forcing a young prophetess too quickly into this peculiar kind of business was as dangerous as ignoring those signs which manifested her special talent to begin with.

It happened just as the mother had feared. The girl grew tired and indifferent, answering questions haphazardly and dispiritedly. Some customers even asked for a refund when Marina fell asleep in mid-question. Thus, when a reporter from the city's most scandalous newspaper came to her masquerading as a famous scientist and asked her if he would win the Nobel Prize for his work on the spontaneous generation of maggots, she answered in the negative but added that his sister's hair would fall out the following month. The next edition of the paper carried an article exposing Marina as a fake. The man's sister had lost her hair the previous month. The morning after, only three people showed up: a blind man, the next-door neighbor's illiterate maid, and a penniless indigent whose mind had been fried by the tropical sun and who asked where he should invest the twenty-five million his mistress, the Queen of Persia, had awarded him for his ardent lovemaking "akin to a locomotive whose pistons have lost control."

The mother resumed her wifely duties—as a woman should,

boasted the father—and bemoaned her fate as cook and cleaning woman for an uncaring husband and woebegone daughter. Marina went back to playing with Felicia, and when the illuminating flashes came to her, she told no one but her dolls and her best friend.

Life went on much as it did for Felicia, and the two became inseparable. They went to the same schools, attended the same parties; they even dated brothers at one point. When they married, their lives diverged, but they still kept in touch, first by letter and, when Marina followed her friend to the capital, by phone. At twenty-eight, after three marriages and four children, Marina decided, with counsel and encouragement from Felicia, to exploit her special gift as a means of supporting her brood and freeing herself from the scourge of matrimony. She apprenticed herself to Estorina la Buena, who remembered her from years back and who understood perfectly the anguish and confusion the child prodigy had suffered during her brief period of forced labor. In three short years Marina had her own practice—by appointment only—and was catering to the folly and vanity of the wealthy.

The route Marina took kept her from being famous like her mentor. She did not appear in magazines and newspapers as Estorina had; she did not have legions of supporters who petitioned the Vatican to canonize her; nor did the police burden her with the gory and unappetizing details of unsolved crimes. She led a quiet life but made enough money to buy a mansion in the city's most prestigious neighborhood and send her children to the best schools. That she sometimes bent her prophecies to suit her clients' wishes, other times kept horrible visions from them, were compromises with reality she was more than willing to accept: she had made of her gift a career, not a vocation.

By the time Marina sat down on Felicia's living-room couch with a highball in her hand, Felicia's dream had undergone several transformations. The angel was no longer an angel but an old man with a white beard who flew off in a winged Buick, and the small creature that had so pleased her had been changed into a blond baby who spoke calculus and out of whose forehead grew two antennae as long as his body. The part about her ascension into heaven, however, remained the same.

Marina took a healthy sip of her drink. A rush of images overwhelmed her, and glass in hand, she leaned back on the couch and closed her eyes.

"What's wrong?" asked Felicia.

"It's too powerful."

"The dream?"

"No, the drink. I'll let it sit awhile until the ice melts."

Before Marina proceeded with her interpretation of the corrupted version of the dream, she asked her friend what she had eaten that day, for food often influenced the sleeping mind and provided the raw materials for visions.

"Fish. I had broiled red snapper, black beans, rice, and salad."

"Was the fish with or without the head?"

"With. You know I like to eat the brains."

Marina's system of dream interpretation was a distilled version of one developed by Casandro Martínez, the old seer who was caught *in flagrante delicto* with a colonel's wife (under pretext of skewering a demon that had fallen asleep in her womb) and was shot in the face by the colonel. According to Casandro, dreams were the manifestations of the spirit force of food, and during his long and tragically active life, he had come to assign symbolic value to every possible source of nutrition, from corn to dog to chicken embryos. Marina had simplified it, as she did not know anyone who ate dog meat or unhatched chickens, by lumping food into seven major categories based primarily on the color, appearance, and texture of the ingestible substances. Thus fish, dairy products, bread, and foodstuffs which were primarily white in color and soft to the touch gave rise to milk imagery, symbolizing birth and regeneration; beef, pork, lamb, and other red meat inspired what she called blood imagery representing violence and death; poultry, rabbit, vegetables, and fruit led to earth imagery, which stood for growth, decay, and the transmutation of substances. As far as liquids were concerned, non-alcoholic clear drinks brought forth wind imagery, symbolic of travel and changes in lifestyle; alcoholic clear drinks produced strong winds (storms and hurricanes), which were equivalent to confusion leading to destruction or loss of good fortune; non-alcoholic opaque liquids produced swamp imagery, symbolic of inactivity and anxiety, especially of a moral nature; finally, at the bottom of her list of ingestibles were alcoholic opaque drinks, which led to satanic imagery—monsters, demons, chimeras, and the embodiments of despair and insanity.

In addition, experience had taught her that unless the dream had been related or written down immediately after waking, it had to be weeded out of what she called reality confabulations, elements of the waking state that had somehow made their way into the dream after the fact. Once Felicia had told her what she had done immediately before and after her nap, the seer was able to discard the Buick and the antennae and, through further queries, culled from her friend a fairly accurate version that included the original angel with the scaly wings, as well as the feathered creature.

Marina saw the dream as basically positive. Tainted as it was with unexpected and potentially negative elements, the vision was also full of hope. The angel figure had difficulty in getting his awkward wings to perform their due function, but work they did, and they left behind a living gift for Felicia, no matter that the creature was not clearly defined. All its metamorphoses were pleasant, and so the being was picked up. In her hands it purred like a kitten when it feels secure. This feeling was transferred to Felicia, who, in acceptance of the bond between the two, ascended of her own power into higher states of the spirit, the combination of water and sky meaning fulfillment not only in this life but also in the next.

"And the dust that blinded me," asked Felicia, leaning over the table that separated the two friends.

"Your hope will be born of the earth. Foresight comes after looking hard through the whirlwind of confusion, after your inner eye surrenders all expectation (outer light) and creates its own light, with which it can identify the forms that fortune presents to it. Only then can you revel in change and see clearly that every transmutation is one more revolution of the wheel of fortune. Once you learn to revolve with the wheel, all time stops, which allows you to leave the horizontal and conduces to vertical growth."

Felicia was more confused than ever. She broke in. "What about the farts? Wasn't that blasphemy?"

"You are allowing your outer light to color the dream. You yourself told me that they smelled sweet, and at no point in the dream were you upset by them. Only in your waking state . . ."

"Yes, but how could God speak that way?"

"God will assume any form, will speak any way to get his

message across. Where is it written, Felicia, that God is indisposed to speaking through the ass?"

"For a moment I thought it might have been the devil in disguise."

"The devil can take any disguise but that of God. You have to trust the dream, the inner light."

"I couldn't understand what the creature said. What does that mean?"

"You have already answered that for yourself."

There was a pause in the conversation and the two friends stared at each other for a long while. The only sounds were the toads singing outside the living-room windows and a breeze fluttering through the venetian blinds.

"My grandson. The baby."

"Yes."

"He's a great disappointment."

"He will surprise you. Trust your inner light—it is telling you something."

Felicia sat back on her chair at odds with herself. Just as she was ready to forsake Antón and wait for a second grandchild, her feelings became suspended in the liquid of confusion. She was angry at herself, embarrassed, and, for a moment, distrustful of Marina. The more she thought, however, the more clearly she realized the accuracy of her friend's interpretation. Her eyes welled with tears, and looking at the floor, she bit her lower lip.

Marina, not without difficulty, got up from the sofa and walked around the table to put her hand on Felicia's nape.

"My friend," she said with the gentleness that forty years of intimacy accorded. "My friend"—she too crying, the bulk of her gargantuan belly keeping her from getting physically closer, yet feeling Felicia's presence as a part of herself in pain, in growth, in the cleansing power of their combined weeping, which infected the house, spread to the garden, and seemed to reach the stars and the very edges of the universe. It was then that God, roused from deep sleep, grumbled, rubbed his joints stiffened by millennia of dealing with human folly, and tossed down the first rays of dawn.

EXPIATION

*T*hat morning, disregarding the rain which other days would have kept her nursing her rheumatism, Felicia went to Fernando's house for breakfast. Her daughter-in-law, who had not expected the return of the grandmother's spirits after eight days of somberness, had not bothered to set a place for her. Rosa called to the maid, but Felicia dismissed her with a quick wave and urged them to start. She was going to check on her grandson.

Felicia returned to the dining room almost immediately and asked her son what a copy of Plato's *Republic* was doing in the crib.

"Antonio put it there yesterday," answered Fernando. "He said the boy should be encouraged early on."

"And your son apparently agrees," said Rosa. "He hasn't let me take the book away. Imagine, the boy is not two weeks old and already they're shoving books under his covers."

"No harm done, Rosa," said Fernando.

"It's dirty. Who knows who handled it?"

"Small risk. Small risk."

The older woman was tempted to interrupt. On the one hand, she instinctively sympathized with Rosa. Yet her brother's simple act appealed to her in a symbolic way, and if it did not mean a thing to the child, it was a sign to all around him. She was about to let her fantasies fly and imagine her grandson as a founder of a tropical Academy of Philosophy when the maid appeared bearing coffee and warm buns.

Felicia stayed long after her son left for work. First she inquired about Rosa's father, who had undergone a gallbladder operation the week before, and then, when they heard Antón awaken in a fit of crying, they rushed together into the bedroom. As the mother was cleaning the baby's rump, his little penis straightened and he peed into her face. Felicia laughed.

"He has a strong spurt, just like his father," she said.

A loud squeal brought her attention back to the child. She offered to care for him while Rosa took her bath, a suggestion which the young woman gladly accepted.

Alone now, Felicia observed the minute mass of flesh and bone, and she placed her right hand softly on his head, her thumb feeling the fontanelle as the child stared at her with eyes that told a long history indeed. The look was the tie to the family she could not deny, and she would carry it with her until her death thirty years later in a foreign land. She picked up her grandson, who blinked twice and squeezed his face into a frown, then opened it into a yawn. She examined the neck, the shoulders, the diminutive arms. Antón squiggled in her hands, and as she turned him to secure her hold on him, she saw the birthmark over his right kidney. At first, she was alarmed, but alarm turned to recognition. It was the mark she herself bore in the same spot. Marina was right: The creature Felicia had picked up in her dream was the same one she was now holding in her hands.

She laid the boy on his back and ran her hand down the side of the small head, feeling the pulsing temple that confirmed her discovery. Her fingers slid over the frail ribs to the belly and came to rest on that mound of organs, warmed by the purr of their functions. The hand, in full communion with the body, followed the downward slope to the garden, where it found a little bud growing. The index finger tickled the underside, and she thought to him: *Here is the future. This will people your land.* Antón gave what she took to be a kick of agreement and gurgled something. *Calculus?* she thought before bringing her hand back to his temple and gently rubbing that thin spot where thought becomes flesh, until the child fell to sleeping.

She stayed by the crib and watched him, naked as he was, too late to diaper him, and was amazed that when Rosa returned, only ten minutes had elapsed. It seemed hours, days, a year, for in those moments framed by Rosa's absence, Felicia and her grandson had discoursed on the meat and matter of life.

Felicia turned to speak to her daughter-in-law but found that she had lost her voice. Try as she could, all that emanated from her grotesquely contorted mouth was wheezes and gurgles from some place beneath her throat. Rosa, noticing the lady's reddening face and crossed eyes, thought her to be choking. She rushed to Felicia's side and struck her three times between the chicken wings, which helped only in changing the hue in Felicia's face from red to deep blue.

Had Munda the maid, who on her way to clean the bathroom witnessed this strange scene, not grabbed Rosa's arm, it was doubtful that the grandmother would have survived the beating her well-meaning daughter-in-law was raining upon her.

"*¡Señora!*" exclaimed the maid.

"She's choking, she's choking," shrieked Rosa. "Call Acevedo!"

Acevedo the pharmacist had just put an album of Donizetti arias on the phonograph and was sitting down to his morning coffee when Rosa's maid appeared urging him in a stuttering voice to save doña Felicia. Most other pharmacists would have resented the interruption, but he looked forward to these emergencies, for they demonstrated to the neighborhood and the world that, except for extirpating diseased organs, pharmacists were as adept in the medical arts as physicians. Of all the neighbors he had treated in the twenty-odd years he had owned the pharmacy, only one had required further medical treatment, and that was a maidservant recently arrived from the country who insisted on applying a homemade herbal concoction to a cut on her foot, instead of the salve he had given her. She wound up losing not only her foot but her job as well. Acevedo's belief in himself as the neighborhood's guardian of science had reached a puritanical fervor, which at one point people ridiculed but gradually grew to respect. For the pharmacist was right in his diagnoses, and when the ailment went beyond his powers, he curtly advised the family—but never the patient—to call the butcher, his euphemism for doctor.

As soon as Felicia saw him, a small frail man with black thick-framed glasses that hung midway down his curved nose, and hands yellowed, not from his alchemies, but from the two packs of unfiltered cigarettes he smoked daily, she grew calm and was able to breathe more freely. He, in turn, assumed the mannerisms of a doctor, speaking jovially and reassuringly, running both his hands gently around the sides and back of her neck. If he discovered something in his examination, his voice gave no hint of it.

"She's suffering from hysteria," said Acevedo to Rosa in the kitchen, where he was offered coffee. "I gave her a sedative. She will rest now. Has she had any great shock recently?"

"I can't imagine what," answered Rosa.

"She should be better in a few days. Don't worry. Keep her calm and put lots of flowers in her room."

Fernando, whom Rosa had summoned from work, arrived. He and the pharmacist shook hands and the situation was explained.

"Shouldn't we call Dr. Figueras?" asked Fernando.

"If it makes you feel any better," answered the man of science. "But no doctor can help her now. She has obviously experienced a trauma which has caused a spasm in the throat muscles. It could have been anything—a bad memory or a sudden scare. According to the great psychologists, hysteria is a condition almost exclusively limited to the female of the species, and the source of the disease can usually be traced to early childhood. I once knew a woman who lost the function of her bowels for one week every time she saw a mouse. Only that creature brought on the condition, not rats or spiders or anything else, and only after seven days to the minute did she regain control. Fascinating, isn't it? And aside from this curious problem, she manifested no symptoms of mental illness. She was a warm, loving wife and mother and lived a happy and contented life.

"If we knew what caused your mother to choke on her words, then we could keep the problem from recurring. In the meantime, you must not allow her to say a single word. If by chance she does speak, have her lie on her back and take twenty-five of the deepest breaths she can manage. Don't give her water or slap her. You will only make things worse. I must go. Goodbye."

Dr. Figueras came two hours after Fernando called him. Rosa had helped her mother-in-law to her house while her husband and the pharmacist talked, and now Felicia lay in bed sleeping soundly. Figueras checked all vital signs and read the label on the medicine bottle: Veronal. He would have prescribed the same tranquillizer. He told Fernando much the same things he'd heard from Acevedo, and while the son was relieved that there was nothing seriously wrong with his mother, he was nonetheless disgruntled that the doctor could do nothing more than the pharmacist. Little could he understand what the doctor, through thirty years of practice, had come to accept: that experience in the field is worth all the degrees in the world.

Fernando put the doctor's complacency out of his mind. He was not the type of man to come to terms with a contradiction. The inquisitiveness and skepticism of his mother's side of the family—qualities that lead ineluctably either to pessimism or to the steady contemplation of paradox—had not been passed on to him. He was more like his father during his prime: taking what was given at face value and diving into the river of life proudly, with Olympian energy. This trait, above all others, had initially endeared him to Rosa and had led her to fall in love with him. That he was no great thinker was no great matter. He, more than anyone else, would prove to be the rock to which the family would cling, not to be swept away by the currents of change.

He could have been a devout priest or a good soldier or, in any other country but this, an able and honest politician. He had fallen into commerce, however, where his ability to accept without a flinch the ways of society and move through it like a fish through water served him well. In his wife's eyes his conformism also made him an ideal husband and, as he was already proving, an excellent father.

Felicia, too, had long ago recognized this trait in her son, and she had been afraid. If her husband had eventually felt shackled by it to such an extent that, once free of it, he had fallen into extremes of dissolution, her son could become the victim of a similar fate. Since Fernando and Rosa had moved next to her, however, she felt more confident, for she could keep watch and act when and if Fernando wavered from what she believed to be his role in life. And so she formed an unspoken conspiracy with her daughter-in-law to encourage Fernando the provider and make his home so attractive, so magnetic, he could not help but return to it day after day and give it all of his devotion.

Fernando talked to his wife about calling another doctor. Even as Rosa tried to convince him to wait a few days to see if Felicia's condition improved, he was running down the list of physicians that he knew.

"There's Calvo Martínez, the man who did your father's gall-bladder. What is it they call him?"

"Silver Hands," answered his wife dutifully. "But he's a surgeon. And it takes weeks to get an appointment."

"And Lionel Urrutia? I saw him on the street last week."

"That's where he belongs. Last year he prescribed the wrong medicine to one of the Icaza girls. The poor thing bloated up like a frog and her face was covered with boils for two months. Her father is trying to sue him, but you know nothing will come of it. Doctors protect each other. He'll go on practicing till the day he dies."

"Well then, Menéndez Hurtado."

"He's in the United States."

And so Fernando mentioned the names, his wife dismissing each with some objection: a bit of gossip or news she'd read in the society pages of the newspapers and, in three cases, pure inventions. Realizing that he would run out of doctors before she ran out of excuses, Fernando stopped after the tenth one, mumbling something unintelligible under his breath, which his wife, having achieved victory and feeling quite proud of herself, easily ignored.

Felicia slept through the night and awoke in the early evening of the following day to a hand-painted cardboard sign, hung directly across from the bed, which read DO NOT SAY ANYTHING. Rosa, who had kept vigil in the room, rushed to the side of the bed with her index fingers to her lips, whispering, "*Silencio, silencio.*"

In spite of the warning, the word *pero* escaped through Felicia's lips. The mere utterance of these two syllables brought on an attack of paroxysms similar to the one the day before and caused her to gasp so powerfully that it seemed to Rosa as if everything in the room—sign, furniture, lamps, herself—would be sucked into her mother-in-law's lungs.

As for Felicia, no sooner had she voiced the word than she felt her tongue swell until it blocked the cavity of her mouth. The sound crystallized in her throat like a piece of crumpled cellophane, and when she swallowed, or tried to, the crystal grew through the gullet and into her stomach. Just as things around her were beginning to blacken, she was pushed violently backward, and she heard a voice through a medieval mist.

"Breathe deep, twenty-five times. Breathe deep!"

Felicia obeyed, trying to break through the cellophane.

"Again!" screamed the shrill voice like a wind through an endless moor. The voice was now closer to her, warmer, a flowering vine entering her ears.

"Keep it up," Rosa urged gently.

At last Felicia's chest filled with a sea of air. The mist was gone and she saw Rosa's face inches away from her own, tense and sweating, break into a smile.

After the twenty-five breaths prescribed by Acevedo, Felicia felt faint, yet she could breathe normally and was about to speak again when Rosa's hand clamped on her mouth.

"You cannot. You will choke."

The lady frowned and made a question with her face, which Rosa answered by pointing to the night table, where a pad of paper and a pencil were lying. She suggested Felicia write down whatever she needed.

Felicia wrote: *I want to go to the bathroom. I want to brush my teeth. I want to take a bath. I want food and water. I want my voice.*

Rosa read what her mother-in-law had scrawled. A look of pity came over her and her eyes grew moist with tears. She tilted her head, rose to her feet, and kissed Felicia on the forehead. The older woman followed her with her eyes. When Rosa said, in a syrupy and condescending tone, that she would get things ready, Felicia peeled the covers off and rose with a start toward the bathroom, fighting off a sudden dizziness that threatened to turn everything black again. Rosa moved forward as if to help, but her mother-in-law waved her off and left the room.

To keep herself silent during the next few days, Felicia stayed in her room and left it only for the bathroom. Anyone visiting was not allowed to speak, and Caridad, her maid, in order to comply with her mistress's wishes, gagged herself with a handkerchief whenever she was in the lady's presence. She had at first tried taping her mouth shut, but this technique left her cheeks gummy, and as her upper lip was somewhat hairy, it was quite painful to rip the tape off. Five, six times a day for the first two days, Felicia heard Caridad screaming in the kitchen, disturbing the sacrosanct silence the lady had imposed on the household.

Whatever communication went on between Felicia and her loved ones was done in writing, and soon there were large drawing pads and boxes of crayons scattered throughout the room so that none of the visitors would feel constrained from expressing themselves. The family took to the system in good enough spirits and grew so adept at handling the crayons that their conversations with her suffered little in the transcription, instead gaining in elegance and logic, the moments between thinking and writing allowing for the formulation of full, eloquent sentences. Antonio, who stopped by almost every day, took the process one step further by devising a series of ideograms that combined words and pictures to stand for complete thoughts. While Rosa and Fernando marveled at the invention, Antonio decided to keep to himself that it was little more than a vulgarized application of some theories on Chinese writing that were then in vogue. Fernando suggested that he patent the process and sell it to the deaf. Antonio countered with a smile and a nod of the head in false assent.

In spite of the family's almost constant companionship and the stream of visitors who were gracious enough to abide by the protocol she had devised, Felicia's medically imposed silence became a burden which affected her both physically and mentally. She grew depressed, a fact the others failed to notice, so busy were they writing their messages; she lost her usually healthy appetite, and her sleep became fitful and tremulous. Some nights she would wake after a bad dream and whole armies of words would struggle inside her wanting to get out; other times two demons, one white, the other black, would chatter in her ear about the pleasures of speech and deride Acevedo and Figueras, whose diagnoses, they maintained, were not only inaccurate but reeked of island provincialism. After hours of these torments in the depth of the night, the rays of dawn, which came like the grace of God, kept her from losing control and spewing forth a flood of words that would have filled the pages of twenty dictionaries.

It was after a particularly vicious harangue by the demons that Felicia asked to see Marina. Disregarding the rule of silence, the seer proceeded to reassure her friend that her present situation was absolutely necessary, nothing more than a soul struggling to right itself. The day would come when the words would flow naturally, graced by inner light, not corrupted by outward ap-pearances and false expectations. Marina advised her to let the demons slobber in her ears all they wanted; before she knew it, they would tire of their antics and go in search of a weaker victim. Above all, Felicia had to find a way of channeling her thoughts.

"Don't let them brew in your head," warned Marina, "or they will rot and their juices will corrupt the light."

Tried everything, wrote Felicia in her pad. *Prayer, knitting, books, solitaire, crosswords.*

"What is the source of your troubles? Address that and you will find release."

How?

"You must answer that yourself. I cannot tell you."

Felicia put pad and pencil on her lap and thought a moment.

Without words, mere thoughts were ether, gas in her brain. She might as well have been a piece of furniture. Or a child.

Marina stayed a while longer, drinking a highball the maid had brought her and relating the difficulties she was having trying to call back her client's dead husband.

". . . but the woman keeps insisting. I have a plan that will rid me of her once and for all."

Felicia barely listened.

A child. A child learns to voice thoughts very slowly. Before that, they simmer in him. That's why he kicks and punches the air, making physical the gas accumulating in his head.

Thought made physical. The word made flesh! The idea stayed with her until she wrote it down. Quite suddenly, looking at the phrase in the book, she realized that the writing of it relieved her.

She continued, putting down anything that came into her mind: sentences, words, letters, names, *Antón*. *Antón*, she wrote again. She looked up to let her friend know of the discovery, but Marina was gone. The empty whiskey glass lay on the chest of drawers, the ice in it melting, and the afternoon stretched away, pulling the shadows with it.

Felicia's expiation, as Marina would later call it, came in the form of a biography of her grandson that she would present to him on his twenty-first birthday. But rather than flatter him, she hoped it would crystallize in him all those qualities that would lead to a full and prosperous life. This newfound project excited her and focused her energies in such a way that she had little time to think about her condition. When Rosa and Fernando, along with Felicia's brother Ruperto, stopped by on the evening of the tenth day of her tribulation, Felicia barely greeted them, preferring instead to fill page after page of her notebook with the smallest details of Antón's brief existence: astrological data, the shape of each extremity, a list of the toys in his crib, feeding times, a lengthy panegyric extolling the virtues of different individuals in the family, and a detailed description of his birthmark. It looked, she wrote, as if someone had spilled a bottle of brown coloring on his lower back. She had been told by her aunt that her grandfather Wellington Turner had been graced with a birthmark in the same place.

Rosa and Fernando received only cursory nods to their written entreaties and grew increasingly alarmed as they sat in frustrated silence in Felicia's bedroom. They were finally moved to action by Ruperto's comment, voiced with exquisite Castilian aplomb, that his sister had at long last gone crazy. Felicia, who was hard-pressed to keep from telling him—as she had countless times— to go to the deepest pit of hell, ignored the comment, and went on with her biography. When they left, she did not even bother to take leave of them.

In the living room, within earshot of the maid, Fernando, Rosa, and Ruperto reviewed what to do next and narrowed their choices to two. One, Rosa's idea, was to call Father González, the decrepit Spaniard who had baptized Antón, but the two men rejected this suggestion as soon as it came out of her lips. Both, but particularly Ruperto, were rabidly anticlerical, a genetic trait passed on to every male of the line. The second option, to have Lucho, their psychiatrist cousin, pay a visit, was subscribed to readily.

That night Caridad stole into the bedroom and apprised her mistress of the plan. The lady was overjoyed, a reaction which, considering the circumstances, greatly surprised the maid. Lucho was one of Felicia's favorite people, and it had been months since she had seen him.

Lucho Turner had been one of the great hopes of the clan—brilliant, witty, dedicated to the pursuit of knowledge, and graced with a self-confidence found only among great men. When it came time for him to attend the university, his passion for psychiatry and his nearly perfect grades won him a state scholarship to study in the United States. Ten years later, medical degree in hand, he returned to the country of his birth, where he attempted numerous times to set up a practice. The competition from seers, herbal specialists, witch doctors, and priests, however, was much greater than he had imagined during his school days, and feeling for the first time in his life the bitter taste of failure in his mouth, he lowered his sights and accepted a clinical position in the state mental hospital of San Cristóbal, a Dantesque repository of the incurably psychotic and the mentally deranged. Ten years there had made him a cynic, and he often said that his mistake was to have been born of such simplistic stock. Had he been a European Jew and practiced among that most complex of races, then he truly would have mingled with the great minds in history. His people had no need of psychiatry. Their superstition and their childlike faith in the powers of supernatural forces made them ludicrously primitive in his eyes; they also happened to be, as a group, enviably sane. Once Lucho reached these conclusions, he found himself professionally expendable. Consequently, he spent as little time as possible with his patients, and whiled away the majority of his working hours in his office reading murder mysteries and Zane Grey Westerns.

His visit to Felicia the next day was brief and pleasant. Unaware of the silentiary vows she had required of everyone else, he asked the usual questions, which she answered by passing strips of paper to him. Soon he grew bored and started fidgeting with the buttons of his shirt. Noticing this, Felicia wrote: *Come by some afternoon and let's play canasta like we used to*. Lucho's thin lips stretched into a smile, but his eyes remained heavily saddened. On his way out he said to Rosa and Fernando, who were waiting in the living room, "She's as sane as a doorknob."

*T*he day Lucho drove up to Felicia's house for the canasta game, a pack of loud children ran about in the front yard trampling on the flowers. Three or four neighborhood dogs, infected by the excitement, hopped and barked under the shadow of the coconut tree. Inside were upward of forty people standing around the dining table or sitting on chairs that lined the living-room wall. On the couch a chorus of silver-haired ladies in black whispered a rosary.

Lucho was compelled to walk out. He did not much appreciate the frivolities and excesses so much a part of the island character. As he stood by the door surveying the covey of cackling women and gesticulating men, Rosa materialized out of the crowd, greeted him with a kiss on the cheek, and told him the news: Felicia's voice had returned.

Rosa took him by the arm and guided him to the dining table, which was crowded with delicacies: large Spanish olives swimming in brine, plates of *chorizo* wreathed with slices of bread, roast plantains covered with melted cheese and sprinkled with brown sugar. In the center of the table was a huge bowl of black beans next to a steaming mountain of white rice, and spreading out from them were trays of sliced fresh ham, roast chicken with garlic, pot roast, cubed pork fried in lard, and every configuration of salad imaginable. The least he could do was stay and eat.

He piled a plate high as gravity allowed and was looking for a place to enjoy the food when he spied the card table covered with liquor bottles. Behind it, Eduardo, Felicia's younger son, was playing bartender, and gathered about were several men, among them Acevedo and Antonio. He would rather have avoided them but Antonio was already motioning to him. Lucho wound his way to the makeshift bar, balancing the plate of food on his right hand and curling his left arm in front as a barrier. The men greeted him. He smiled back faintly and asked if they had seen Felicia. Eduardo nodded in the direction of the bedroom and made a space on the table.

Involved as they were in their discussion—the pharmacist defended Italian opera while Antonio, whose knowledge of opera was in inverse proportion to his capacity for needling, touted Mozart and Wagner—they ignored Lucho and allowed him to eat in peace.

As he picked through the food, he remembered how he and Antonio spent whole afternoons together in their youth silently reading on their grandfather's bed, passing each other books as they finished them. And so they went through all of Verne, Hugo, and Dumas. They also read Fielding and Dickens and Defoe and any other writer who crossed their paths. Then after their sessions were over, they would sit at the supper table and confound the rest of the family by speaking in the style of their books— the assumed objectivity of Verne, the elliptical addresses of the eighteenth-century English, the restrained elegance of the Victorians, or the dark ominous voice of Dostoevsky.

Their families lived on the same block, in houses owned by their grandparents, once powerful landowners whose vast holdings had been destroyed by countless battles during the War of Independence. "It was as if," the grandfather would say before he died, "those bastards had agreed ahead of time they were going to ruin me." In spite of their losses, the old couple had enough money remaining to buy several houses in the town of Corral Falso and to give one to each of their sons when he married.

The two boys liked to pretend that the grandparents' house, by far the largest and most labyrinthine, was a novel and the family the cast of characters invented by the author, a role they assigned to the octogenarian groundskeeper, an ex-slave who had lived in a room behind the larder ever since anyone in the town could remember. Several days a week they went to him and asked when Felicia would elope with Ceniciento the ragpicker, or how they would unearth Boabdil's treasure from the back yard, or whether it would not be more in keeping with her station in life to have the cook attack the cleaning maid with a meat cleaver rather than an ax. The groundskeeper was at first mortified by these questions, but each time dismissed them, grumbling and yelling after them always the same warning: "The day will come when you will find out what life is!"

Lucho looked down at his plate. The fat on the remaining pork was congealing into white globules. He asked Eduardo for a whiskey and walked outside. The heat had made him sleepy and he wanted a place to rest away from the crowd. He found it under the royal poinciana at the far edge of the yard. He sat against the trunk, drank his whiskey in one gulp, and dozed off.

Through a dream of gardenias and trolleys he heard a maiden's voice call his name. He opened his eyes and saw Felicia's face hovering over him and for a moment he thought he was in a novel. As soon as he stood up, she embraced him, pressing the side of her face against his chest. Lucho felt his heart quicken and pushed her to arm's length.

"How did it happen?" he asked.

Felicia explained that she had overheard a commotion from her bedroom and had gone to the kitchen to investigate. The two maids, Munda and Caridad, were arguing with Luciano the grocer, who, they claimed, had delivered a sack of rotten potatoes. Munda turned to her and complained that Luciano was up to his tricks again.

Felicia looked at the grocer. Luciano assured her in the most deferential tone he could manage that the potatoes were fine when he delivered them. And then it happened. Calmly and naturally, as if she had never stopped speaking, she said, "Luciano, please bring us another sack."

Munda crossed herself and Caridad fell to her knees, invoking the graces of the Most Blessed Virgin Mary Mother of God, St. Ursula and the Eleven Thousand Virgins, and a host of saints and martyrs to whom she had prayed for a cure. Felicia told Lucho that her own voice hit her like a wave rippling through every muscle and vein and that she had to use all her strength to keep from collapsing onto the kitchen floor.

"Over a sack of potatoes, can you believe it?" Felicia said, and noticed that Lucho's eyes were turned down.

He congratulated her, then quickly took his leave, claiming that he had to go back to the hospital.

Felicia did not believe him. She well knew the hospital did not count for much in his life, but she was also aware of his discomfort. His frivolity had abandoned him when his ambitions crumbled. All she said was "Next Tuesday" and it seemed enough, for her cousin's face lightened and he offered a faint smile.

Later on, after the guests had left and only family remained in the living room, Eduardo said in a voice slurred by drink, "That Lucho is a strange bug. The crazies he deals with must be melting his brain."

Felicia defended her cousin. There wasn't anyone in the family, she maintained, who had gone as far as he. And no one had suffered so at the hands of fate.

"Had he stayed in the United States . . ."

"Had Grandmother had wheels, she would have been a bicycle," interrupted Eduardo, waving his drink in the air and spilling some on the couch.

Lucho was at Felicia's door promptly at two the following Tuesday, and likewise the next week and the one after that, and so on for the better part of nine years. The only interruptions were a hurricane that flooded most of the area around the hospital and kept Lucho at his desk grumbling disconsolately and a general strike against the government that paralyzed the city as effectively as the storm, without the water and wind, and prevented people from venturing into the streets for fear of being shot at by snipers or arrested by marauding gangs of police. In less than a month's time, the canasta game became a pause in the sentence of their week to which they came eagerly and left refreshed, the promise

of another lurking just beyond the stagnant waters of Sunday
and the duty calls of Monday.

Sometimes Antonio and Marina joined them, and then the
games became parentheses in which four middle-aged people
regressed into childhood battles pitting the men against the
women. Antonio, Marina and Felicia agreed, was the worst player
they had ever known, incapable of keeping a straight face when
dealt a good hand. On the other hand, Antonio claimed that his
sister and her friend cheated, but, when challenged, could never
come up with any firm evidence. "I hope you do better in the
courtroom," Felicia would mock him. Lucho, for his part, did
not say much—he had never been a child of many words, and
as an adult, he had turned his taciturnity into an armor only
Felicia, and one other woman in his life, could ever breach. The
foursome invariably ended with Antonio storming away, cursing
the two witches of canasta who had stolen another game from
under his nose.

Mostly, Lucho and Felicia played alone, and that was the way
they preferred it. Lucho would arrive flushed after a quick lunch
in one of the downtown bars and sit at the card table, where a
demitasse of coffee and a glass of water awaited him. She shuffled,
he cut, and the game would begin.

After months of play, they knew each other's strategies perfectly. Lucho liked to meld and leave quickly, hoping to catch
his cousin with all her cards in her hand. Felicia opted for a
patient game, watching her cousin's every discard until the pile
was fatter than the pot, then taking it to win hand and game in
one swoop. As each tried to outdo the other, the matches lengthened well into the evening, and during the epic doldrums of the
middle game, they entertained themselves by chatting. At first
their conversations turned around superficial things—Lucho's

daughters' birthday parties or Felicia's neighborhood gossip or the latest infirmities of family members—but as their interest in these matters leveled and the talk increased, rather than relieved, their boredom, they quite naturally and unconsciously fell into revealing their innermost secrets. Winning became secondary and the cards acted as a conduit for their intimacies.

This is how Felicia learned of Lucho's other woman. It was not a secret in the family that Lucho was miserable in his marriage. His wife, uneducated and obese, was interested only in good clothes, jewelry, and in her doting and adder-tongued mother, who had lived with them since the day, many years before, when her husband had committed suicide by jumping into a vat of boiling tallow in the soap company he owned. The old man, a self-made millionaire who had started out as a country peddler selling colognes he mixed in their kitchen, had a weakness for young men which had come to light a few days before, when his wife received in the mail a brown envelope containing some rather compromising photographs.

Since that day Sofía and her mother had turned their claws on Lucho, the only man at their disposal, and conspired not to let him have a moment's peace at home. They not only questioned the worth of his person, calling him epithets like lazy porker and plucked hen, but also his manhood; the mother once had the nerve to mention to some of their friends that he was a homosexual, for he had not satisfied his conjugal obligations to Sofía in at least five years, that she was aware of.

Had they stopped at verbal attacks, Lucho would have found ways of circumventing them, but mother and daughter made his home life a purgatory. They purposely ate early, so that he had to sit alone without the pleasure of speaking to his daughters at the table; they stopped sending his laundry out, so that more than once he found himself without a clean shirt in the morning; and when they left to visit some relations in a faraway town, they changed the locks on the house and conveniently forgot to leave him the new keys. Understanding the mechanics of transference, Lucho had hoped he could help them confront their rage. What the psychology books did not tell him, and he sadly learned himself, was that anger, particularly the sort that arises out of extreme circumstances, can be a delicious thing, difficult to part with when it helps people cope with the workings of a vicious and unrelenting fate. His failure to bring the curative powers of his profession to bear on his own life—he was well aware that he wanted to help his wife and mother-in-law, not out of Aesculapian altruism, but only to keep from going insane himself— served only to add more fuel to the fire of his cynicism and to undermine any sense of control he might have had over his personal life.

During their one-hundred-sixty-second game, when Lucho needed 150 points to meld and Felicia waited for the discard pile to reach an irresistible size, she inquired, innocently, as if to make conversation, about Sofía. Lucho, whom she had never known to use vulgar language, even as a young man, answered, "The fat bitch is fine," and then without any transition which might have eased Felicia's shock, he divulged that he had a mistress.

"It was all I could do to keep from being devoured by those two harpies," he said, reaching for the pot and discarding a black trey. He mentioned her name, Jill Goldsmith, and confirmed that she was American, but dropped the matter altogether when he was able to meld, closed two canastas, and won the game.

Felicia's curiosity was not satisfied until three Tuesdays later. The game on that day ended early. On the second hand Felicia took a gargantuan pile and made canasta of canastas. Lucho stayed for a last cup of coffee and brought up Jill Goldsmith again.

She was a masseuse and had lived in the country for seven years. She loved books, and gave him novels by Faulkner and Hemingway and all those Americans who took life too seriously. He detested them but read them out of a sense of forbearance. She also liked the sea and spent hours taking the sun.

"American women love the sun, but our women hate it," he commented. "They think it makes them age faster."

Jill Goldsmith had been married before, to a government lawyer in Washington, D.C. The decision to divorce had been a mutual one, arrived at after a series of calm, rational discussions. They were still good friends and corresponded with each other often.

"Americans can be so amiable," interrupted Felicia. "Our people would be sending each other poisoned letters."

Jill Goldsmith worked at two of the beach clubs in Plaza del Mar and complemented her meager income with an allowance her father sent. Lucho described her as independent and headstrong, yet kind as an autumn breeze. And that kindness, which grew naturally and was given freely with no expectations to be paid back in kind, was rare indeed, at least for Lucho, to whom it seemed more certain by the day that women were the handmaidens of Satan.

Felicia had at first thought this "mistress" to be an adventure, a much needed one given his situation, but a temporary escape nevertheless. As she heard her cousin's voice grow thick and excited with emotion, however, she realized that this was no midlife tryst but an affair of the heart. She was moved and asked him why he didn't leave his wife once and for all.

The only reason he stayed with Sofía, he admitted, was his two daughters. As Felicia saw them, however, they were little fat sows, imitations of their mother, on whom he threw all of the attention that should have gone to a deserving wife. The two or three times a year Lucho brought them to visit, she felt she was face to face with the worst that human nature had to offer. They whined, they complained, they spilled ice cream all over their expensive dresses, and all their father would do was humor them and promise trips to the amusement park or the movies as recompense for good behavior. Most of all, Felicia wanted to ask why a man, to whom nature had afforded so much more freedom than to a woman, was afraid to take advantage of it.

The maid brought more coffee. Lucho took small sips and followed them with gulps of ice water.

Lucho and Jill met at a party given by Paco Verdún, better known as Tadeo Latraso, the most prolific author of serial romances in the country. His novels circulated like forbidden manifestoes through the finishing schools and kitchens of the capital. Felicia, for one, had read all 253 of his works.

Felicia lit a cigarette and exhaled upward. She asked Lucho how long he had known this Jill. He answered a year, but she shouldn't take it badly. Jill wasn't just anyone. What he meant to say was that Jill Goldsmith was at Paco's party quite by accident, brought there by a friend, and even Paco had dismissed her as being too straitlaced. Felicia was not convinced and drilled him with all sorts of questions regarding Jill Goldsmith's background. He responded as best he could, but could not answer why she was working as a masseuse when her father was so rich, other than to say, quite correctly as it turned out, that she liked to work. Lucho kept to himself the fact that he was spending a fair amount of money on her, going as far as paying for the redecoration of her apartment, and concluded the conversation with the one statement that encapsulated all that a person can feel for another and that carried with it all the justification he would ever need for leaving his wife: "She's the best woman I have ever known."

As the years passed, Jill became such a regular part of Lucho's life that he spoke of her more often than he did of his own daughters, and he related to Felicia, to the utmost detail, almost everything that they did together. He usually saw her on Thursdays, and his late arrivals home caused Sofía to go into such fits of rage that the lard on her neck quivered. Once she waved a kitchen knife under his nose and said that if he had any balls she would cut them off. In time, however, the wife, facing a storklike indifference on the part of the husband, gave up trying to make him account for his absences.

Lucho spent more and more time away from the house, sometimes whole weekends when he and Jill went on trips to other parts of the island. His attitude toward his work changed; he became concerned about his patients and was instrumental in instituting outpatient treatment in the hospital. He wrote two articles, one on the care of mentally disturbed children, the other on the segregation of the retarded and the mentally ill, which were published in journals in the United States. He also became more talkative in the few family gatherings he attended, discussing politics with Antonio and decrying the amoral practices of American big business with Fernando, who staunchly defended the military-industrial complex as the United States' greatest contribution to economic development. He even surprised his cousin by presenting her with a leather-bound volume of love poems. The gesture was particularly significant in view of the fact that, not long before, he had considered love to be the basest of human emotions—the phantom of vanity, as he liked to call it—and lovers the most pitiful creatures on earth, driven to find in others a mirror for their own delusions.

When not playing canasta, Felicia spent much of her time providing her grandson Antón with the moral and ethical values which his parents had no time for. Antón's homeliness had not entirely left him, but in him she saw the future of the family. She reminded herself that the narrow, sloping forehead was the mark of a disciplined mind. The thin lips and diminutive chin were certain signs of shrewdness. Only in the eyes did she see something disturbing—a hardness, an edge. And so she set to teach him all the virtues few of the men she knew actually possessed: honor, courage, honesty, and selflessness. She made the boy believe that the world was made of kindness and that God was invisibly perched on every shoulder.

Though Antón was pliant and obedient, she did not know for sure if he understood what she was saying. Again his eyes disturbed her, and a queer passivity that kept him sitting before her in silence with hardly a question or complaint. Nevertheless, the attention she lent to her grandson kept her busy and balanced, and the teaching of those values had the added benefit of renewing them within herself. Whatever obstacles came between her and contentment she was able to overcome with serenity. Her life seemed graced at last with the peace and sense of purpose due all human beings who enter the wane of their lives.

At the age of seven, the boy started school, and her mornings turned into empty stretches laced with anxiety. When she thought she was done with waiting, there she was, doing it again. On his return, Antón seemed flushed and feverish with new excitement, and not so willing to sit and listen to her expositions on the "virtuous path that leads to manhood." His head filled with school matters, and when he learned to read, books supplanted her: at first the school books she deemed appropriate for a boy his age, then more adult books, like those his father read, which she feared would make her grandson a skeptic before his time. She brought her concerns to Fernando, who waved her away. Books, he believed, were harmless. Mere entertainment. If the boy wanted to flip the pages of Ortega y Gasset or Unamuno or Hemingway, or any other book in the house, for that matter, then let him.

Felicia could not have disagreed more. On weekends and vacations, when Antón would once again fall into her sphere, she worked furiously, countering the attractions of the secular life. She had him over for breakfast, and they spent Saturday mornings together in the garden, tending to her roses—the flowers of the saints—and Sunday mornings at Mass, so that her grandson would be well acquainted with Latin, the language of God. Though the boy went along with her attentions, the tinge of diffidence in his eyes was not lost on her, nor the way his lips tightened and turned downward as he dug into the black earth of the rosebeds.

The October after Antón entered second grade at the School of the Most Holy Sisters of the Resurrection, Felicia heard of the death of Cándido Barrientos. The game that day was another short one. She gave Lucho enough hands to win the game and not notice her trick. Then she told him all: her first encounter with Cándido at the beach club two years after Luis's death and his subsequent visits to the house; the marvelous stories he told about the three-eyed women of the Congo and the ruthless pirates of Cochin China that had so endeared him to her sons; and how, throughout it all, he had exhibited a gentlemanly respect and a sense of propriety that had gradually won her affections.

"How did it end?" asked the psychiatrist, staring at the empty demitasse before him.

One week she had taken the trolley to the club expecting to meet him there, but he had not shown up. She waited in vain all that week for him to call, and she returned to the club on Sunday. It had rained and the beach was empty but for an attendant who sang to himself under an umbrella. At home she locked herself in the bedroom and wept a soup of rage and pain while the children listened outside the door. She never heard from Cándido Barrientos again, but a few weeks later Marina, the only person she had told about the affair, brought her a newspaper clipping announcing the engagement of the distinguished accountant Cándido Barrientos to the delicate and delightful Gabriela Zúñiga y Caballero, precious flower of Creole society. Felicia stopped attending the club, in spite of the boys' entreaties, and never again trusted a man outside her family. Her only consolation was, she admitted to Lucho, that in the picture printed with the announcement, the bride-to-be looked like a mulatto pelican.

"So, you're human after all" was Lucho's comment.

Somehow she had expected more from her cousin, perhaps some psychological insight that would lift her out of her depression. Instead, Lucho went on to relate to her the story of one of his patients who had occupied much of his time the previous months and about whom he was writing an article. She was a woman of means, and her family, embarrassed by her bizarre behavior and fearing ostracism from their social circles, had interned her in San Cristóbal under an assumed name. The woman, whom he chose to call Ana, believed she had lost her womb and carried a flashlight which she pointed under beds, inside closets and cupboards, and into garbage cans in search of her organ. She also asked anyone who happened to be in the ward at the time —other patients, nurses, orderlies, unwary visitors—if they had seen it and would they please bring it back to her, handing them bits of paper with her real name and address.

Lucho felt increasing pressure from the directors to have her isolated, and doubtless he would have done so had the woman come under his care in the days before Jill. Now, however, while well aware that she was beyond help and would remain in her state for the rest of her life, his newly found scientific curiosity drove him to an exhaustive analysis of the patient. On her last session with him, Ana had squatted on the leather chair before his desk and raised her dress, asking him, "Can you hear the winds? Can you see the emptiness?"

Felicia wanted to know how the woman came to be that way, and Lucho said that he was eager to know himself, but speaking to a schizophrenic was like trying to fill a hole in the sand with water. Ana's parents refused to cooperate. When he called, the mother at first denied ever having an insane daughter, but then more or less admitted the fact and cursed her to hell for having brought such anguish to the family. From information he obtained from Ana during her few lucid moments and the sketchy history in her file, Lucho was able to piece together that at fourteen she had had an affair with a mature man and that, as a result, the mother had kept her a virtual prisoner in the house for ten years. At some point during that time, the young woman had first heard voices coming from the toilet bowl announcing to her the loss of her womb. After the mother discovered the gardener trying to prove to Ana that her organs were intact, she was brought to the hospital. The father left a generous contribution to ease the director's mind for falsifying the admission papers.

"The parents are to blame! They are the cause of her misery!" said Felicia, realizing as she spoke the consequences her rejection might have had on her grandson. "Could it be?" she added more hesitantly.

Trying not to be condescending, Lucho explained the complexities of such cases. The parents' behavior was inexcusable, granted, but it wasn't necessarily the cause. Other people had suffered similar indignities, if not worse, and, although traumatized, had not become psychotic. On the other hand, there were inmates in the hospital who were hopelessly insane but whose histories exhibited no such parental abuse or neglect. The problem was, he explained, that there was no pattern. Rich, poor, black, white, happy or miserable, madness preys on some but not others. Only two maladies show us, he concluded, that human beings are more equal than not: lunacy and death.

Drinking sage tea for her unsettled stomach at bedtime that night, Felicia was no longer depressed, and Cándido Barrientos's death was not the emotional catastrophe that had threatened her for a week but, rather, a casual footnote in the history of her life. Ana became the focus of her concern, and over the next few weeks Felicia pestered Lucho with questions every opportunity she had. For some reason she did not care to explore, but which her cousin identified as the unspoken sorority of women whom the male gods have abandoned, Felicia's empathy for Ana was unshakable. She prayed for her and even offered to pay her a visit, if her cousin thought it would do any good. He almost agreed to it, considering the effects of human warmth on the psyche, but decided that such a tactic would only raise false hopes. Warmth could never help Ana find her lost uterus. Felicia then shifted her attentions to the article he was writing, and inquired with like insistence as to its contents.

The article, as it turned out, was never finished. In the absence of support from Ana's relatives and unable to circumvent administrative pressure, Lucho was forced to send his patient to the asylum in Corrientes, in the eastern part of the island, where problem cases inevitably wound up.

If San Cristóbal was a metaphor for hell, Corrientes was the real thing. Nestled in the mountains thirty miles from the nearest town, the asylum was free of the constraints of civilization. Madness there turned into a contagious disease that infected nurses and orderlies as well. Syphilis and other venereal diseases were passed from patients to staff and back to patients. Nurses carried nightsticks and beat inmates mercilessly for the merest offense. On his one visit, Lucho had witnessed an orderly break a patient's arm for retrieving a piece of stale bread from the garbage. The psychiatrist in residence, Dr. Zacarías Velázquez de la Vega, still held Wilhelm Fliess's theories as to the causal connection between the nose and the sexual organs. He considered Freud a Victorian lackey and his followers mere sycophants lusting after fame and money. Putting Fliess's theories to practice, the mad doctor of Corrientes, as he was called by his urban colleagues, had performed nasal surgery on a third of the inmates at the hospital.

The results of these amateurish operations—faces mangled into grotesque, phantasmagorical shapes—added a chilling texture to the hopelessness of the place. Lucho, still a young, unjaded doctor in those days, had returned to the capital with the shakes and, after a period of recovery, had written countless letters to his superiors and to higher authorities in the Ministry of Public Health reporting on the conditions he had witnessed and urging an immediate investigation.

He received three bland bureaucratic responses that the matter was being looked into, but burdened by his own unhappy home life and growing cynicism, Lucho gave up his reformatory pursuits. The place was still in operation, but Dr. Velázquez had at least desisted from performing any more surgery due to a painful case of arthritis that had all but crippled his cutting hand.

"What will become of Ana?" Felicia asked.

"She will turn gradually madder and madder until only the outer shell is left—a body with no soul."

As he found new purpose in his profession and grew less despondent about his inability to make a significant contribution to psychiatry, Lucho became more brazen in his criticisms of his wife and bolder in weighing the alternatives life had placed before him. A will made of something resembling hard metal materialized in him. He spoke to Felicia of leaving Sofía and moving in with Jill, who was now, for all intents and purposes, the center of his life. It was she who filled his mind, she whose health he worried about, and she whose opinions acted as counterpoints to his own.

Felicia had finally met her, four years after her cousin had first alluded to her in the middle of a game, at a lunch date arranged by Lucho. Felicia found Jill a pleasant woman, distant and guarded but sincere. They spoke of flowers, a topic they were both genuinely interested in, but broached few others. There would never be any intimacy between them, yet both instinctively recognized the bond they had to this man who sat with them nervously sipping his drink.

The lunch ended well. Felicia promised Jill some cuttings from her garden and Jill suggested an afternoon outing to the botanical gardens. Neither of these things would ever come about, but

Lucho saw them as signs that the two women had found a common ground to deal with each other.

While Felicia tried to help Lucho with his crumbling life, she had the benefit of watching her son's thrive before her. Through the years Fernando had risen from his initial position as office clerk to general manager of the National Shoe Company. He had become—in the language of the islanders—a "personality." Mention of his name was enough to open any door in the business community; credit was instantly available in the numerous banks on Piedra Street, the financial center of the city; socialites vied for the privilege of having the handsome couple, Mr. and Mrs. Fernando García-Turner, appear at their functions. The company itself was a model of efficiency and steady growth. In the four years under his leadership, it had increased profits by 75 percent. It seemed that anyone of distinction wore Nacionales, the trademark that became so popular it appeared in the lyrics of a bolero of the period:

> . . . through the streets of the city
> I searched until I wore out my Nacionales.
> I found only darkness and pain
> and the wind blowing without pity.

The owners of the National Shoe Company, Calixto Bergaña and his wife, Asuncíon, felt blessed. Not only was Fernando making them obscenely wealthy; they also found in him a surrogate for their worthless sons, the older a homosexual florist living in Paris, the younger a poet with Communist leanings. The Bergañas gave Fernando generous yearly bonuses and presented him with a late-model Oldsmobile. They offered his family full use of their beach house and motorboat in the exclusive resort of Caracoles, and one Christmas sent him and Rosa to New York for a one-week stay at the Plaza so that they could spend the holidays "in style."

In spite of his success, Fernando remained a man of simple tastes. He much preferred the company of his family gathered around a home-cooked *ajiaco* to the elaborately formal dinner parties which he and Rosa were more and more often obliged to attend and where they were served food "prepared by people who have lost their taste buds." It never occurred to Fernando to refuse the Bergañas' largesse, just as it would never have entered his mind to expect their special treatment to begin with. He accepted their gifts innocently and enjoyed them fully, while they lasted. Whatever maliciousness lurked in his character surfaced only during his weekly poker games, the one vice he inherited from his uncle Antonio.

If the Bergañas became Fernando's benefactors, it was not beyond don Calixto, in his prime a ruthless and inveterate businessman, to consider that in gaining a son and practicing the generosity which is one of the few delights any parent has, no matter his age, he was at the same time making it next to impossible for any rapacious competitor to lure his manager away. He would have named him the primary beneficiary in his will, as his wife had urged, were it not for the laws of the land, which maintained the supremacy of biological survivorship. The best he could do for Fernando was to set up a secret trust fund that would start him on the way to becoming wealthy upon the death of his mentors.

While Fernando accepted the signs of his success lightheartedly, it was another matter altogether with Rosa. She saw them as proof that they had finally arrived where they belonged. She began to look down at those whom fortune had passed by and resented the beggars and cripples who gathered at her mother-in-law's front porch every afternoon waiting for the leftovers Felicia was only too happy to give them. Rosa's manner with Munda her maid became so brusque that the poor woman appealed to Felicia and asked her to intercede.

Fernando took his wife's petulance with his usual aplomb. He convinced himself that Rosa was going through a stage, as all women do at some time in their lives, and that soon she would be her old self again. He listened to her complain that their names were not appearing with regularity in the society pages of the papers, and that her wardrobe was hopelessly inadequate, and he nodded condescendingly when she pleaded with him to go on an ocean cruise to el Norte. His patience finally gave out during a conversation soon after he bought a plot in the new American development of Sea Haven.

She wanted to start building their new house immediately. He did not see the rush. They were perfectly comfortable for now. She added that the house was becoming crowded, and it was difficult for her to entertain her friends. It was not a proper house for that sort of thing.

"Besides," she continued, "Antonio and Eduardo and your other relatives are always dropping by unannounced, being vulgar and telling dirty jokes in front of our son. It's embarrassing."

"Listen, Rosa," he told her, staring at her with fierce eyes like his mother's. "The day you start shitting rose petals I will build your house, but you can move into it by yourself."

Antón heard the argument in his room. His mother was contradicting herself. She was always cheery around his uncles and was the first to laugh at their jokes, no matter how off-color they were. Whether the subject of discussion was the lot in Sea Haven or the way his father had looked at a woman at a party, Antón concluded that his parents were inconsistent creatures, full of love one moment, full of hate the next. He turned inward, became more impassive, and took to speaking in monosyllables.

Felicia brought the boy's taciturn nature to the attention of Fernando and Rosa, but they paid no heed, busy as he was making money and she spending it. They passed it off as one more of the lady's numerous worries. Felicia continued with her grandson's moral lessons, though she often felt she was speaking to a stone, and with her canasta games with Lucho, which she played as much out of habit as out of pleasure.

The Wednesday after the four-hundred-seventy-eighth game was a school holiday. Antón was sitting on his grandmother's rocking chair waiting for her to finish applying some rouge so they could go to the library when Marina flew into the room without knocking. Her hair lay flat on her head and she wore no makeup. Her eyes were bloodshot and the lids were swollen. She threw herself on the edge of the bed with such abandon that Felicia thought the frame would crack.

"Get me a whiskey," Marina said, ignoring Antón.

Even though it was eight o'clock in the morning, Felicia did not question her friend's request. She brought her a tall glass with lots of ice and a sprinkle of water.

Marina drank half and then spoke. "I have had a terrifying vision, the worst of my life."

Felicia noticed that her temples were flushed.

"I saw the city burning and people rushing everywhere trying to escape the flames. They were being pursued by demons waving short pointed swords. The ones caught were disemboweled and the demons threw their guts into wagons that came along pulled by old women dressed in black. My mother was among them, and yours, too. On the seat of each wagon were other demons with long beards and . . ."

She stopped and wiped her brow with the back of her hand.

"What? What?" implored Felicia, sitting next to her.

Marina took another swallow of her drink. She glanced at Antón, then back at her friend.

"They were naked and had long red penises wrapped around them like hoses. They screamed at the women and spat big gobs of phlegm that landed on their heads. In the harbor there were thousands fighting to board Spanish galleons to get away. I saw children trampled by the mob. I saw old people cast aside like garbage."

Felicia wanted to send her grandson away, but it was too late. He could not hear any worse. She tried to reassure her friend. "Maybe it does not mean anything. You've said nightmares . . ."

"I was wide-awake, Felicia. I haven't slept a wink all night.

"All along the streets there were students and revolutionaries waving banners and screaming, 'Long live Freedom' and 'Death to the tyrant.' It means something all right."

"Yes!" said Felicia, her voice rising. "It means that Sotelo will soon fall. Imagine that. After all these years we can have a legitimate government. What is so bad about that?"

"I tell you. If you think Sotelo's regime is bad, what is coming will make it seem like Paradise."

Marina's voice had reached a pitch of intensity that scared her friend. Her eyes glowed vivid blue.

"We will see the end of our families and the end of the country, too. Prepare yourself. In a year's time Sotelo will be out of the country, and soon after that, we will follow."

As much as Marina's hysterics upset Felicia, her prophecy was so extreme that she did not bother with it much. The seer had been wrong before. The truth was that even Antón could have predicted the fall of the dictator at this late date. Everyone had had enough of Sotelo's corruption and brutality, and even Felicia had voiced her opposition before Antonio, to which he responded, quite simply, "What did you expect from a man whose favorite avocation is raising fighting dogs?"

She watched the political developments around her with a certain detachment. And while she decried Sotelo's ineptitude in occasional discussions with her brother, her daily attention was focused almost exclusively on her family, particularly Antón.

Her awakening was sudden enough. It happened, in fact, at three one Friday morning when she heard a succession of pops, as if someone were setting off firecrackers, followed by a siren and brakes screeching. She peeked through her window and saw, directly in front of her house, a policeman illumined by car lights shooting at a body on the ground. Then two others came and dragged it into the car. Hearing them drive away, she rushed next door, where she found Rosa and Fernando in the living room with eyes as big as billiard balls. No one was hurt and Antón had slept through it all, but a bullet had gone through the door and was encrusted in the wall. She found Munda in the kitchen, a whimpering mass of nerves, and ordered her to make coffee. Then the four of them sat on the couch whispering softly all manner of conjectures and waited for the dawn to come.

The canasta games continued, but Lucho lost more and more of them in the last six months before circumstances put an end to them. His concentration was distracted by thoughts of Jill, who, because of the tense political situation, was considering moving back to the States, and by his own attempts to extricate himself from his marriage in the least damaging way. The decision was prematurely forced upon him when he came home one night to find his books and clothes in a pile in front of the house. As he walked through the door, Sofía, who had been waiting in ambush in the darkened living room, attacked him with a broom and hit him on the side of the head with such force that the handle broke. Lucho felt the world start to spin, but afraid that if he blacked out she would surely take his life, he shook his head back to consciousness and grabbed his wife, who was about to jam the stick into his bloodied ear, by the throat. They fell to the floor and were rolling around over and under each other when the two daughters came out of their room. Thinking that their father, who was now holding the splintered handle, was the attacker, they came to their mother's aid. They clawed and kicked him without letting up until Sofía called to the girls to hold him while she went for a knife. The daughters, startled by their mother's command, let go of their father, who flew out the door and into his car.

The game after the altercation was memorable, not because it was the last, but because it never took place. As Felicia was about to start dealing, Lucho put his hand over the deck and announced that he was going to America with Jill. They had tickets for the following Saturday.

Fighting back a sorrow that threatened to overcome her, Felicia embraced her cousin. She went to her room and brought out a bottle of port Cándido Barrientos had given her and which she had been saving for a special occasion. After the third glass they became drunk and spent the rest of the afternoon toasting the future. At dusk the wine was finished and they grew silent, watching the red sun drop behind the coconut tree out front and listening to the toads intone their mournful songs.

B E S T I A R Y

*B*y the time he was eleven, Antón García-Turner had heard from his grandmother the life stories of twenty-seven saints, fifteen holy men and women, and seventeen children who had led exemplary but disturbingly brief lives. Felicia began her hagiographies when her grandson was seven, the age at which, in her estimation, one first confronts the world. The night before he started first grade she told him the story of Pascual Babilonia, the shepherd boy who learned to read by asking passersby to teach him a word or two from a book he carried with him. The moral of the story, Felicia said to Antón, was that one learns from everyone, and one should not be afraid of asking questions, even of strangers. This last piece of advice went contrary to his mother's warning about speaking to people he did not know, but the boy listened in his usual passive way, much more anxious than attentive. The following day he was to be surrounded by strangers.

From then on, Felicia always had a saint ready for any eventuality in Antón's life. After he once disobeyed his father and sneaked away to play by the stream, she told Antón the story of St. Vitus, whose father had cooked him in oil for doing much the same thing. Antón could not imagine his father throwing him in a vat of boiling oil, so he dismissed Felicia's warning and continued with his visits to the water's edge to catch tadpoles and launch his paper boats. On another occasion, when she discovered that Antonio, her own brother, had given the boy a copy of the *Odyssey* for his tenth birthday, she told Antón about St. Jerome, the holy man of letters, who had been forced by God to spend a year in Purgatory to atone for his undue love of Plato.

Some of the tales had the clear purpose of teaching Antón a lesson; others, however, she told for the simple pleasure of putting the fear of God into him. Her favorite saint was St. Francis, who loved music, animals, and flowers. She always referred to him when she gardened. "According to St. Francis," she would say, "you may find the face of God in those petals." Antón would look very hard but saw nothing but flowers before him. One time he got so close to a bloom that a bee came out of it and stung him on the nose. For days his right nostril was red and puffed up. Sneezing was agony, and crying was out of the question. His grandmother called it mortification, and she alluded to yet another saint, a beekeeper who was attacked by a swarm of ten thousand bees; such was his agony that God instantly forgave all his sins and assumed him into heaven.

But it was a cat that acted as an antidote to all the holiness and made the seed of doubt sprout like a black flower in Antón's mind. He and Felicia were working in the rosebeds when he looked up and noticed a bony, dirty, and, according to Felicia, very pregnant female staring at them. Despite its appearance, its eyes burned with a yellow fire, and it made no attempt to move when they stood up.

As soon as Felicia determined that the cat was free of rabies, they prepared a corner of the garage and led it there with a plate of milk, so that it could give birth in peace. Three days later his grandmother met Antón at the door after school and told him the cat had given birth to six kittens. He ran past her, through the dining room and kitchen, and into the garage. He saw the mother lying on the towel, but the kittens were gone. She was preoccupied with something in her paws—a ball, a piece of cloth, a mouse? He peered directly over her and saw that she was gnawing on what looked like a kitten's head. Strewn all about the garage floor were the half-eaten remains of her brood—tufts of hair, pieces of tail, and the fleshless oblong forms of five skulls.

That night Felicia tried to console her grandson as he lay in his bed, but she could not invoke a single saint whose life might put the situation into the proper perspective.

"The mother ate her babies," Antón insisted.

"It was God acting through her." She knew she was on shaky ground.

"It's like Munda's story."

"What story?"

"The one about the lady who cooked her children and served them to her husband. It happened many years ago, when the devil's daughter was getting married. That's what she said."

"She should not tell you those things. Say a prayer for the soul of those kittens and go to sleep."

"Sr. Etelvina said animals don't have souls."

"That's true. Go to sleep. You must forget what happened to-day."

"I can't."

"Go to sleep," she said uncertainly, pulling up his shirt and running her hand over his birthmark. Antón was embarrassed by her interest in his anatomy and perturbed by her constant reminders that he was special, when he felt, and was quite happy to feel, quite the opposite—common, regular, average.

He slept deeply but woke up early the next morning with the taste of disenchantment in his mouth. He had had enough of his grandmother's stories, her piety, and her rosebeds, and he learned to avoid her by going to the grove of banana trees in the rear of the yard, where he could concern himself with matters of true importance. There he captured creatures—lizards, frogs, spiders—and put them in shoeboxes, sometimes individually, sometimes together in different combinations, spider with lizard, lizard with frog, frog with spider, hoping some battle would ensue. Mostly they tried to escape, but sometimes, after an initial flurry of activity, they lay motionless in the bottom of the box. They did not fight or try to devour their companions, and they crawled over each other without the least recognition that another living being was in the box.

What Antón could not witness he imagined, and he came home brimming with battles which he described to Munda the maid, the one person in the household who listened in rapture to his inventions. And so he told her of the encounter between wolf spider and lizard: how they measured each other, keeping their distance at first until the spider felt the lizard's head with one of her legs. The lizard only blinked. Then, when it seemed they would both go to sleep, the lizard pounced on the spider, tore off one of her legs, and devoured it in one gulp. This the reptile did with two more legs until the spider, sensing that if she did nothing she would soon be without limbs, leapt onto the back of her enemy and bit it at the base of the skull, paralyzing the attacker with her poison, after which she proceeded to strip strands of flesh off the helpless lizard and suck them through her lips like spaghetti, until all that was left was the bare skeleton. When Antón saw that Munda's eyes were wide open and that she had crossed herself three times during the narration, he knew he had an eager audience.

Every few days he came to her with another still more terrifying story. She countered with tales of her own about ghosts and apparitions in Piedra Negra, the place of her birth. Except for the one about the mother who cooked her babies, most of these were innocuous and not nearly as bloody as those Antón made up. There was one, however, which so impressed him he would remember it in all its details, as if he had lived it, for the rest of his life. The story, in its essence, went like this:

In Piedra Negra there once lived a cattle rancher, a Spaniard by birth, named don Ernesto Sánchez de la Vega. His ranch was the largest in the province and his herd was so numerous it was said that every inhabitant on the island had eaten at least one steak carved from one of his animals. Don Ernesto's bovine passion was such that he traveled to the farthest corners of the country in search of the best-looking animals to add to his herd. When the train bearing him home reached the town, all activity stopped and people gathered in the station to see what marvels he had brought: handsome, white and gray zebu bulls and tender virgin heifers. Don Ernesto took great care of the animals and oversaw their unloading, making sure none was hurt or damaged as it was led out of its specially padded wagon and into the holding pen. He paid his hands better than any other rancher, but God pity the man who mistreated one of his prize heifers. Rumor had it that he had shot a fellow for kicking a cow. The men who worked for the Spaniard took better care of the cattle than they did their families. At the ranch they were all love and tenderness; at home they beat their women and whipped their children and ordered them about with clicks of the tongue.

At this Munda made a noise with her lips between a clack and a chirp.

With all that land and all those animals, don Ernesto was a very powerful man. He was small but attractive, and people always knew when he was coming because the birds stopped singing and the sun hid behind a cloud. Some folk claimed they heard thunder pealing in the distance. He kept two mistresses in town, whom he visited several times a week, and four on the ranch, one at each point of the compass, so that there was always a woman close by when he needed one. The men in the bodegas looked up to him like a god, and after a few drinks, they bragged that he was insatiable, like his bulls. He had so many illegitimate children he couldn't keep up with them, and it happened that one night, as he was walking down the street behind the slaughterhouse—the Street of the Thieves they called it, because the people who lived there were all good-for-nothings—he saw a young man beating another. The Spaniard intervened and, holding the attacker by the neck, asked him who his father was. The boy answered, "You are, sir." Don Ernesto gave the barely conscious victim two hundred pesos to keep quiet about the incident and went on his way. Next day it was all over town.

Munda stopped, rubbed her hands nervously, and looked all about. She made Antón promise never to reveal the source of the story to anyone.

Not long after that, the Spaniard went to el Norte in search of more cattle to upgrade his herd and brought back with him the most beautiful, the strongest, the largest bull Piedra Negra had ever seen. The day don Ernesto was scheduled to arrive, the whole town came to the station. The vendors put up foodstalls and a trio of barefoot musicians played country songs. Finally the train pulled up and gave its sigh, as they do when they're tired after a long trip, and don Ernesto's men brought the animal out. Everything grew quiet. Even the cicadas stopped chirping. The bull stood twenty-one hands at the shoulder and its testicles were as big as watermelons. It walked down the reinforced plank don Ernesto had ordered by telegraph and trotted around the holding pen, eyeing each person standing at the fence with its big black eye. The face, which had a human nobility to it, was like dawn, half light, half dark. That's why they called it Matutino. After trotting around a few more times, it moved to the middle of the pen, lowered its head to show off its silvery horns, then suddenly raised its neck and gave out such a bellow it made the onlookers shiver with fright and admiration. There had been nothing like it in Piedra Negra, ever.

Don Ernesto kept his new bull by itself in a corral within walking distance of the main house and there brought to it his best heifers. His ambition was to create a herd so pure and perfect that he would be the envy of ranchers the world over. Every morning, five days a week, three or four cows entered the corral, and the untiring bull performed its duty with great gusto. In less than a year, several dozen cows had calved, and the Spaniard's ambition was on its way to becoming reality. He started receiving inquiries from other farmers who wanted to breed the bull with their stock, and the President himself sent his personal representative to buy the bull, but the Spaniard, who was a staunch liberal, did not give the emissary the courtesy of a meeting. "Let the President come and kiss my ass," he bragged to his friends at the Lyceum.

Now that the bull was so famous, don Ernesto grew worried that someone might try to steal it or do some other harm, and so he assigned his best farmhand, Perico Mas, to guard Matutino. Perico attended to the beast all day long and slept in a hut outside the gate. It was he who noticed several nights in a row a strange creature like a small stiff cow with a square rump making its way through the corral toward the bull. Matutino would trot to the creature, mount it, and hump it so recklessly and for so long, bellowing and panting the whole time—like a man who falls hopelessly in love and loses all his pride—that Perico felt compelled to tell his boss of the apparition, for that is what he felt the creature to be—a bovine ghost that was robbing the bull of its vigor and strength.

By this point in the story Munda's eyes were flushed and her voice was agitated and breathless. Antón pressed her to keep going.

The following night, after sending word to the mistress of turn that he would not be visiting, don Ernesto went to Perico's shack and waited. Three, four hours went by, and just as the rancher started to curse the cowhand about his drinking, the figure appeared from behind the barn at the far edge of the corral and waddled along to the center of the pen. There the bull met it, nudging its sides gently with its snout, then walked around and mounted it as it had done every night for a week. Fully satisfied, Matutino went off by himself and left the creature shivering in the moonlight.

Don Ernesto ordered Perico to follow him. At close range they realized that it was no animal but a contraption on wheels covered with cowhide. It had horns on one end and a tail on the other.

When the Spaniard pulled off the hide, he uncovered doña Concha, his wife, totally naked, lying facedown on a wooden cart. She was whimpering quietly and her face was covered with mucus and tears. Don Ernesto gave a scream so loud people later claimed it had shaken the walls of their houses, and they thought it was the devil flying over Piedra Negra. Then he took his wife by the hair and dragged her through the mud in the direction of the house.

Perico thought that that was as good a time as any to leave. He knew it was not beyond his master to silence the one witness to the debasement. The cowhand stayed in town long enough to tell the story and disappeared. The bull disappeared, too, and doña Concha was never seen in public again. As for don Ernesto, he fired all the people in his employ and let his ranch go to ruin. In less than five years, only a few wild, half-starved cows remained of the once proud herd; the rest were poached by the cowhands the Spaniard himself had dismissed. When he died, several of his sons entered the main house and found doña Concha, old and wrinkled and barely alive, on a filthy bed in one of the back rooms with the bull's dried-out testicles hanging from her neck.

That night Antón could not sleep. He had, ever since becoming conscious of his physical self, associated emotions as arising in one of three places in his anatomy. The chest, he knew, was the seat of love and joy and hatred, for whenever he experienced any of these, his thorax seemed to want to burst and his lungs never filled with enough breath. When he grew curious about something, it was the head, especially the forehead, that took control, and the rest of his body fell away. Humiliation affected the eyes; everything grew dark and he looked through a tunnel that led directly to the source. Now there was a cat in his gut that had just awakened and was scratching the walls to get out. The more he thought about doña Concha being mounted by the bull, the more restless the cat became, its tail curling around his heart and its whiskers catching in his throat.

Not long after she told the story, Munda was called away to care for her ailing mother and left her niece in her place. A shy, untutored seventeen-year-old who had never ventured beyond the town limits of Piedra Negra, the girl had none of the social graces deemed necessary for a domestic in the service of an ambitious woman like Rosa García-Turner. At first, Antón's mother had refused to take her in, claiming that it was a mistake to hire someone sight unseen and based solely on the recommendation of Munda, whom Rosa had never trusted to begin with.

"What if she's a thief? What if she's promiscuous?" Rosa asked her mother-in-law.

Felicia suggested that she assume full responsibility for the girl, and as her suggestions had the power of commands to anyone who knew her, Rosa agreed to take the country girl in on a trial basis.

When Felicia met Mirta, she was struck by her unearthly beauty. Her face was round and innocent; her eyes, which she kept lowered most of the time, were a vibrant green, like the sea before it deepens. A child still lived in her, but her body was that of a woman. It was obvious from the few simple answers that came from her lips that she did not yet know the power of her beauty. Were she lighter-skinned, the older woman thought, she would be an angel.

Mirta replaced doña Concha and the bull as the focus of Antón's passion. After seeing her, the purr in his belly metamorphosed into an ardor in his groin. He spent days lost in reverie, making and remaking her eyes, her perfect face, her glowing skin, and those parts of her he could only imagine. School, parents, his grandmother were mere distractions that took him from what he knew to be the essence of his being. For the first time he felt the shame of uncontrolled desire, but shame was a weak antagonist to the excitement pulsing in his veins. All he had he would have given to Mirta, and he dreamed he brought her a precious goblet full of bright liquid and spilled it at her feet.

On the night of San Juan, shyness finally let go of him. The family was gathered in Felicia's porch, and at nine o'clock, the hour at which Mirta took her shower, he sneaked away into the dark behind his house. He stood under the maid's bathroom window and heard the voice of reason—Felicia's voice really— recede into a corner where it was drowned by the beating in his ears and the gush of water inside as the shower went on.

He waited for the water to stop, then he crept onto the ledge under the window. He pulled himself up and looked in. Mirta had a towel around her head and was drying her hair. Her breasts were glazed with water, which beaded on her dark brown nipples and fell away as she rubbed her head. When she straightened, he could see the slope of her belly and a line of down from the navel to where her coiled hair grew wet and profuse. Antón's body was shaking and he wanted to swallow her breasts and be fed by them, and to jam his face against the dark mound she was now drying. Everything blackened and he felt his groin being pulled away, the goblet of his dreams spilling out, joining his memories to his body, his body to the night, the night to the song Mirta was singing:

¿Cuándo volverá mi amor,
aquél que me trajo flores,
cuándo probaré el sabor
de sus labios y sus fulgores?

A boy's first love is a sacred one, finding no outlet other than the paths of the imagination which will turn and twist on themselves in pursuit of the beloved, fleeting ghost of the self. Antón forsook his search for truth, thinking he had found it in his loving, and he neglected the two lizards he was keeping in a box under his bed until they died and filled the room with an intolerable stench. He went into such a state—his eyes red and swollen, his appetite gone—that his parents thought he was gravely ill. They put him in bed and called Acevedo the pharmacist and Dr. Figueras, neither of whom could find the slightest sign of disease, suggesting that the problem was perhaps psychological. Deep depression brought on by the onset of puberty was Acevedo's exact diagnosis.

Felicia, remembering the story of Ana, was convinced that the boy was manifesting symptoms of schizophrenia. After the doctor and the pharmacist had made their visits, she called Marina to arrange an exorcism for the next day, when her daughter-in-law had an appointment for her weekly manicure and hairdo. The seer appeared with branches of basil, an incense burner, and a vial of holy water. As she entered Antón's room, Marina turned to her friend and said she smelled love and death, then went over to the boy and stroked his forehead. She lit the incense, and giving the censer to Felicia, she started a chant in an indecipherable language, all the while sweeping the bed with the basil and sprinkling holy water on him.

After an hour the room was so full of smoke Antón could barely breathe. He had the covers up around his neck and had not moved since the two ladies marched in. His eyes teared and he started sweating. He saw his grandmother transformed into a person from another world, comical and terrifying at the same time, and he did not know whether to run out of the room to the nearest adult or join in the mirth.

Felicia did not expect Rosa home until noon, but a small fire in one of Remi of Roma's new hair-drying machines had forced the early closing of the salon. Rosa was still wearing hair curlers when she walked through the bedroom door. Her sudden appearance caused Felicia to stiffen, the censer swinging from her outstretched hand. Marina looked Rosa up and down with eyes half-closed, like a diva whose aria has just been interrupted by an ill-mannered patron. Antón pulled the covers off and stood on the bed, frozen by the cold wind his mother had brought with her.

Rosa rushed to him crying, ¡Mi niño! ¡Mi niño! She put her arms around his waist and tried to whisk him away. But an eleven-year-old boy, no matter how small and gnomish he might seem, is an awkward bulk to lift, and where she thought in her outrage she would find a feather, there was a heavy stone. Mother and son lost their balance and toppled over, Antón putting out his unrestrained arm to break the fall, a simple and instinctive act that kept his mother's head from landing squarely on the tile floor and saved Acevedo and Figueras another visit to the house. Dazed on the floor, the boy heard his mother, who had bounced right back on her feet like a rubber toy, berate his grandmother with such language that he thought the flames of hell would consume her on the spot. When Rosa was done, she lowered her voice to a simmering snarl and ordered the two ladies to leave and never set foot in her house again.

If Fernando noticed the sepulchral silence in his home when he arrived for dinner, he gave no indication. Antón watched him sit at his place and wait for Mirta to bring him his glass of wine.

He took a sip and, wrinkling his nose, said, "The house smells like a church."

That was enough to open the faucet of Rosa's wrath. She growled, she screamed, she hissed, she whimpered, she wept. She called Felicia a witch, a manipulator, a *santera*, a gossip, a simpleton, a grouch, a busybody, a flatterer, a harpy, a hound dog, a snake, a wasp, a monster, and the very incarnation of evil, who was now using her son as an initiate in demonic rites.

Fernando sat with a forkful of food suspended between mouth and plate, and as the litany of epithets grew, his jaw hardened and his eyes glazed. Antón, on the other hand, ate voraciously, as if he were attempting to muffle what he was hearing with what he was eating—a battle of the senses that ended in stalemate. In ten minutes his plate was empty and his stomach hurt. Rosa had paused and was weeping loudly into her napkin. Fernando's final words were "The food is cold," after which he pushed his plate away and walked outside.

Neither parent realized that Antón's appetite had returned, and as the boy watched his mother whimper and gasp at the table, he felt a force beyond his control contract his torso and tighten his throat so violently that a jet of half-digested food gushed out onto the plate, tablecloth, and lap. Rosa rushed to his side and once again intoned her cry, ¡*Mi niño!* ¡*Mi niño!*

The boy tried to free himself and assure his mother that he was all right, but every time he opened his mouth, vomit, not words, blurted out. Soon his mother's dress, and his head, were covered with a gray, odorous ooze that affected Rosa as well, so that she, too, started heaving. Since she had skipped her dinner in favor of her bilious harangue, the only thing that came out of her was a series of rhythmic batrachian sounds, not unlike that which bullfrogs make during mating season.

Alarmed by the croaking, Fernando rushed back in and was witness to a scene that would have put Dante to shame: *Peristaltic Pietà, Child and Virgin of the Vomitorium*. His initial reaction was as far from the sympathy his wife expected as human emotion can get. Rosa noticed the revulsion in his face and, in between croaks, gave him a steely look that should have melted what she believed to be the stone of his heart. Fernando fought back the nausea that threatened to make him the third point of the triangle—an unholy family swaddled in intestinal glop—and called meekly to Mirta, who stuck her head through the kitchen door with eyes swelling their sockets. He ordered her to clean up and, taking his wife and son at arm's length by the elbows, led them into the bathroom.

Later, after mother and son were cleanly in their beds, Fernando found Felicia in her room sitting in her rocking chair with her back to the door, knotting and unknotting her handkerchief. He called to her from the doorway.

"The child is better, isn't he?" she responded, and said nothing more, leaving Fernando stranded in an ocean of helplessness.

For two months he bobbed between wife and mother, an experience that allowed him to formulate a piece of advice he would, years later, pass on to his son: *Never get caught between two warring women*. Nevertheless, it was he who mollified his wife's determination that their son should never be alone with his grandmother, and it was he who wrenched the promise from his mother never to "cure" Antón without permission and bore it to Rosa with the fervency and dispatch of Hermes himself. What brought the two women together finally, however, was not Fernando's mediation, nor Antón's birthday, for which they had planned (before their conflagration) a large family gathering, but an incident which ended Mirta's stay with the family as suddenly as it had begun.

Antón was not the only one who had been struck by Mirta's beauty. Her mere presence left men's jaws loose and twitching, and the smell of hay and wild fruit which emanated from her awoke in them a glandular urge to home and hover around her virginity. Inside a week of Mirta's arrival, Rosa's kitchen filled with men. Luciano the grocer, Joaquín the gardener, Zacarías the mailman, and at least a dozen others came at all hours and lingered about trying to make conversation with the girl, who responded in monosyllables and whose demeanor, shy and self-effacing as it naturally was, actually whetted the men's appetites. A fleeting movement of her eyes in their direction was enough to encourage their return the following day. Mirta served them coffee and glasses of water when they asked, and otherwise went about her chores, accepting the visits with the unquestioning innocence she had brought with her from the country.

Soon the two homes were the best kept, best tended to in the neighborhood, while other houses began to suffer from the neglect of the workmen. Toilets remained plugged, walls unpainted; gardens were left unkempt and ornamental bushes overgrew their beds. Once the model of middle-class civility and tidiness, the block now acquired an aura of decay reminiscent of the older, less prestigious neighborhoods on the other side of the city.

The Sunday night preceding Antón's party there was a great commotion in the house. Rosa had rushed out of the kitchen, arms flailing over her head, and told Antón to get his grandmother next door. Felicia arrived, with Antón and Caridad her maid at her heels. She peeked around the door and saw Mirta lying naked on the floor of the kitchen. On one side of her were her uniform and her shoes; on the other was a half-empty bottle of firewater. Her eyes were fixed on a point on the ceiling, and on her lips a thin film of saliva bubbled as she breathed.

Rosa, bordering on hysterics, stood by the refrigerator, while in the shadows of the corner closest to the door was Fernando. His face glowed with an expression somewhere between the demonic and the beatific. His body wavered as if standing on the deck of a ship, and no doubt he was using his considerable reservoir of fortitude to keep from pouncing on the drunken girl.

Felicia acted quickly. She went into the maid's room and brought out a bedcover, which she draped over Mirta. Then she knelt over the girl and asked softly what the matter was. Mirta moaned a word the lady could not make out. She asked again, and on the second try, she was able to make out the name Mariano.

"Who's Mariano?" asked Felicia, really to herself, but everyone in the room, except Mirta, who was now moaning continuously and moving her head from side to side, answered in chorus, "I don't know."

Felicia directed the same question at the girl with no better results, and Rosa, somewhat more composed now that the matter was less raw, volunteered that Mirta had received a long call from Piedra Negra that afternoon, after which she had locked herself in her room without a word of explanation.

"Munda," exclaimed Felicia. "We must get hold of Munda."

"My God," said a voice from the corner. Fernando was still on the deck of the storm-tossed ship, but he was at last able to speak. "How do you propose to do that?"

The mother ignored her son's question and, with Caridad's help, took the girl to her room.

After two days of calls to the telephone dispatch office in Piedra Negra, word got to Munda, who was staying at her mother's shack five miles out of town, that her employers were asking for her immediate return. Confident that her mother's nephritic crisis had passed and more than eager to leave the stagnant backwaters of Piedra Negra, Munda took the train that same night and was back in her old kitchen at exactly 5:32 the following morning. Felicia did not let her unpack before demanding an explanation, and Munda, who had never lost an opportunity to tell a story, no matter the circumstances or the time, obliged.

Mariano Zayas, an ex-seminary student, had been Mirta's platonic paramour. Their relationship had been a strange one no one in town was ever able to figure out. Mariano spent whole afternoons reading to Mirta from the Bible; she sat by him smiling, staring off into the distance. The men mocked him, claiming that the priests in the seminary had cut off his balls, while the women marveled that there was at least one man in Piedra Negra whose mind was not exclusively on sex. When Mirta went to the capital, Mariano Zayas was so dejected that he joined a group of anti-government guerrillas in the cordillera that ran across the northern part of the district. This bunch of slovenly boys had gone to the mountains for any number of reasons but revolution. Their acts were limited to robbing livestock from poor farmers and occasionally blocking the one road in and out of Piedra Negra. On one of their sorties, Mariano, weighed down by four fat guinea hens, had tripped and fallen, and the farmer in pursuit had hacked him to pieces with his machete.

All that could be done now, Munda and Felicia agreed at six in the morning, was to send the girl back to her parents, which they did that same day, hiring for the job a taxi driver who, neighborhood gossip maintained, was homosexual and would thus be immune to Mirta's bewitching beauty.

Middle-aged, timeworn Munda stayed behind. The workmen resumed their previous lives and came to the house only when called, the neighborhood was soon restored to the composure and order that had long been its trademarks, and the animosity which had threatened a breach in the family left as with the tide. Rosa and Felicia made their peace and fell back into their instinctive complicity, maintaining the domestic concord which Fernando would find impossible to betray, at least openly.

Antón returned to his creatures. But while he collected his specimens in the scorching afternoon sun, Mirta hung suspended just beyond him, so that when he looked up from his labors, she was the first thing he saw; and at night, as his eyelids drooped with sleep, her naked body floating at the foot of his bed was the omega of his days. In a few months, time eroded her features and flattened her figure. Much as he tried to sharpen the focus of his vision, memory betrayed him: Mirta was gone from his days, leaving behind a blank space framed by his imagination, into which henceforth he tried to fit every woman he loved.

As far as Felicia was concerned, the exorcism had worked like a dream.

PART

TWO

STORM

*A*ntón awoke to a day heavy with clouds. The air was still and sodden, and the late August heat, which normally blazed and made everything sparkle with life, was a wool blanket that dropped on birds and flowers and left behind the barely perceptible smell of catastrophe. He had had a dream that he was at the seashore and a giant wave like a mouth had curled over the beach and swallowed him. He slid down a narrow red tube to a concrete swimming pool the size of the city, in which two wedding-cake figurines floated. A whirlpool formed between them and he was sucked in. When he reached bottom, his body stuck headfirst in the drain hole. On the other side was a huge brown birthmark the shape of Iceland and on it was his grandmother, watching him squirm through.

He kept the dream to himself. When Munda brought him his toast and *café con leche*, she announced that a hurricane was heading straight for the capital. His mother was buying provisions, and his father was at the shoe factory securing it against evil winds. Antón gulped down his breakfast and went outside.

The poinciana drooped sadly and the roses by the side of the house had refused to open. He walked to the grove of banana trees by the far hedges where no one would see him and sat on a stone bench streaked dirty green with mold, a relic Felicia had brought with her from Corral Falso. He saw a cat cross the far corner of the yard, and he threw a stone at it.

He recalled the mother cat who had eaten her babies and a bad taste filled his mouth, which he tried to overcome by whistling. Munda had taken the cat to the stream and drowned it. She came back saying that it had the devil in it, and you can't kill the devil, so it would return sooner or later.

A strong breeze had picked up and the banana trees were rubbing together, making a rasping noise. He heard rain thudding on the broad leaves above him. His mother's voice, dim through wind and water, called his name. For some time he ignored her, like a tropical hero challenging the caprice of the gods. The sky turned black and the rain grew stronger. He held on to the bench until the rushing wind drowned out his mother's voice. Finally he ran, the water stinging his face and the wind pulling at his clothes.

In the back porch Rosa waited, transformed from soft, resplendent flower into the flaming bush of righteousness. She cursed, she yelled, she asked where he'd been and if he didn't know she was worried sick. The boy waited in silence for her anger to subside, all the while fixing big liquid eyes on her who was his mother no longer but sister to the wrath intensifying outside. When she was finished and her attention was diverted by the preparations, he changed his clothes and went to the living room and looked out the window toward the street. Felicia had told him that during the hurricane of 1926 the wind had blown all manner of things past her house: cows lifted up out of their fields, porpoises that had been sucked out of the sea, cars with people still in them, a sailboat that was later found lodged in the belfry of a church.

The boy expected similar marvels of this storm, and he waited for anything unusual that would reward his patience. He saw only crumpled newspapers and a cardboard box rolling down the street.

Absorbed in his newfound belief that the world was a lie, Antón went into the kitchen, where he found his grandmother and his great-uncle Antonio drenched to the shoes sitting at the table drinking a bowl of fish soup.

"What's up, boy?" asked his great-uncle.

He loomed like a mythical figure before Antón. Something about the man and his manner—fearless, constant—drew the boy's attention like a magnet.

A revolver lay next to the water glass. Antonio noticed the boy looking at it and, after a slurp of soup, pulled the napkin from his lap and covered the gun.

"It's for mosquitoes," Antonio said through his Buddha smile. Then he spoke of the storm: how the streets next to the port had flooded and the city looked like a tropical Venice; how the plate glass from a store window had flown into the countryside, where it decapitated a palm tree; and how a nun praying in the garden of her convent had ascended heavenward in a column of wind but was released short of her destination and had landed, still clutching her breviary, on the roof of a bordello in the town of Arañas.

"Nothing like that ever happens around here," said the boy.

"I should say not," said the uncle; then speaking to Felicia he added, "I told Fernando this is no place to raise a boy. He'll grow up to be a boor."

Antonio finished his soup and tucked the gun into his belt. Felicia met him by the door and whispered something in his ear, which Antón, much as he craned, was unable to hear.

Before leaving, Antonio asked the boy what he was reading.

"*The Sons of Captain Grant*," the boy answered.

"On the twenty-sixth of July of 1864, with a strong breeze blowing in from the Northeast, a magnificent yacht steamed full speed ahead over the waves of the English Channel," Antonio recited from memory. He stood up and, with a final wave of his hand, disappeared into the rain.

When he was fully gone, that is, after Felicia closed the door and picked up the empty bowl from the table, Antón asked what the gun was for. Felicia's answer, that he had received death threats from one of his clients, was too quick, as if she had prepared it ahead of time. Was she lying again? He thought he saw tears in his grandmother's eyes and decided against challenging her. Instead, he asked for a bowl of soup. Of all the people he knew, his great-uncle was most like the world, unpredictable and full of mystery.

Antonio reappeared at Felicia's house two weeks later. Rosa and Fernando were away on a trip and Felicia was teaching her grandson the game of canasta. Brother and sister embraced. Antonio sat at the table and asked for the bottle of whiskey. The boy listened.

It happened that Paco Verdún, the hack novelist better known as Tadeo Latraso, had persuaded Antonio to join him in one last adventure before the ravages of senescence fell upon them. Paco had learned through a nephew of his that several underground university groups were planning an attack on the presidential palace, an almost impregnable edifice in the shape of a pyramid Sotelo had ordered built after the tenth attempt on his life had almost succeeded.

Had the invitation come a year or two earlier, Antonio told his sister, he would have declined. Now, however, the mood of the country was different. The middle class was outraged at the dictator's corruption and at his overweight and vulgar wife. In addition, the guerrillas operating in the countryside were demoralizing the regular army. Intelligence reports had it that the palace guard was ready to drop its weapons and join the rebellion at the least instigation, and that the police were none too willing to protect a government that had not paid them in six months. It was only logical that the attack on Sotelo's pyramid would bring about the fall of the government.

Antón was dizzy with excitement. He had never known a conspirator before. He suppressed the urge to give a whoop and instead tried to become invisible.

Paco figured that he and Antonio would be in minimal danger. Their role would be primarily defensive—watching over the left flank of the main force of one hundred students. Given the speed with which the attack was to take place, there was little chance that the two men would be involved in any confrontation.

The planning meetings were held at Paco's ranch, the one

where Lucho had first met Jill. According to Antonio's description, it was a garish place with suggestive Grecian statues sprouting amid the overgrown bushes of what had once been a Louis XIV garden. In the back, toward a pool surrounded by fake Corinthian columns, a half dozen goats roamed loose, munching on whatever flowers still grew. The students spent their time as the young will, feverishly planning, arguing, and discoursing on their aims. Antonio gave his advice only when approached. Paco, on the other hand, joined the spirited discussions, which went on for days and nights without respite and which ranged in topic from the layout of the uncountable rooms and secret passageways inside the pyramid, to Hegelian dialectics, to the most fitting way of executing the despot once they captured him.

One of the leaders, Alberto Johansen, a disturbing fellow with icy blue eyes, suggested that Sotelo be walled in the palace so that his pharaoh complex could be fully satisfied; his rival, Federico Ortega, who had the pink cheeks of a mama's boy, was of the opinion that Sotelo should be thrown to the sharks in the harbor and that all presidents and leaders of the world, including the Pope, should be invited to witness the fate of those who violated the trust of the masses. Finally, after a thin dark girl with too much sadness in her face screamed that Leandro Sotelo should be hung from his penis outside the cathedral and all those he had imprisoned and tortured be allowed to carve their initials on his body, Paco stood up, stretched his arms before him in a magnanimous gesture, and quieted what had, by now, turned into a Jacobin rabble.

He was smiling broadly, so that his gilded molar gleamed with the light from the candelabrum overhead. His thinning hair was slicked back without a part. His nose, broken by a policeman's club during his activist days, was flat and meaty. He wore his usual garb, a blue blazer over a tight white shirt that accentuated his bulging stomach. The shirt was unbuttoned to just below the sternum, exposing a solid gold crucifix as big as an archbishop's nestled on an unruly mass of gray chest hair. He looked more like a boxing promoter than a literary man, yet the young upstarts looked on him as a legend. They had all heard of his exploits in the twenties during the rule of Liscano Gautier, when he had rightfully earned the epithet "macho."

Paco Verdún's speech was a grandiloquent piece of oratory that began *Friends, compatriots, colleagues* and went on to allude to all the lofty ideals that sprouted like weeds from the gutters of history. Only a man who had never believed in anything since he took shape in his mother's womb could have given such a speech; only Paco Verdún, with his stubby grocer's fingers and his peasant's paunch and his 253 novels and his trysts with mysterious elegant women in the bars of the city—*I haven't paid for it yet*, he liked to brag, *and I never will*—could have lulled the crowd of bloodthirsty bourgeois youth with his song of vacuous sentiments and worn-out platitudes. He invoked the fatherland; he praised the spirit of democracy to which so many of the country's youth had sacrificed their lives; he pleaded with them to remember the founding fathers—"and mothers," the sad girl in the back rejoined—whose struggles for liberty they were continuing. He urged them to keep in mind the purpose at hand, not to seek vengeance for wrongs done against them or their comrades, but to ensure success by putting their bodies, their souls, their very blood, into the enterprise. If we succeed, he said, the whole country will rally behind us and tyranny will have breathed its last. If we succeed, our names will stand alongside the great heroes of history—"and heroines," the sad girl insisted. And heroines, he added. Leandro Sotelo will be tried in court and he will be subject to the laws of our constitution. Let his crimes, not our actions, condemn him. Let him live with the horrible truth of his life, and when he dies, let our outrage go with him to the grave, then let us pause and look to our future, as bright a star as ever shone over the sea.

When Paco finished there was a momentary silence, which was soon followed by a roar of hurrahs. Tears fell, eyes blazed, arms waved, fists shot into the air, and all hearts beat to a single pulse. All but Johansen's, that is. Antonio watched him from the rear of the now empty hall. Johansen leaned against the corner smoking, his lizard eyes shifting this way and that. Paco approached him, transformed back into the pudgy, balding man who feared routine as much as he feared death, and they said words to each other, too low for Antonio to understand.

The students resumed their preparations with even greater zeal after Paco's speech. Antonio pitied them. Many would lose their lives, and if the attack on the pyramid failed, others would be captured and sent through the torture mills of the Sotelo regime. While every step of the attack had been choreographed, they had neglected to consider failure and retreat.

Good revolutionaries, mused Antonio, pouring himself another whiskey and speaking directly to his grandnephew, must temper their idealism with the instinct for survival. Temerity leads to death and death to the grave. Here then the paradox: The best revolutionary of all is the one who is in it for adventure or for personal gain, like Paco and him. They had survived countless street battles in their youth, not because of their lofty goals but because in wanting to touch the face of death—the ultimate adventure, the ultimate power—they had also known when to pull their hands away and run for cover.

And so the effect the speech had on the group compounded

Antonio's skepticism. It was Paco, after all, who had dragged him into this affair, and he could not quite come to terms with his friend's empty rhetoric, the silly call to sacrifice, not from a man whose credo, whether fighting governments or seducing women, had been *Dulce et decorum est in lecto mori*. Then there was the intimate exchange with Johansen; that disturbed Antonio most of all, for he saw a shadow spread across Paco's forehead and his eyelids droop with the weight of a secret too heavy to bear.

Later, Antonio approached his friend and said, "It smells like the underside of an outhouse."

Paco agreed and looked openly at him. For once his face showed despair, smothered by shame.

"You must go," Paco said. "There is a bus leaving town at eight in the morning."

"How do you propose I get there? That's five miles."

"Walk. If you leave now, you'll make it in plenty of time. There won't be anyone on the road at this hour."

"And you?"

Paco did not answer. Instead, he avoided Antonio's gaze and focused on a plaster bust of a Roman emperor—Hadrian? Marcus Aurelius?—on the broad classical forehead of which one of the students had scribbled *The empire of fools is over*.

When Antonio reached San Juan del Llano, he was walking on the water of blisters. His feet were gnarled and swollen inside his Nacionales, awful shoes for walking which he wore out of some twisted sense of familial allegiance. It was four in the morning and the streets were empty but for three half-starved dogs that tormented him on the way to the bus depot. It had not rained since the hurricane, and the hot wind from the countryside blew down the main street like a river of misery. The depot was closed, but there was a light on in the café next door. Inside, two travelers were sleeping on benches against the wall. The attendant, a boy no older than fifteen, sat on a stool behind the counter reading a comic book.

"Give me a brandy."

The boy wiped a shot glass carefully with his apron and set a bottle on the counter. Antonio took bottle and glass to a table and tried to make himself comfortable. The brandy dulled the pain in his feet and he was able to rest somewhat. At six-thirty, as the light of dawn broke the shadows of the establishment, a man woke him.

"Passing through?"

He was a big mulatto with a wide face and faint lines of gray in his hair. His suit was streaked with red dust.

"Yes. What's it to you?"

Antonio put his feet down and a double current of pain shot up his legs and coalesced in his groin.

"Just curious, man. Mind if I sit?"

He spoke with the lilt of the eastern part of the island. He took his hat off and called to the boy for a glass. The shape of his smile had not changed.

When the boy came, Antonio paid for his drinks and ordered a coffee.

"I'm a salesman, but in this town I might as well be a pauper," the man said.

"What do you sell?"

"Anything I can—ties, notions, costume jewelry, you name it, I can sell it. Anywhere else but here. Jews without Christ, these people are. They wear the same clothes year after year and pass the rags on to their children when they die. Right, boy?" he called behind him. "When was the last time your mother bought you a shirt?"

"Leave my mother out of it," the boy answered.

"Where are you headed?" the salesman asked Antonio. "You look like a city man to me."

Antonio stood up to leave and tried his best not to give away the discomfort in his legs. He felt dizzy from the drinks.

"Watch it out there. The wind smells of death," the man warned him. And then to no one in particular he added, "Just passing through. He doesn't even have a suitcase, but he's just passing through."

"What if they followed you here?" Antón spoke up for the first time.

"Boy, you have to be a weasel in these matters," said the great-uncle. "Whoever tried to follow me is just now chasing his tail somewhere east of the city."

That same day, Felicia joined in, while he zigzagged across the province, the army had surrounded Paco Verdún's house and crushed the conspiracy. According to the latest reports, only two conspirators had been captured, one of them Paco. The rest were dead.

"They say the house is in ruins. The army brought in tanks and mortars, and those who surrendered were mowed down mercilessly, including a pregnant woman," Felicia said.

Antonio nodded and smiled bitterly.

"My feet are killing me," he said. "Help me off with these shoes."

Felicia rubbed her brother's feet and washed them with olive oil and alcohol. She tried to get her grandson to go to bed, but the boy protested and Antonio sided with him. He made Antón promise that he wouldn't tell a soul about what he'd heard.

"Do you think Paco was the one who informed?" Felicia asked her brother.

"It seems obvious."

"Why did he do it?"

"I don't know. Rub my feet."

Antonio added that he was too tired to move. He would go home to his wife, Julia, in the morning.

The official announcement of the government's victory over the terrorists was made the next day at a televised press conference given by Colonel Zalariaga, the officer in charge of the operation.

He described the sortie to the last detail, illustrating his narrative with maps and charts and blown-up photographs of Paco Verdún's house. He boasted that the enemy had suffered severe casualties and that his fearless men had uncovered the largest cache of arms and ammunition ever in the history of the nation, as well as letters of support from the governments of China, Vietnam, North Korea and a list of assassination targets that included not only the great leader himself but also all members of his cabinet and Bebita Santa Ana, the Queen of the Bolero. Standing over the table and saluting the flag with his field marshal's baton, he bellowed that the effeminate and cowardly opposition had breathed its last sigh. He demanded that the few gangsters still at large give up their arms and surrender to the authorities lest a similar fate befall them. Then he did an about-face and marched out of the room, his oversize haunches quivering to the beat of his clicking heels.

At the same time, the newspapers of the city, which vied unscrupulously with one another for the most scandalous and sensational news, printed graphic photographs provided by the authorities depicting corpses riddled with bullet holes and burnt to cinders. Rather than deter any more acts of terrorism, however, the gory publicity had the unfortunate effect of wounding the insurgents' pride and precipitating a spate of bombings and assassinations that made the city tremble. Every night dozens of explosions kept the residents awake and shaking in their beds; every morning bodies appeared in pools of blood on street corners, outside churches, in front of the Lions' Club Central Office, or else hanging from the streetlamps that lined the Boulevard of Fallen Heroes. These events became so common that the newspapers relegated them to the back pages under the obituaries and filled their front pages once more with the reports of multiple murders, nefarious robberies, and bizarre births that had previously been the mainstays of their style. Inside a month, the sale of newspapers was up to what it had been, and the citizens, having all but forgotten the revolution, were able to sleep at night and carry on their daily business convinced that the world was not coming to an end and that life was moving along on its proper course.

By then, Antonio had resumed his usual activities, disregarding the death threats that his wife and secretary handed him on a daily basis along with the mail and phone messages. He walked the streets oblivious to the dangers around him and enjoyed the sunshine and the shapely girls strolling by on their lunch hour as if he were an anonymous citizen.

His sense that bullets might come and go but that none would ever have his name was shattered one Wednesday morning when José María Unanue, his personal taxi driver, told him that Paco Verdún had been found in a woman's apartment with his throat slit. Rumor had it that the secret police were behind it.

The news would not have been so much of a shock—after all,

Paco had, of his own initiative, opened the wolf's mouth and put his head in it—were it not for the fact that Antonio was on his way to visit a widow whose estate he had settled and whom he had been "consoling" on a weekly basis for over a year. The possibility that he, too, might be found lying in a pool of blood in a lady's boudoir was more than he was willing to concede to his bravado.

Antonio had José María Unanue drive him straight to Felicia's house, where he could hide in relative safety. He directed the driver to let Julia know that he was safe and to bring back some clothes and his pet parrots.

For her part, Felicia invented a story, which she spread through the neighborhood, that her brother's wife had thrown him out, and she embellished it by making Julia out to be such a miserable and vengeful wretch that all the neighbors treated Antonio with special kindness. Sometimes he put on a face so full of the sorrow of existence that the women's eyes welled with tears; other times he made believe he was writing poems to his wife, sitting in the back yard with pen and pad and looking wistfully at the sky while the ladies visiting his sister sighed with sympathy. His acting was so effective that they came to agree with Felicia that Julia was the worst woman that ever lived.

Brother and sister enjoyed the charade and reveled in Antonio's sequestration, which returned them to the golden years when all that mattered was the daily machinations of their youth, but it was another matter next door.

Despite the political turmoil, the National Shoe Company, which Fernando managed, had prospered beyond anyone's expectations. Demand for Nacionales had reached a point where the company could not keep up with it and people were paying upward of fifty dollars a pair in the black market. Billboards had sprung up all over the countryside with the face of Bebita Santa Ana, the one and only Queen of the Bolero, saying MY LOVE WEARS NACIONALES. The advertising campaign, designed by Fernando as a way of countering an American company's incursion into the national market, not only destroyed the competition; it also made Fernando a marketing genius among the business community that had long and reluctantly deferred to the powers of American big business in such matters, and increased his and Rosa's visibility, bringing them a stone's throw away from the highest social circles. The day after Antonio came to hide at Felicia's house, Rosa and Fernando received a personal invitation from the Minister of Commerce and Industry to a gala reception honoring the president of the United Fruit Company. They were to sit at the table of honor, next to the American ambassador and his wife.

Fernando was troubled, and more than a little anxious about having his uncle, a political renegade, hiding out at his mother's house. Rosa was incensed and spent three days in bed with an attack of nerves and rage, which subsided only after Dr. Figueras injected her with enough codeine "to drop a horse."

They attended the reception, and much as Rosa's beauty had enchanted the American ambassador, they were all but ignored by the other officials there. The Minister of Commerce had difficulty remembering who they were, and apart from the initial greeting as they passed through the reception line, he did not speak to them. He spent the whole evening ingratiating himself with the president of the United Fruit Company, a bulldog-faced man who had never learned to smile and whose only words during dinner were complaints about the salty food and the strong coffee. Rosa was elated that she was able to teach the ambassador some new dance steps, and seeing her excitement, Fernando kept from her his disappointment and his suspicion that he had been shunned because of his uncle.

The next day, unable to contain himself any longer, Fernando went next door to confront Antonio. The uncle was feeding his three parrots, which he was training to recite poetry. One could already say the first four lines of a sonnet by Góngora. The other two, Antonio feared, were too stupid or too vulgar to learn more than a few random phrases from Poe's "The Raven."

"The government is not interested in me," said Antonio, passing a cracker to one of the stupid ones.

"In me, in me," echoed the parrot.

"So long as I stay out of their way, nothing will happen. Besides, I needed the vacation."

"Vacation, vacation."

"Well, they killed Paco."

"Paco was in the thick of it. Nicolás Campión and his gang sent word from the mountains to get rid of the university group."

"University group, university group."

"Why?"

"If the attack on the palace had been successful, the students would have taken over the government and Campión would have been left in the wilderness with nothing to do but put down his arms and kiss their well-educated asses. Listen to this."

Antonio gave the intelligent parrot a cracker and snapped his fingers. The bird gave a squawk, followed by "When in disgrace with fortune and men's eyes . . ."

"That's amazing," exclaimed the nephew. "It has an English accent."

"He learned it from a record," said the uncle. He continued. "They played a trick on Paco. Johansen, most probably, got him to have the meetings at his house, then blackmailed him into betraying the students."

"Blackmail?"

"It wouldn't have been difficult."

At this point Felicia, who had overheard the conversation from her bedroom, appeared in her nightgown.

"If Paco had been such a good friend, he wouldn't have involved you in this madness," Felicia said, waving her index finger at her brother.

Fernando remembered the reason for his visit. He asked Antonio why he had joined the plot; why the police, not the rebels, had killed Paco Verdún; how, knowing the dangers he was exposing them to, had he the gall to force himself upon them?

Antonio sat back on the couch. He gave them a tired smile and lit a cigarette.

"A man gets to a point in life when his faculties are no longer what they were. His mind gets brittle, his body sags, he can barely get himself out of bed in the morning. When this happens, there are two things to do. Either he lets time flatten him into an amorphous shape, without sex, without mind, without spirit . . ."

He paused, looked at the ceiling, let the smoke out slowly through his nostrils, then gave a bleary look to his nephew.

". . . or he tries to recapture, at least for a moment, the surge of energy he felt as a young man. A man wants to be immortal. My last hurrah. My last sigh."

"That's ridiculous," said Fernando.

"I'm getting old. The police won't come. The rebels won't. Leave me to my parrots and prepare yourselves. The government is going to fall soon. All those guys you saw at the reception— they were jockeying for position like rats about to abandon ship, and if you don't think the Americans knew it, then you don't know the Americans. Worry about Nicolás Campión. He is what's coming."

Notwithstanding Felicia's complaints about the birds' racket, which made the house sound like a primeval jungle, and the animal smell that hung in the air and was absorbed by the walls and furniture so that no amount of air freshener or pine cleaner or, when neither of these worked, gasoline sprinkled in the corners, could eradicate it, Antonio kept the parrots and continued their training, determined to make them the most literate birds on the island. For hours at a stretch, he drilled into them the sonnets of Shakespeare, the satires of Juvenal, and the odes of Pindar.

Whenever he could, Antón sat with his great-uncle. After his grandmother's saints, the beautiful green birds with red heads were a welcome change. Soon Antón's attention was diverted to the literature Antonio recited and the boy inadvertently became the fourth pupil in the afternoon sessions. At first he lagged behind the stupidest of the three parrots, but in a few days he was competing with Sophocles, the most learned bird.

Felicia was justifiably concerned that poetry would lead her grandson away from the path of holiness, but there was little she could do to contain her brother's infectious enthusiasm. The immediate results of the lessons charmed Rosa and Fernando. Antón could recite at will, before company, sonnets by Góngora and Quevedo, a poem or two by Mallarmé, and whole sections of Milton's *Paradise Lost*. His teachers were unimpressed and after a few weeks, his parents began receiving notes from them regarding his bizarre behavior in class and his declining grades. The last note, direct from the principal's office requesting a conference, came when the parents were away on one of their trips, and it fell on Felicia to visit the School of the Most Holy Sisters of the Resurrection.

The principal, a brittle old nun who looked as if she owned all the goodness in the world, warned her that the boy's sudden change from ideal student to lazy ne'er-do-well, coupled with his constant recitation of poetry too sophisticated for his young mind to comprehend, was a sure sign that the devil was playing with his spirit. If such a thing was not stopped as soon as it was detected by those who knew best, he would lose the path to God forever. They were all praying for him, the saintly woman said, but prayer alone could not do it. Someone was corrupting him. It was up to Felicia, who, the principal could tell from her demeanor, was a lady of great moral stricture and devotion, to protect her grandson from the evil that was stalking him.

When Felicia arrived home, her brother was taking his after-lunch siesta in the bedroom. Normally she would have waited for him to wake, but her agitation that day was such that she barged into the room and shook him by the shoulder, ignoring that most irksome habit of his of sleeping without his clothes on.

She ordered him to dress, then went into the kitchen and asked Caridad to make coffee and serve it to them in the living room.

By the time Antonio showed up, the coffee was lukewarm. He refused to drink it and complained that she had spoiled a most wonderful dream. He was living in a big white house surrounded by vast expanses of green and perfect lawn in a suburb of Detroit, Michigan. Next door, in an even bigger house with a swimming pool in the shape of the Caspian Sea, lived none other than God Himself. He was just about to cross the yard and introduce himself to his distinguished neighbor when he felt the cold hand of the Angel of Reality calling him back.

Felicia told him about the meeting with the principal.

"She knows you are here, I have no doubt. Mercedes Garcés must have told her."

"The world would be a grand place without religion or politics. It would be like heaven, like Detroit, Michigan."

"Detroit, Michigan," squawked the stupidest parrot.

Antonio turned to it and gave it a peanut. It was the first time it had spoken since Antón joined them.

"I will teach him geography, I will teach him arithmetic, history, science. I will teach him the twenty-three lessons for a superior mind. In no time he will know more than his teachers! And curse the lot of them!"

Antonio started with his nephew's lessons that same afternoon. Each was named after a famous person, real or fictional, and contained any number of postulates derived from a central theme. The first lesson, for example, he titled "The Lesson of Descartes"; its theme stated that the self was the center of all perception, even the perception of God. To diminish one's self, then, would bring about the diminishment of God. The second lesson was "The Lesson of the Duchess of Alba"; the third, "The Lesson of W. C. Fields"; and so on. In this manner, the uncle proceeded to teach the boy a vast body of eccentric facts and obscure anecdotes that bore no relationship to each other other than that they occurred to Antonio during the hour of instruction.

As a result, Antón was able to list Euclid's ten postulates at the same time that he could recite the complete lineage of the House of Hapsburg, down to Carlos the Bewitched. He could also relate to his dumbfounded teachers that Archimedes had found a way to express the number of grains of sand that it would take to fill the whole of the universe; that Philip III of Spain had died because the proper palace functionary could not be found to remove the brazier he was sitting next to; and how Louis XIV had said, after his army was defeated at Blenheim, "How could God do this to me after all I have done for Him?"

The last was more than the principal of the school could tolerate. She convinced the parish priest that the boy was a heretic in training and should be expelled as soon as possible, before he tainted the other students. Had political events on the island not intervened, it is doubtful that Antón would have remained in the school much longer than a week.

THE FALL

*N*ews of the fall of Sotelo reached the family as all important news did, by word of mouth, at dawn, before newspapers came out and radios were turned on. By six o'clock the family was gathered in Felicia's living room drinking coffee and rounds of whiskey, toasting the end of the old order and the beginning of the new. Only Antonio looked glum, refusing to praise Nicolás Campión and complaining about having been awakened at such an uncivilized hour.

By ten in the morning the family had received eight different versions of the facts, and it took the men, their faculties slowed by the fog of whiskey, until early afternoon to discard the rumors and piece together a fairly accurate version of the events. They learned that after a battle in which half the regular forces defected to the rebels, Sotelo, complacent with age and wealth, finally acquiesced to his wife's wish to leave the country. He struck a deal with Campión whereby he would relinquish the presidency as long as he was allowed to escape. And so, on the night before the rebel leader declared his victory, the President of the republic flew out of the country with his wife and children, a half dozen of his closest associates with their families, two mistresses and thirteen illegitimate children, five fighting dogs, 175 suitcases, fifty million dollars, and his personal valet, an old black man rumored, but never proven, to be his father.

Campión marched into the capital city without a single shot being fired. Policemen and soldiers burned their uniforms, buried their guns, and joined the crowd that welcomed the rebels. They arrived in tanks, trucks, convertibles, motorcycles, mule carts, bicycles, scooters; in short, anything that moved. The column grew as it approached the city, so that it seemed that half the young men in the country had been in the mountains. At its head, riding the turret of a Sherman tank festooned with flowers and rosaries, was Nicolás Campión, the glory and triumph of the revolution himself. That same night he settled into Sotelo's office at the top of the pyramid. From there, he would proceed to undo the old society and create the new.

He wasted no time and gave his first balcony speech the following morning. It was an extravagant oration that lasted from seven until ten. Unused to political events starting so early, a large portion of the population of the city missed most of the speech, engaged as they were in waking, washing, dressing, and other activities that civilized society deems fitting for the morning hours. As Antonio had once said, "Politics and prostitution are pursuits of the deepest dark of night."

Up early as usual, Antón had turned on the television while

the adults slept off the previous day's celebration and heard it all: the humble beginning during which, in a barely audible voice, Nicolás Campión thanked all those who had fought alongside him and mourned those others who had given up their life for the mother country; then the long description of the armed struggle against Sotelo, from its inception in the rooming house where Campión lived as a university student to the insurrectionist period in the mountains. He called himself a simple servant of the people and the "Messenger of History." He said there would be no more hatred and no more war. The flag of peace would fly next to the flags of justice and equality. In almost the same breath he dared anyone to challenge those flags, and he added that the country had to be ready always to repel any foreign or native attempts to control it. "We must root out our enemies. The rivers will run red with their blood." He concluded with the slogan that became the cry of the revolution: "The land will stand."

Antón, infected with the surge of emotion the speech aroused in him, for once did not complain when his father sent him to the pharmacy to buy the papers. Acevedo had taped a large poster of Campión on the window with a hand-painted sign under it reading, ¡VIVA CAMPIÓN! ¡MUERTE AL PEZ! The pharmacist met him at the door, flushed and excited in a way Antón had never seen before. He treated him to a Pepsi-Cola and refused to charge him for the three newspapers. Donizetti was blaring from the back room. Gutiérrez the constable sat in his usual place, his cap and nightstick on the table, drinking brandy from a beaker. As Antón left the store he could hear the two men singing in Italian. Outside, the street was awash in January light, everything cleansed and new and in place. Someone yelled from across the way, *¡Viva la libertad!* and he heard himself echoing back the phrase without misgiving.

Back home he handed his father the papers and he heard the steam cooker already going in the kitchen and he smelled onions frying as he had every day of his life. Felicia was on the phone. Antonio sat on the sofa frowning. The revolution, it appeared, had passed like an angel over the family.

In the afternoon after lunch, Fernando suggested they all take a drive downtown to see what was happening. Rosa objected, claiming it was too dangerous, all sorts of ruffians out with guns, but her warnings fell on deaf ears. Antonio went back to bed and the rest drove away: Fernando at the wheel, Eduardo next to him, and, in the back seat, Antón and Felicia. As they sped down the boulevard, people shouted slogans and waved flags at them and they waved back. At the entrance to the port, as close to the presidential palace as they could get, the streets were clogged with cars honking and young couples dancing and rebels in their fatigues with their weapons slung over the shoulder, looking heroic and posing for cameras. The García-Turners left the car and spoke to several of the soldiers. One of them, barely out of his teens, was reluctant to talk about his experiences in the mountains but eagerly signed an autograph for Antón. Another, with his long black hair tied in a ponytail, gave him a wooden crucifix he had been wearing around his neck.

As the crowd grew, so did Fernando's discomfort. He said he was concerned about the traffic on the way back and, after some prodding, managed to get his son, mother, and brother in the car. They returned late to a worried Rosa, who refused to speak to her husband and made Antón go to bed right after supper.

The next morning Antón went to Felicia's house, eager to show Antonio his souvenirs and resume his lessons, but his great-uncle was not there, nor were the parrots. Felicia explained that

Antonio had gone back to his house now that it was safe, and she tried to console the boy with milk and toast, which he declined. His brain was at best half full with a soup of facts, numbers, poems, dates, formulas which bore no connection to each other. What did it matter that he could trace the evolution of man from Australopithecus through Cro-Magnon, or that he could list the twelve labors of Hercules? The world was still an unknown, and in the soup floated question marks like flaccid, overcooked noodles.

He left his grandmother's house and went home to the back porch. There, in the shade, memories came to him like leaves falling off a tree: Matutino the Bull and Mirta the Beautiful, now a featureless shadow, and one of his teachers at the school who had mocked him in front of the class for not praying in the proper manner, with hands clasped in front of him and eyes upturned —*like a Murillo Madonna*, Antonio had said when he heard of it. But there was something hanging over him just beyond his reach. It had to do with his grandmother—an ominous and bitter thing, too far back in the past to recall. The effort left him in a daze, and he felt as if he was being sucked into a deep hole and there was no one around to pull him out. Half the city was still celebrating; the other half, including his family, had returned to their normal lives. There was work to do and business to take care of. It was then that Antón sensed momentarily that radical change is illusory, and that the slow current of time flows on unimpeded by the earth-shatters of history. This last seed, covered over by the loam of his youth, was planted in him by Antonio, whose one true gift to the boy was the belief that the only thing we can count on is the irremediable passage of time, which does not stop with one's death but continues in spite of it. Understanding that, Antón would understand everything.

He would understand, for example, why Campión was in such a hurry to impose his changes, why his "Statement for a People's Mandate," delivered in another of his epic speeches merely one week after he took power, called for the complete restructuring of the society inside a year and imposed severe penalties for those who slowed the pace of the revolution.

In one of his occasional visits to Felicia's house, Antonio called Campión the most dangerous ruler in the history of the island, not really explaining his statement but adding that every promise he made was not to the people but to himself and that he was turning the country into a monument to Nicolás Campión. Then Antonio changed the conversation and asked Felicia for a cup of coffee. His great-uncle's comment sounded harsh and cynical to Antón and threatened the excitement he had felt the previous week. Wasn't everyone saying that Campión had saved the country? When the boy asked what had become of Sophocles and the other two parrots, his uncle replied that he had sold them for stew, an answer that further confirmed the man's cynicism and kept Antón from ever approaching his uncle in quite the same way again. Antonio would have sold him for stew, too, if he'd had the chance.

Not long after Antonio's visit, rumors began to circulate that the government had started arresting and executing former members of the Sotelo government. The García-Turners were not overly upset. Some measure of purgation seemed not only necessary but, given some of the individuals in question—henchmen, torturers, executioners—it was laudable. Other stories came to the family, of people whose houses and cars had been expropriated and whose businesses had been shut down. It appeared that Campión was making good the final sentence of the "Statement for a People's Mandate": "The bourgeoisie has breathed its last."

In the following weeks, the face of Nicolás Campión began to appear everywhere in the city with disturbing regularity. It loomed on billboards where once Bebita Santa Ana had smiled, plugging Nacionales, "the shoes of the nation." It replaced calendar prints of the Sacred Heart of Jesus on the walls of the poor, and it flashed conspicuously on television in the middle of a soap opera or a variety show. Political speeches went on for hours, and the radio waves were crammed with endless discussions which, Fernando maintained, had cured his insomnia. Two months into the new regime, Antón came home using phrases like the "struggle of the proletariat" and the "curse of capitalism," which he had learned in a new course at school called "Political Awareness," taught not by the nuns but by a lady in uniform, who told the children that religion was no longer necessary and that from then on their future would be assured by Papá Nicolás. Such a development may have worried the boy's parents, but not Felicia. She was secretly glad that the principal had gotten her just deserts.

Felicia's attentions were more immediately focused on the food shortages. Meals, which she had previously planned weeks in advance with military efficiency, were now haphazard affairs, using whatever ingredients were available at the last minute. The aggravation she suffered as a result and the almost daily spats she had with Luciano the grocer got to be too much and led to a breakdown that put her in bed for two days—neurasthenia was Acevedo's diagnosis—after which she agreed to Munda's suggestion to have Luciano, who was well aware of the family's eating habits, deliver whatever the wholesaler happened to bring in.

"Tell him I want no liver, not even if he gets a truckload," she advised Munda. "And no *bacalao*. And if the *chayotes* are brown around the edges he can feed them to the hogs. If he brings corn, check the husks for worms. The fresh fish—make sure the eyes are clear, not milky."

And so she continued her instructions. Munda disregarded them and, except for the liver and the *bacalao*, took what the grocer brought unquestioningly and prepared it as best she could, using plenty of spices and bathing it in sauces of her own concoction.

The García-Turners viewed these changes with no small amount of distaste and with disapproval tempered by resignation, but unlike many other people in their circle who were leaving the island in droves, they lacked the acumen and the political intuition to see the inconveniences as signs of something larger and darker growing just under the surface of their existence. Fernando was especially prone to blinding himself to the realities of the new regime. The National Shoe Company had received an order from the Army of the Revolution for fifty thousand pairs of marching boots, but it did not occur to him to question why there would be so large an army when Campión himself had coined the slogan "Peace before and above all." And so Fernando made the first major mistake of his life: he enthusiastically diverted a significant portion of the company's resources toward meeting the order one month before the deadline.

Then the inevitable happened. Antonio was arrested on a cold February morning as Marina was complaining to Felicia that she was losing all her well-to-do clients. She had had to cut her fees in half and take on middle-class housewives who wanted all their problems solved in a one-hour session.

"When they realize I can't do it, they leave and never come back. I can't stand their ignorance. You know what they see when they look at me? A witch!"

No sooner had Marina spoken than Fernando rushed into his mother's living room with news about Antonio. For an instant Felicia lost her breath and everything before her turned black. She recovered quickly enough so that her son failed to notice, and after drinking a glass of water to compose herself, she called Julia, Antonio's wife. From her Felicia learned that the secret police had shown up at their door that morning and refused to say where they were taking him. Considering the political climate, an arrest was as good as a guilty verdict.

The trial, which Felicia attended with Julia the following week, was mercifully brief. It lasted three hours, during which thirteen witnesses were called to testify, charging Antonio Turner with everything from anti-revolutionary activities to moral turpitude to corrupting youth. When Antonio heard this last claim, he turned to his sister and wife sitting three rows back in the gallery and gave them a bitter smile.

The thirteenth witness, a graying mulatto in army fatigues, identified himself as Commander Orestes Miranda of the Revolutionary Army. He told the tribunal that on October 16 of the previous year, in the Café del Centro of the town of San Juan del Llano, at approximately 6:30 in the morning, the accused, after imbibing a substantial amount of brandy, told him that he had informed the local police office of the gathering taking place at the ranch of Paco Verdún. The accused also bragged to him that he was directly responsible for the elimination of one hundred student heroes and that he expected to be rewarded with a judgeship on the Supreme Court as a result.

"Do you have any doubt in your mind," asked one of the judges, "that this man is guilty of the crimes charged to him?"

"None whatsoever," answered the commander. "Ninety-seven of our bravest youth were massacred by his doing."

During the testimony, Felicia had kept her eyes fixed on her brother and noticed that, as the man testified, Antonio's head, which he had kept raised and arrogant as a rooster's throughout the proceedings, drooped lower and lower, so that when the last words were said, she could see only his hunched shoulders and a half-moon of balding skull suspended over them, nodding in disbelief or despair, she didn't know.

After the commander left the witness chair, the chief magistrate gave Antonio an opportunity to speak. Antonio stood and leaned on the brass bar that surrounded his chair. His lips were trembling, but his words came out forcefully, old hand that he was in court.

"I will not burden the court . . ."

"The tribunal," corrected one of the judges.

"Excuse me. I will not burden the tribunal with a lengthy defense of my innocence, which is as clear as the water in the pitcher before you. Nor will I attempt to undo the web you have woven around me for reasons which are beyond my knowing. Innocence and guilt are masks hidden in the closets of the heart. Sometimes they are interchangeable; more often than not they are identical. The thirteen witnesses brought to testify against me have charged me with certain crimes. I know I did not commit these crimes. I have robbed no one; I have corrupted no one; I have killed no one. I have informed on no one. There is no need to convince you of that; nor can I convince you to let me go free. You have your orders. Capricious as they may seem, you have chosen to obey them. This is a choice I can understand, can sympathize with. Failure to do so on your part will place you where I am now. So we are all victims: I of injustice, you of a will much greater than your combined ones can ever be. All I ask is that when you sentence me you show mercy. I am old and tired. Neither my mind nor my body is capable of doing your government harm, if that were my wish. I want only to be left alone."

After a ten-minute consultation with the other two judges, the chief magistrate read from a statement prepared ahead of time. The accused was guilty of the crimes alleged against him and was sentenced to death by firing squad, commuted to thirty years of imprisonment.

Much later, after Antonio was led away and the crowd had dispersed, the two women were led by a guard through a long hallway to the rear of the building and into a room where Antonio sat in shackles, smoking a cigarette. He greeted them with a shrug of the shoulders. Julia started to cry.

"Don't waste your tears. We have only two minutes. You know what to do."

"No, I won't," said Julia.

"I'm not leaving the country until you are free," said Felicia sternly.

"Not so loud," said Antonio.

"Let them hear. Bastards. Sons-of-bitches."

Then the three of them grew silent until the guard opened the door.

"And they didn't even give me the chance to be a martyr," said Antonio as he was led away.

As Julia and Felicia walked out of the courthouse, they noticed that José María Unanue, Antonio's driver, was parked right in front, in a space reserved for official vehicles. Felicia accepted his offer to drive them home. The two women sat in the back seat and nothing was said until Julia was dropped off in front of her apartment building.

"Felicia," said the driver in a Castilian accent, "things might get dangerous for you. You and your son's family should leave as soon as possible."

"I'm not leaving. Even if I wanted to, there's no way. The planes are full, the boats are full. Everybody is going."

"I can arrange it."

"How?"

"I can arrange it," he repeated, avoiding her eyes in the rear-view mirror.

"Trust is a luxury these days, José María."

"Señora, Antonio has been like a brother to me, my one true friend. You put a knife into me when you doubt my intentions."

They turned on Vistalmar. To the left rose the city, the buildings shining with the last light of dusk. To the right was the sea darkening toward the horizon and the entrance to the harbor; rising out of the rocks on the far point was the Fortress of the Rock, the impregnable prison into whose bowels men had disappeared for three hundred years.

"Do you think he's already there?" Felicia asked José María. And then she added, almost as an afterthought, "He won't come out alive. Death will cut short his sentence."

Notwithstanding Antonio's imprisonment, Fernando was still reluctant to accept what to his mother and to his wife, whose social life was in shambles, was a reality clear as glass: Nicolás Campión was a ruthless tyrant in populist disguise. Next to him, Sotelo was a venerable man. Fernando went about fulfilling the government's order for fifty thousand pairs of marching boots with an energy that dumbfounded the two women. He still held to the maxim that business begets business.

The truth hit him eight days after delivering the order. Three government functionaries, followed by five union leaders armed with carbines and shod in the company products they themselves had worked on, took over the office and declared the National Shoe Company the property of the people and the state. Fernando arrived home in a state of shock, carrying the few personal papers they had allowed him to take. After a sleepless night in which he blamed no one but himself for being tricked, he showed up at the breakfast table with a calmer face, and when Antón left for school, he announced to his mother and his wife that they had to leave the country. Felicia refused, but commanded Rosa and Fernando to go, if only for the sake of the child, whose mind at that very moment was being corrupted with lies.

"And you better hurry. You've wasted enough time as it is."

Too much time, as it turned out, for when Fernando went to the Ministry of the Interior that same day to obtain exit visas, he was curtly informed by the clerk in charge, after waiting two hours in a line that curled around the block, that travel out of the country had been suspended on direct orders from Nicolás Campión. Fernando asked for an explanation and the woman responded that an order from Nicolás was explanation enough.

At home he found the jalousies drawn and the front door locked. He had not taken a key with him in all the years they had lived on the street. He knocked and heard the quick shuffling of feet on the tile floor and whispering he could not make out. He knocked again and identified himself. The door opened a crack, then more fully as Rosa's hand reached out and pulled him in. Sitting on the sofa were Felicia and Acevedo. Fernando asked what was going on and his mother told him that the pharmacist had brought a pound of coffee. Contraband from the countryside, she added, pulling out her cup from under the seat.

Munda brought Fernando some, which he drank in one gulp.

Acevedo told him that two men had come to the pharmacy asking questions about him.

"What questions?"

"All sorts. What time you left in the morning, when you returned, if I had seen strangers driving by. I said that the only strangers I'd seen in the neighborhood were the police. They got rid of Gutiérrez, you know. Then they asked me if you had bought any drugs lately, and I answered the truth, that the only drug you or anyone else could buy in my store was aspirin, that I'd run out of everything else. The Ministry of Health sees fit to supply me only when it occurs to them. And they send only aspirin and alcohol. I have enough to get all the elephants in Africa drunk and cure their hangovers after. They even asked if you used prophylactics, and how many you bought a week."

Rosa gasped at this and covered her mouth with her hand.

"Acevedo, please, some respect."

"It wasn't my question, Rosa," said the pharmacist.

He turned to Fernando. "It all leads to one conclusion and one conclusion only. They are building a case against you."

"They don't need to build a case, they can invent one," Felicia broke in. "Look what they did to my brother."

Fernando stood up unexpectedly and ordered Rosa to open the blinds. He was not about to become a prisoner in his own home. He went to the door and flung it wide, then closed it immediately.

"There are two men in a car across the street," he said, trying to speak without alarm.

Acevedo peeked through the blinds.

"They're the ones who came to me this morning." Releasing the slat, he added, "It's hot in that car. I hope they fry like sardines."

"They weren't there when I came in," said Fernando.

"Of course not," said the pharmacist. "They were following you. From now on they will stick to you like remoras."

"They must suspect you, too," said Felicia to Acevedo.

"It is an honor," replied the pharmacist, pointing a cigarette at the ceiling.

Still standing by the door, Fernando grabbed the knob.

"Where are you going?" Rosa asked him, straightening up in her chair.

"To speak to them."

He waited until his eyes became accustomed to the glare, then he looked.

"They're gone."

"They'll be back," said the pharmacist. He explained to Fernando what lay behind the cancellation of exit visas. A bomb had been planted in the seat of Nicolás Campión's favorite jeep, and instead of exploding, the homemade device had fizzled and burned his buttocks. Campión had become furious. The pain around his haunches was such that he could barely walk around his office. Sitting on the toilet, it was said, reduced him to tears. Campión blamed the United States and the CIA and was heard to exclaim while still in the hospital that they might have gotten his ass but he still had his balls, and that he would not let another bourgeois piece of turd out of the island if it killed him. The authorities had kept the story off the airwaves, but they were as yet unable to stop the gossip network which had been around since the city was founded four hundred years earlier, and which was, by this point in history, part of the genetic makeup of the island race.

"The day they cut off our tongues," said Acevedo before leaving, "that's when they have us."

Two events led Felicia to take control of the situation. The first of these was the appearance at her son's house of Mercedes Garcés. Their once solicitous neighbor, she was now a full-fledged member of the militia. She came accompanied by two strangers, also in militia uniform, who proceeded to take inventory of all the goods in the house—clothes, china, silverware, even the used tires Felicia stored for Antonio in the garage. While the men filled form after form and slapped labels on the side of things, Mercedes Garcés stood in the middle of the living room, a bit too rigid for Felicia's taste. On the way out, Mercedes Garcés told Felicia, not as an excuse, but by way of letting her know where her allegiances stood, that she was acting under direct orders of the great leader. Felicia blew smoke in her face and the woman growled back, *"¡Viva Campión!"*

A few days later another event hit the family broadside. Fernando was on his way to the American embassy, following the last threads of his once ample optimism, when he was picked up by the secret police. When he walked in the door of his house at ten-thirty that night, Rosa and Felicia were at their wits' end. He looked pale and exhausted, and there was a bruise on his temple. His jaw, set tightly in his face, quivered ever so slightly. He refused to talk about the experience and went straight to bed.

Felicia remembered what José María Unanue had told her. She called and asked him to be at her house at seven the next morning. Afraid that her phone was tapped, she added that she needed to deliver some clothing to Antonio. Fernando and Rosa, ready now to do anything to leave the island, were at her house at six-thirty. There was no sign of the sinister men out front, and the neighborhood was still in the thrall of sleep. José María came in through the back door. His face had a gruff look about it, but he spoke quietly and calmly.

"It will cost five thousand American dollars," he said to Fernando.

"You are mad," Fernando replied. "Where am I going to get that kind of money?"

"I have it," Felicia interrupted.

Fernando looked hard at his mother. What money she was offering was all she owned, saved dollar by dollar for thirty years and stashed somewhere in the recesses of her armoire. He felt as if he were taking part of her anatomy, but he had no choice. Finally he spoke.

"What are the plans?"

"It is best if you don't know," said the Spaniard. "I'll pick up the money tomorrow. It will take a few days to make the necessary contacts. Pack a duffel bag with clothes for the three of you. You'll have only a few hours after I give you word."

Fernando had the worst of the wait. Never having been a man to while away his energies at home, and unused to the honeylike properties of domestic time, he bloated with anxiety. He spent the days pacing back and forth in the living room or peeking out the window observing those who were observing him. A thousand doubts filled his head, and on the third day he concluded that José María had duped them, was probably now counting the money and basking in the glow of his thievery.

Felicia looked at her son and understood that patience was a virtue bestowed on women to help them withstand the weight of domestic routine. On the street time was horizontal, pushing men toward success. The fastest ones brought home the laurels of their race, to start again the next day. That's why men worked so hard at making roads smooth and their vehicles efficient. At home time was vertical, pressing down like heavy air to flatten the spirit, and all a woman could do to keep from being overwhelmed was to fill each moment with herself, make time the bowl of her existence. *Speed is of the essence*, she had heard the men say and, saying it, become enslaved. For her, the only meaning lay in stasis and in the freedom it brought to do things at the pace of each day. In the end, man and woman were creatures of time, and their final and irreversible position would be the same: supine, breathless on the ground; in a word, dead.

"Remember the star-apple tree in your grandfather's yard?" she asked her son.

Fernando sat at the edge of the bed and nodded, very much like a child.

"You could climb up to the highest branch and eat fruit, and when you had your fill, you would perch there for hours, remember?"

"Yes," said Fernando. "I used to make believe I was on a ship's mast and was searching the horizon for land. One time I fell and threw up all the fruit and you thought I had busted my gut."

"And your father took you from me and forced you to go back up so you would lose your fear."

"I haven't tasted a star apple since. That was a long time ago."

Felicia put out her cigarette and picked up her handkerchief. She rolled and unrolled it with a nimbleness that was a mystery to him.

"Things were simpler then," he said.

"They always are when one is young. Your son is so excited about going to el Norte he can barely contain himself. He thinks it's a great adventure, but I have a pain in my heart that won't go away."

It was Antón who noticed the note slipped under the front door two days later just after sunset. It read *Be ready. 1:00 a.m.*

and nothing more. They ate their supper and packed the duffel bag and spent the remaining time with Felicia, who kept herself from weeping by a superhuman effort only she was capable of. Not so Rosa, who cried rivers, lakes, whole oceans, until the house filled with the salt waters of sorrow. Fernando sat stone-faced on the easy chair, speaking in short breathless phrases, trying to console his wife. Such quiet Antón had never before experienced in the family. Inside him his heart rattled, his ears popped, and he felt lightheaded. He asked his father again how they were getting there, and Fernando answered the same as before: not to worry, everything would be all right. The son protested he wasn't worried, he just wanted to know, and the father this time smiled feebly and suggested he try to get some sleep.

Eyes closed, the boy thought of what he was abandoning—his books, his toy soldier collection, the house—but his attention did not hover over any of this long enough to cause pangs of remorse; his mind was too young for nostalgia and his imagination was crowded with visions of the coming adventure. He was taking with him only one book, *The Sons of Captain Grant*, and the baseball glove Eduardo had given him but which he had not yet used. The realization that he was leaving, possibly for good, the most important person in his life did not yet strike him.

Some time before midnight Rosa's parents came to say goodbye, followed a few minutes later by Ruperto, Eduardo, and Julia, and lastly, preceded by the jingling of her bracelets, by Marina, who announced that she had consulted the saints.

"The streets are quiet," she said. "There will be no danger."

"The police don't listen to the saints," Fernando responded, dropping on the sofa by his son's feet.

Eduardo offered him a drink of contraband rum and they

resumed the wait, the only light a candle Felicia placed on the coffee table. When José María arrived at the back door, he grumbled at Felicia that she might as well have invited Campión to the party. He then picked up the duffel bag and ordered Fernando, Rosa, and Antón to follow him, allowing no time for the drawn-out farewells everyone was secretly dreading. Only their eyes said goodbye.

Outside by the royal poinciana Antón turned to take one last look at his grandmother, but it was a moonless night and he could see nothing. The darkness had swallowed her.

José María led Antón and his parents single file down the trail by the creek to the bridge. There, an army truck waited. Rosa complained that she had worn the wrong shoes. Fernando asked about the vehicle and the driver who sat at the wheel singing and smoking. José María reassured him that the driver was trustworthy and, after helping them onto the back, said it would be a long drive, and tied down the canvas flap.

Resting was impossible in the back of the truck. The wooden benches they sat on communicated every dip and bump of the road through their bodies. They sat still, nevertheless, and said nothing to each other for two hours. Even Antón dared not speak, as if doing so would give them away to the authorities of darkness.

Well into the ride, the truck went down a slope and the road got much rougher. Antón's teeth started chattering and his head shook so violently he felt his thoughts thud against the walls of his skull. Several times Rosa slid against her husband, who pushed her away and said nothing except the last time, when her elbow dug into his ribs and he groaned.

Finally, the truck stopped. A strong breeze picked up and

made the tarp flap against the metal supports. They waited until José María came around and untied the flap. Then they climbed out and followed him through a thicket of sea grape.

As they walked, Rosa once again spoke up about her shoes, and Fernando, letting go of the reserve that was his trademark, told her to shut up. José María walked over to her and asked her for her shoes. He broke off the heels and handed them back. Rosa began to say something, but the Spaniard was on his way already, and all she could do was put the shoes on and keep walking.

The path led to a cove. On the beach, just out of the water, a small rowboat rested. Before them spread the sea, shining with the light of the stars. The Spaniard walked to the boat and dropped the duffel bag in the bow. He called Fernando and pointed to a bright star over the horizon.

"From here on, you are on your own," he said. "Keep the prow of the boat pointed at that star. Around three miles out, you'll see a yacht with the name *Tigre Juan*. They're expecting you. The tide is out. The rowing will be easy, but don't delay. They won't wait forever."

José María patted Fernando on the back and rubbed Antón's head. Then he disappeared into the trees.

Of all the possibilities that had coursed through Fernando's mind the previous five days, rowing for his life had not been one of them. He looked to his wife and son for reassurance but instead found their need. He breathed deeply and helped them into the boat, putting Rosa for good ballast in the stern and Antón as a lookout in the bow.

The rowing went easily at first, and he was encouraged that he still retained some of the strength from his youth. Soon he could feel his heart drumming in his ears, but afraid that the *Tigre Juan* would leave without them, he did not let up.

"Let me row, let me row," Antón kept saying. Every time Fernando heard him, he increased the pace so that the creaking wood and the splashing oars drowned out the boy's voice. Finally the right oar jumped out of his hands and he fell backward, his head hitting Antón's rump.

"Let the boy row for a while," said Rosa from the stern.

Every muscle and tissue in Fernando's body was in rebellion. He could no longer wrap his hands around the oar handles, and his back felt as if an elephant had stepped on it. Beaten down by the realities of age and desk work, Fernando gave in and told his son to take over.

Antón rushed to the oars and almost toppled the boat. After a few awkward strokes he established a smooth rhythm, and within minutes they were alongside the *Tigre Juan*.

The captain was a gaunt man with a deeply creased face who introduced himself as Arturo. He had lost all his teeth and spoke as if he had swallowed a spoonful of molasses. He went barefoot and his feet were calloused and much too wide for a man of his frame. With him he had a boy barely older than Antón whose elongated, narrow face, prominent ears, and bulging black eyes gave him an undeniable resemblance to his father, who was now helping Rosa on board. The boy, too, had no shoes and seemed to work instinctively alongside his father.

The captain and the boy pulled the rowboat up with a winch and set it on the deck; then the captain asked the three of them politely to go under into the cabin and wait there until they reached open sea. If he gave word, they were to crawl into the hold. The patrols went by at three, but one never knew. Rosa asked what if they were caught, and the captain answered that if they were caught they were caught, but he, for one, was not being taken alive.

While the deck had been lit by the light given forth by the sea, the darkness in the cabin was absolute and the smell of stale fish overpowering. Antón held on to his father's arm, afraid that if he let go he would lose him forever.

"It is the belly of the whale," he said, remembering one of Antonio's lessons.

Rosa added that she thought she was getting seasick and Fernando told her once again to shut up, from now on they had to be quiet. He would have said more, but the sputter and roar of the motor interrupted him, and the smell of diesel blended with the fish odor as the boat gave a sudden lurch forward.

They were exhausted and fell into a sleep that nothing disturbed—not the soup of smells or the discomfort of the damp wooden floor on which they lay or the chug of the pistons under them or the heat the engine gave off.

They were awakened by the captain's voice calling them up. Fernando was the first one on deck. He held on to the side of the canopy. There were purple rings under his eyes and he seemed forlorn. Rosa crawled out next. Her face was pale and her eyes darted back and forth as if searching for something to focus on.

The last was Antón. In the morning light he realized this was no yacht but merely a crusty fishing boat. The paint was peeling on the gunwales and the wood on the deck was rotted and warped; on the starboard side of the stern, a fishing net lay in a bundle. Around him was the flat, calm sea. The landmarks that had once defined him—the trees of the back yard, the kitchen where he would sit and listen to Munda's stories, the very ground

he walked daily from his house to Felicia's and back—were gone
and the only solid spot left to him was a thirty-foot pile of weather-
worn wood, which could, at the merest swell, fall to pieces. What
had he left behind? All that led to him and held him in place.
What was he going to? The unknown and the infinite possibilities
that it presented—from being devoured by the sharks of the
Florida Straits to driving down Hollywood Boulevard in a con-
vertible with a beautiful blonde at his side. Antón could not have
anticipated this feeling of displacement, but the effect it had on
him was small compared to the beryl-blue immensity that spread
outward to the horizon. For now, it was geography, not anxiety,
that held.

The captain gave the wheel to his son and brought them a
thermos out of which he poured *café con leche* into three small
tin cups. He pulled out a loaf of bread from a paper bag and
broke it with his creased, oil-stained hands into five equal pieces.
Rosa declined the breakfast, but Antón and his father ate and
drank their portions with the desperation of castaways.

The captain was in better spirits now and told them they were
making good time and should be within sight of Florida in twelve
hours. He sat on the net and added that he had made the trip
ten times and that he knew these waters like his own wife. During
the ensuing conversation, or rather monologue, for Arturo gave
the others little opportunity to talk, it came out that he had been
the famous Tiburón, who had amazed and horrified American
tourists during the thirties and forties by wrestling sharks in the
waters of the harbor. Fernando remembered hearing of Tiburón's
feats. Young men praised his courage and made him a legend in
the bars and bordellos of the capital. Shark wrestling had almost
made Arturo a rich man, and he enjoyed the attention and the
American women who came to him in the middle of the night,

wanting to make love to a killer of sharks. But it happened that one of his young and brash imitators had a leg torn off at the socket by a twelve-foot tiger shark, and Arturo, shocked by the event, gave up his occupation.

"One thing is to take your own life in your hands," he said. "But when you watch a kid bleed to death because he's trying to outdo you, you start to think. I killed fifty-two sharks in my time, and the only weapon I used was a knife."

He spoke with pride, but there was an undercurrent of remorse in his voice.

"I told my boys that if they ever considered doing anything like that, I'd break their fighting hand. They are all fishermen like me. That's the youngest one there. I'm teaching him the sea. He will be the best."

Arturo had been able to buy the *Tigre Juan* with the money he made killing sharks and had returned to Puerto Santo, his native town, and had a good life. He loved fishing more than anything. He'd learned the trade from his father, the best fisherman he had ever known, so good he could fish without bait. Sometimes he would whistle and the fish jumped on deck. One day the old man went out and never returned. Some of the neighbors claimed that he had left, abandoning his wife and children for a woman in another town, but Arturo was convinced that the old man was dead. Sometimes when he went out alone, he could hear his father whistling over the waves, and he would reach port loaded to the gunwales with catch.

Arturo's narrative would have lasted the whole trip, eager as he was to tell his life to so captive an audience, were it not for the appearance of a ship on the horizon, so far off only the captain and his son could make it out. To avoid being seen, Arturo veered to the northwest, thus extending the crossing by several hours.

When Rosa heard this, she turned suddenly to her husband and growled under her breath that she had had enough. She was tired, she was hungry, her nerves were like needles, and she had to relieve herself.

"How does one go to the bathroom?" Fernando yelled to Arturo at the wheel.

The captain, his eyes fixed on the horizon, pointed to a bucket behind him.

"Ay, no!" exclaimed Rosa, whose lifestyle had never led her more than a few steps from the most modern conveniences.

"Don't worry, lady," replied Arturo. "We won't look."

And so Rosa, who would have given her life to have the bladder of a horse, was forced to crouch precariously over the bucket and, for the first time in her life, relieve herself before an audience. Although the men had turned away from her, she could not keep from thinking that the sound of the stream and the last spasmodic plops of the golden liquid—final punctuation to her embarrassment—were reaching their ears.

As the day lengthened and the sun intensified, the parents sagged against the cabin wall and tried to rest. Antón grew despondent and the slowness gave way to boredom. He grew tired of counting flying fish and looking out for sea turtles or watching the swells for porpoises.

"What will we do when we get there?" he asked his father.

"We'll call Lucho," his father said.

"Then what?" Antón asked. His boredom had turned to fear. He wanted to approach his mother, whose eyes were fixed on him.

"We'll see," his father said.

"Things will work out," added Rosa with much more caring than conviction.

"They have to," said Fernando. "We cannot go back if they don't."

Antón said nothing more. He lay against his mother, resting his head on her shoulder, and tried to sleep. He thought that his father was right. Leaving the island was like waking from a dream. Bad or good, he didn't yet know.

*W*hen Antón awoke and lifted his head off his mother's shoulder, he saw reality stretching along the horizon like a long, somnolent snake. Slowly, almost imperceptibly, the dawn light brightened and the coast appeared, gray and indistinct. He made out a few coconut trees and wooden houses, decaying, oddly familiar at a distance. Farther back was a water tower, and behind that three radio antennas, flashing red warning lights.

Antón stood and realized they had made the crossing safely. *Key West*, he heard Arturo yell over the chug of the engine, and Antón felt as if he had broken through water into air. His eyes teared and his chest filled with longing and dread.

"We have arrived!" Rosa said, and as she said it, the land

seemed to stand still and the bobbing of the boat became more pronounced.

Fernando asked why they had stopped and Arturo answered that if it were still night, he would take them all the way in and give them a tour of the city to boot. But now it was too risky.

"I'm a smuggler," he added. "You can row the rest of the way. It's only a few hundred yards."

Arturo put the boat in the water with help from his son. Antón sat in the bow and Rosa astern, hunched and shivering. Fernando crawled down on the rowing seat and pushed off. Despite his blistered, aching hands, he rowed with strength he did not know he had. The tide was coming in and the boat flew over the water. Antón directed his father to the closest landmark, a wooden pier that seemed about to fall into the water.

Realizing their speed would take them under the pier and into a concrete breakwater behind it, Antón threw his arms around one of the pylons and stopped their forward motion. He was the first one up the ladder, followed by his mother, who clambered up the last step and rolled sideways onto the dock. Then, without warning, his father threw the duffel bag up. Antón caught it to keep it from landing on his mother, and as he did so, he felt a pain and burn on the inside of his arms. He dropped the bag and looked. His forearms were scraped and bloodied from the barnacles and raw wood on the pylon. By the time Fernando made it over the side, Rosa had taken out a handkerchief and was patting the scrapes. She said they had to get him to a doctor and Antón pulled away, dismissing her concern with a man's phrase, "*No es nada*," and meaning it.

Rosa took off her heelless shoes and threw them in the water. Then she pulled a pair of canvas espadrilles from the bag and slipped them on. When she turned to look at Antón, he was smiling in a confident, open way she had never seen before.

The pier led to a residential street lined with large wooden houses. It was almost seven and the street was beginning to stir. Someone was watering bushes. A man walked his poodle while reading the paper. An old woman rode by on a bicycle. A few cars whooshed by, disturbing the freshness and leaving behind the smell of exhaust. No one was surprised to see them or stopped to question them or asked if they needed help.

Fernando walked ahead with the duffel bag slung over his shoulder, like a seaman returned from a voyage. Rosa and Antón followed, trusting that Fernando knew where he was going. In reality, he was merely following the urbanite's instinct that all streets of all cities are the same: they lead where one wants to go.

As they walked, the neighborhood changed and more storefronts appeared. They passed by several bars, a newsstand, a clothing store with beachwear in the window. The buildings were weathered and unkempt, the sidewalks cracked and weedy, and Antón was disappointed that el Norte looked no better than Corral Falso on a bad day.

At the next corner, Fernando put the duffel bag down and wiped the sweat from his forehead with the palm of his hand. The sun was well up now and hitting them square on their backs. Rosa suggested that they ask for directions to the nearest hotel. Fernando surged ahead, and mother and son followed a few steps behind. They passed a grocery store and Rosa called out to her husband that they might as well get some food and drink. Fernando turned around and began to say that it was better to find a place to stay first but interrupted himself. There, on the other side of the street, was a motel, small and wooden and recessed away from the traffic, its sign almost fully covered by the branches of a poinciana tree.

Inside the office, Fernando explained in broken English to the man behind the counter that they needed a room. The man was squat and bald, but he had hairy arms and thick tufts growing on his neck out of the shirt collar. He responded in perfect Spanish to please fill out the card; then he smiled down at Antón and asked about his arms.

"I fell," answered Antón without hesitating, sensing he couldn't tell the real story. It was the first of many lies.

"Yes," the man said without changing expression. He excused himself for a moment while he went to the back.

"Maybe he is suspicious," Rosa said quietly.

"Of what?" asked her husband.

"Of us, of why we are here, how we look."

Fernando moved a step away and looked Rosa over.

"You look like a tired tourist."

"You don't think he believed Antón when he said he had fallen. He could be calling the police at this very moment."

Just then they heard some stirring in the rear, and the clerk appeared. He had with him some iodine and gauze and cotton in a plastic bag.

"Here," he said, handing it all to Rosa. "For the boy's scrapes."

The room they were given was two doors down from the main office. Fernando opened the door and dragged the duffel bag in.

"It's starting to weigh like a dead man," he said. He added that he was going out to get some food and left Rosa and Antón in the room by themselves.

It was the first time Antón had been in a motel, and he immediately went to the TV and turned it on. Only static came through.

His mother called him to the bathroom so she could clean and dress his arms. He had to clench his teeth and shut his eyes to keep from crying while she applied the iodine, which gave his skin a sickly, cadaverous hue. Then he lay on the bed closest to the wall.

Directly across from him over the dresser was a cheap print of boats sailing calmly in a bay. The picture was a lie. The sea was not like that—peaceful and full of color. The sea was a desert. The sea was darkness waiting to swallow boys.

He turned sideways toward the night table and saw a metal box with the word *Vibra Bed* on it. Under a coin slot the following was written: "Insert quarter, turn knob slowly, and relax your troubles away."

Antón asked his mother what a quarter was. Rosa, who was pulling clothes out of the duffel bag, said, "A what?"

"A quarter," Antón repeated, lifting the metal box in her direction as far as the cord allowed.

Rosa walked over to the bed and took the box from Antón. She read what it said out loud.

"A quarter!" she said. "I have some coins in my purse."

She went to the dresser and brought a quarter to the bed. Antón made room for her.

"What will it do?" he asked.

"I don't know," she said, putting the coin in and turning the knob.

Suddenly the bed started vibrating under them. To Antón it felt as if his whole body, including his mind, was bubbling. He laughed. Rosa lay down and began laughing, too. She said she'd never felt anything like it.

By the time Fernando returned with a bagful of groceries, Rosa had just used up her third quarter. She had her husband lie on the bed, which he did reluctantly, hungry and ill-humored as he was. The result was magical. In a matter of minutes, Fernando was his old self again, patient and tolerant and kind as a palm tree.

He wanted to put another quarter in, but they were out of them. For now, he had to resign himself to saying something about American ingenuity, which Antón misunderstood. He thought his father was making a disparaging remark about Americans, which did not make sense considering the marvels of the Vibra Bed.

It was not a thought over which he could linger. His mother had set the food out on the kidney-shaped table by the window and was calling them over to eat. Antón saw the strange breakfast of hot dogs, canned sardines, potato chips, doughnuts, and Coke, but he didn't complain. He had not thought about food up to this point, but now that it was before him, he realized he was famished.

As they ate, Fernando mentioned that he had called Lucho, the psychiatrist, from a public phone outside the grocery store. Lucho said he was coming the next day to pick them up and that they could stay with him and Jill as long as they needed.

Rosa asked if they should not call the authorities.

"What authorities?" asked Fernando.

"There must be a law against what we have done."

"No one cares who we are or why we are here," he said, intrigued momentarily by the idea of leading an underground life. "At this point we can do anything we want."

"What we do now," she said, "will affect us for the rest of our lives. Either we do things legally or the three of us will be renegades. There must be some authority. Haven't you always said that this is the country of law and order?"

Fernando was surprised at his wife's vehemence and said he would deal with the situation tomorrow, after consulting with Lucho. Right now they needed some sleep.

Later, while his parents were sleeping on the bed next to him, Antón tried to think what lay ahead. He wanted grand avenues and skyscrapers, bridges and factories. He wanted America in all its industrial power, its democratic arrogance and Wild West roughness. He wanted Wyatt Earp and Doc Holliday, Billy the Kid and the James Brothers, Eliot Ness, Al Capone, Baby Face Nelson, Mickey Mantle, and Warren Spahn. He wanted right and wrong to do battle out in the open where he could see them. He wanted a baseball, white and hard and perfect, to come flying in his direction so he could catch it and save the game. It was the early sixties and he was in the country where all of this was possible. He knew it from the movies and from television, Key West and its sad streets notwithstanding. He knew it, too, from someplace inside him neither his parents nor his grandmother had ever touched: el Norte was the way into the pure self.

The room started spinning. He felt himself growing smaller, until he was the size of a pin in the middle of the bed and a drain hole was sucking him in. He tried to hold on to the sides, but the force pulling him through the hole was too strong. Finally, he slipped through to the other side and there, sitting in her rocker, was Felicia, his grandmother, smiling, knotting and un-knotting her handkerchief. He asked her what she was doing and she answered that he was getting what he deserved. "Look what you have done to me!" she said in a scratchy voice. She ripped open her dress and exposed a hole in the middle of her chest where the pulp of her entrails slithered over and around itself like a giant worm.

He awoke suddenly, sitting up. Next to him he heard his parents' hard breathing and, behind that, the hum of the air conditioning. Light was seeping in through the sides of the heavy curtain that blocked the window, and he could see the outline of their forms, like snowy cordilleras. He was safe. He lay back and thought of a photograph he had seen in a picture book of the Rocky Mountains in mid-winter. That is where he wanted to be, away from the heat of Key West, away from grandmothers and nightmares, as far away from the island as he could get.

Lucho was at their door early the next morning. He was wearing a red-and-green flower-print shirt, yellow Bermuda shorts, and white tennis shoes without socks. Varicose veins added the only color to otherwise pale and bony legs. His smile, which was constant, seemed the result of inner peace rather than outer stimuli. Lucho's life was an open book, and he didn't care who read in it. Quite simply, he was happy. The moment Antón saw him he felt reassured.

They drove to Miami in a station wagon that seemed as if it might disintegrate at every turn. From the back seat, Antón could see the blur of asphalt through the floorboard. Luckily, the road up the Florida Keys was straight and smooth and they were at Lucho's house before noon. Jill waited for them at the door. Tall, freckled, with reddish hair tied loosely in a bun, she looked comfortable and uninhibited. She was wearing shorts, one of Lucho's shirts, and no shoes. It was the first time Rosa and Fernando had seen her.

The house was decorated in the most disparate way. A Peruvian weaving hung next to an African mask on the wall of the foyer. In the living room, between two easy chairs, was a three-foot black statue ·of a smiling Buddha with an uncanny resemblance to Lucho. On a glass table in front of the couch there was a bowling ball with three ostrich feathers sticking out of it. On the wall by the kitchen hung a suggestive drawing of a nude couple embracing.

The back yard was shaded over by huge ficus trees, so that no grass grew on it. A series of snaking gravel paths led through overgrown ivy to the rear, where, in an old dog run that abutted the canal, Lucho kept a lioness, a sorry creature he had rescued from a bankrupt traveling circus. Every night after dinner, he and Jill would sit before the cage, drinks in hand, and watch the lioness devour the chunks of alligator meat they bought from a hunter down the road.

Jill disliked housework and there were coffee mugs and high-ball glasses left where they were last used and books and news-papers in teetering piles everywhere. In the mornings, she faced the sun for hours in the lotus position, after which she tended to her flowers and sang old show tunes in a voice too reedy for her corpulence. At five-thirty she would wait by the door, dressed, washed, smelling of all the flowers of the earth, for her husband to come home. After a long embrace and a passionate kiss, the two would go into the kitchen to drink, talk, and prepare anomalous but strangely delicious dinners.

Antón loved the ambience where everything was accepted and where anxiety dissipated like an ill wind. He helped Jill in the garden, learned the names of her flowers and plants, and sang with her the few songs he knew. She baked him cookies and taught him English terms he didn't know, like doorjamb, jalopy, and laundry hamper. She made him try peanut butter, which he gagged on, and hot apple cider with cinnamon, which he loved. At night she pointed to the stars and made him repeat their names. When Lucho was home, Antón helped him cut up the alligators for the lioness to eat as a mortified Rosa looked on from the back porch and wondered aloud to her husband how much longer they would have to tolerate this insane asylum.

They stayed long enough to get temporary papers from the Immigration Service and for Fernando to reach his contacts in the shoe business. In a month's time, he had a job offer from Brazilian Leathers, Ltd, and the García-Turners were on their way to New York. Only Antón was disappointed to leave Lucho and Jill.

When they arrived, the city was in the thrall of winter and the landscape was a chaos of brick, steel, and dirty snow. It was a Monday in the late afternoon, and they took a taxi from the airport to an address in Brooklyn where, Marina had told them, a friend of hers ran a boardinghouse. As they rode they passed huge graveyards in the dim light of dusk. "This is the bone land," Fernando said under his breath.

The taxi left them on a street lined with dark brooding town houses. A faint smell of burning rubber hung in the air. When Antón stepped out of the cab, he felt the cold air fix on his face like a vise. He was wearing a light jacket, unzipped, and in a matter of moments his chest was invaded by the cold. Instinctively he hunched and walked on, liking the sensation, for in this weather the warmth of the self was asserted, and he realized how much more than water and breath he was. It had snowed two days before and the snow from the sidewalk had been shoveled onto the curb. Thinking it solid, he stepped on it and sank to his knees.

They walked to Number 32, as sad and hermetic-looking as

the rest of the houses, and up the steps to the door. At first no one answered. The windows were dark, and Fernando started to say that no one was home when the door swung open and a small, frail woman appeared before them.

Lala la Brava had met Marina when both frequented the parapsychological circles of the capital. She had become a *santera* and moved to New York, where her practice flourished until the death of her husband, a jazz trumpet player with a fondness for cocaine. She had bought the house then and retired. She nevertheless kept a small altar to Santa Barbara with fresh fruit and a candle burning at all times.

Lala let the García-Turners two rooms in the back for fifty dollars a month and left them alone. She took a liking to Antón and spoke to the nuns at the convent down the street so that he could attend their school free of charge. Often, in the afternoons when Antón came down to the living room to watch television, she would pester him, in between puffs of her cigar, with vagaries about his future life: "Next week your hair will grow half an inch." "One day you will cross great water, but you will not drown." "I see ashes and wings in your eyes." "You must elect what you cannot avoid." Eventually she would fall asleep and leave her chomped-on cigar smoldering in the ashtray.

The García-Turners tolerated the cramped quarters, the constant smell of cigar smoke, and the sinister guests they sat with at dinner as best they could. In April, when the weather warmed, Fernando found them a two-bedroom apartment in the Bronx and they moved again.

That fall Antón started attending Jesuit school. At first the boy, who had been taught by Antonio that the only good priest was a dead priest, mistrusted his teachers. They seemed marked by their faith and driven by dark forces he did not understand.

In time, however, he grew to accept them and to avoid their righteous wrath at all costs. Rosa learned to cook and took to decorating the apartment with the odds and ends she could afford. Though Fernando worked as a mere bookkeeper, he was nevertheless happy to have the job and felt confident he could advance. It seemed the García-Turners would be able to settle into a semblance of a life.

Then Fernando's brother Eduardo came with his pregnant wife, Lidiana, and their young daughter, needing a place to stay. They sat around mostly, he watching television and drinking Scotch, she playing solitaire on the dining table and complaining about the stifling heat in the apartment. After two months, Fernando found his brother a factory job in Connecticut, far enough away so that they had to move.

Not long after, Ruperto, Felicia's younger brother, showed up with a suitcase as large as a sarcophagus and planted himself in the apartment. His wife and daughter had gone to Puerto Rico, where she had relatives, but he swore never to be trapped on an island again. He would sit by the window with an empty coffee can and spit into it, confiding to Antón that this was as sure a way as could be found to pacify one's sexual appetites. He also told him of his exploits as a student revolutionary, compelled as he was to compete in that arena with Antonio, his older, more lustrous brother. Those anecdotes, however, were fabrications mostly, and served as introductions to others dealing with women and sex. The happiest year of his life, he said, had been the time he successfully defended the madam of a bordello against a tax evasion charge and, as payment, received a year's services free of charge.

In order to avoid his great-uncle's constant chatter, Antón spent most of his free time walking the streets of New York. He listened to the roar of the city's intestines under his feet, the rattle of pneumatic drills, the choir of klaxons, and the wails of the sirens until there were no other songs luring him out of the past or toward the future. Everywhere he went he found the same energy, the same passion for the vertical, the same beat of the heart of work which was hope which was freedom unbounded which was what those people who came to the apartment were looking for but had not yet found. He had found it, or so he thought, not in the womb of the family, but in the anonymity of the streets, where only his name, when he had no option but to give it, and the presence of his parents, when it was unavoidable, betrayed his origins.

Once Ruperto realized that the canyons of New York were not as blessed with wealth and opportunity as American cinema had led him to believe, he packed his bags and bought a plane ticket for Puerto Rico, where his wife had opened a beauty parlor and was in need of an apprentice beautician.

"Imagine what a job I'll have," he boasted to his grandnephew, "making beauty out of ugliness, glamour out of plainness!"

Six months after Ruperto, Arístides Berza appeared. He was Felicia's distant relative, whose plantation in Corral Falso Antón dimly remembered visiting. Family lore had it that he had been a gangster as a young man and had done business with Capone and Lansky and other figures of the American underworld. With money from his dealings (rum and women, it was said), he had bought ten thousand acres and retired to the town of his birth. Now he was an old, semi-literate grouch without a penny to his name, who depended on the charity of others to keep himself clothed and fed.

As was usually the case whenever an adult stayed with them, Antón slept on the living-room sofa. Arístides Berza awoke before anyone else, and by the time the boy opened his eyes in the morning, he invariably saw the old man's figure on the easy chair, dressed in a black suit, white shirt, and gray tie, the stone face with a gargoyle's scowl perched atop his red, creased neck.

It was always the same phrase out of Arístides's mouth: "That son-of-a-bitch Campión," repeated twice, followed by silence until Rosa brought him coffee and he lit his morning cigar. Then he'd add, "These Cameroon niggers don't know how to handle tobacco." Never once did Antón remember the old man getting up from the chair during the day, except to eat. Arístides did not own a watch and did not look at the clock in the kitchen, but at eight o'clock, as if summoned by a biological imperative, he would say good night and retire to his room.

In a few weeks Arístides Berza had hopscotched to another relative's house and the García-Turners invited Miriam Marrero and her two young children to stay with them. A dim acquaintance of Rosa during her socialite days, Miriam was tall, with alabaster skin and a shock of lightning-gray hair streaking from her forehead back into the glimmering black waves that fell loosely around her neck. She moved and spoke with the confidence of the well-born, which poverty had not taken from her and which her charity clothes, plain dresses, and worn shoes could not begin to conceal. In the afternoons, Antón listened to the conversations between the two women, enraptured by Miriam's mellifluous voice and the way her eyes sparkled and skirted to punctuate her words, no matter that the talk centered on the most domestic and, to Antón—shadow of his father—most trite of matters. She could have been a movie star, or a consul's wife. To his permanent disappointment, Miriam Marrero stayed only two weeks.

Others passed by after Miriam, but they fell into the afterglow of his infatuation and so were barely memorable. Only Samara, Lucho's oldest daughter, who on her way to school in Boston spent the last days of summer vacation with them, remained clearly in his memory. She was seventeen, and not nearly as beautiful or entrancing as Miriam Marrero, but was more accessible, the way spoiled girls often are. One Saturday night when Rosa and Fernando had gone to the movies, Samara had unbuttoned her blouse and shown him her breasts, small pink buds pointing up.

The following year Antón put aside his mistrust of clerics. It began with his religion teacher, a young Irish priest with a hunch to his back and something like hellfire in his eyes. He charged at the students from the front of the room, speaking with an undiluted and fierce passion. "No one asked you to believe in the virgin birth," he would scream. "How can rational individuals accept such a thing? What's in it for you, fear of eternal damnation?"

Antón sat at the edge of his seat, entranced by the man's convictions. "Faith," the priest would say. "Each day you question is each day you must make an act of faith, leap into that darkness where reason falters and the only guide is love of Christ. Leap and burn with His love. Leap and burn!"

The other boys made fun of the priest and called out to each other in the hallways, "Leap and burn! Leap and burn!" Nevertheless, the phrase stuck with Antón, and the priest's words rooted in him. He started taking Communion daily and prayed for an hour every night, as the priest suggested. Sin and virtue became the parallel lines that guided Antón's life. A glance at an adult movie marquee or at a beautiful woman on the street was all that was necessary for his heart to race and his groin to jump. The week before his fifteenth birthday he lost control and fol-

lowed a woman in tight black pants down Fifth Avenue, from
Fifty-seventh Street to Forty-second. The woman noticed him
and quickened her pace. This excited him all the more and he
cared only about the satisfaction of his urge, a red thing without
a shape but with the heat of hellfire. Almost panting, he stopped
at the corner and imagined her without clothes as she climbed
the stairs to the public library, her buttocks rubbing against each
other with each step, the dark pink parts below taunting him.
At the top of the steps she looked back with vulnerable, troubled
eyes. It was then that he felt an explosion into his underwear
that buckled his knees and made him reach for the streetlamp a
few feet away. He went home drowning in shame that day and
did not leave the house all week, feigning a sickness his parents
did not believe and spending all his time praying with the desperation of a condemned man.

The drone of orations behind their son's door became a torment
for his parents. When Rosa one night found Antón doing penance
by kneeling on hangers and reciting the Lord's Prayer in Latin,
she had had enough. She told her husband that the priesthood
was too high a price to pay for salvation and that no one ever
got rich from holiness. She demanded that Fernando take control
of the situation and do something. Antón had to be saved from
the Jesuits.

It was at this time, when the García-Turners were at wits' end
about their son, and Antón was blind to everything but his fervor,
that Tico Brahe Alouf, Rosa's second cousin, called them from
Idlewild Airport. His parents, amateur astronomers with a fondness for drink, had managed somehow to send him out of the
island on a Canadian airplane. He was waiting for Rosa and
Fernando to pick him up.

At nineteen, Tico was one of the most endearing young men

in Rosa's family. He was thin, about the same height as Fernando, with a small chiseled head that made him look at times like Jeff Chandler, Rosa's favorite actor. He had had a reputation as a dandy and a ladies' man on the island, although neither Rosa nor Fernando had ever heard him boast of his conquests. Whatever ravages his young personality had suffered from the trials life put before him he kept well hidden. At dinner he was all smiles and jokes, and whenever he could afford it, he bought flowers or a loaf of bread for the dinner table. His only fault was his lack of ambition. Fernando had urged him to go to night school and get a degree. With the proper credentials and his personality, there was no end to what he could accomplish in the business world. Tico had laughed and waved him off.

Before Antón had a chance to learn what was going on, Tico settled into the extra bed in the room and switched the radio on to his favorite station. Antón asked how long he was staying. Tico answered that he didn't know; the sooner he could get a place of his own, the better. In the same breath he asked Antón if he had a girl. Antón answered no and, not to lower his cousin's opinion of him too much, added that there was a girl he had danced with a few times at school dances.

Tico held his fist in front of his face and pumped it up and down, asking if she gave any. Antón shrugged his shoulders. He didn't know, she had a boyfriend.

"All the more reason you should go after her," the cousin said. "He's warming her up for you."

Tico was not one to skirt a subject, and his next question made Antón feel as if his soul had been split open.

No, Antón mumbled, aware that there could be no lying now, he had never done it. Tico leaned closer to him, smiling.

"Why not?"

"Because it's a mortal sin," Antón answered.

The cousin fell back on the bed and said, "We have to do something about this."

An Everly Brothers song came on the radio. Tico, who was an ardent rock fan, reached out and turned the volume as high as it would go.

Two months passed and Tico found himself a job at a bakery downtown. Often he would stay out all night and return the next day boasting to Antón about his conquests or his visits to this or that bordello. "You're wasting your time with all that praying," he would say to Antón. "Come out with me." Antón always said no, but he knew it was only a matter of time before his cousin's insistence wore him down.

One Friday night in midwinter it happened. Tico didn't ask so much as tell Antón they were going out. Antón wanted to refuse, but he knew the time had come. Any more denials and his manhood would be suspect. All he could hope for was that fate would interfere with an obstacle: an accident, a cold, a power outage.

They took the Third Avenue El and got off at 163rd Street. It was cold and blustery on the avenue, the weather Antón had taught himself to like. He zipped his jacket as high as it would go, put his hands in his pockets, and hunched his shoulders forward into the wind. On the corner, a group of men huddled under the lights of a liquor store passing paper bags to each other; some had broken away from the bunch and ambled down the block, arms limp at their sides. Across the street someone was laughing, but for the most part things were hushed and yellow. Antón could have invoked religion and forced a quick retreat, but this was a place beyond religion. He had no option but to trust his guide.

They turned the corner onto a street the cousin called *la calle de las mujeres* and were immediately accosted by a woman with a blurred face who rushed at them out of a doorway.

"Ten and two," she said. "Ten and two."

Tico looked her over and waved her aside.

The woman mumbled a curse and went back to the shadows. Other women appeared before them calling out numbers. The cousin explained that the first was the charge for sex, the second the cost of the room. One girl, with a pockmarked face and her left eye barely open, stood under a streetlight and raised her skirt, then asked Antón if he liked it. He did not answer, frozen as he was somewhere between terror and lust, watching the triangle of thick hair glistening with cold light. His legs grew weak and he felt a strange animal taste in his mouth. The prostitute smiled at him in a motherly way, but she addressed Tico.

"Ten and two, the boy half price."

The cousin gave her a two-dollar bill and moved on.

"They think those bills bring good luck. Next time you come bring some."

At the end of the block they reached the House of Love. There was no light over the door and the first-floor windows were boarded up. To the side of the steps lay a half-spilled garbage bag. Antón thought he saw a rat scurry out of it. His teeth were chattering, whether from cold or fear he could not tell, and his mind raced through a list of excuses.

They opened the unpainted metal door and were met by air damp as breath and the smell of garlic and cigar smoke. An old woman with a scarf tied around her head was sitting to the left of the entry. Tico had words with her and the woman leaned forward on her rocking chair and asked in garbled Spanish if the boy was old enough. Antón was about to reply that no, he wasn't, but the cousin was already waving money in her face, which she took without counting and stuffed in the drawer of the old school desk she had in front of her.

"*¿Quiere trago?*" she asked.

Tico answered yes. The woman pulled out two paper cups and a bottle from a shopping bag behind her and waited for Tico to put five dollars on the desk.

"Whiskey," said the cousin, to which the old lady added, "Linda, third floor."

Tico raised his cup and sipped. Antón followed suit, but he took too much in his mouth and his eyes bleared. He forced himself to swallow.

By the time Antón was able to focus, the cousin was on his way up the stairs. There was no banister, and where the paint had not peeled, the plaster was stained with handprints. Next door someone banged on a conga drum and behind that were the dim cries of children playing. Antón caught up with his guide on the third floor.

Tico was standing by a door with the name Linda written on it in red crayon below other names—Nena, Angela, Jane—that had been hastily crossed out. Antón joined him and they continued sipping their drinks. Although the whiskey dulled Antón's anxiety somewhat, it had the corollary effect of loosening his senses. The air around him turned to water, the floor under his feet was like clay. His tongue was a woolen scarf that grew in his mouth and swaddled his breath. The beating drum had grown louder, faster, closer, until it entered him and joined with his heart, and he became aware of a voice in the thick-mangled undergrowth of his thoughts that told him there was nothing else; the rest of the world—parents, friends, school, God, his grandmother—had fallen away beyond the edges of his memory into a blank and omnivorous emptiness.

The door opened and a man hiding his face with his hat slid past them. It was Antón's turn. He pulled his feet out of the clay and entered.

Before him on the floor lay a bare mattress with a sheet twisted on it, and in the corner to the left was a girl—Linda, he presumed—squatting over a washbasin splashing water on herself. She smiled at him; then she picked up a towel and wiped herself dry. She was young, not a year older than he, with small breasts and full hips. He watched as she moved to the bed and spread herself on it, her head leaning against the wall. She called to him, "*Ven*," and tongue between her lips, she turned her attention to her left breast and began to pick at the skin on the nipple.

Antón did not move. The clay had turned to glue and there were tremors in his gut. He wanted to talk to her, wanted to ask her real name, her age, where she lived, how many times she'd done it tonight, what she was doing after work.

She spoke again. This time she was brusque and businesslike. "*Vamo*, man. I don't got all night."

He went to the bed and kneeled on it, tried to undo his pants, but the tremors had moved to his hands. She sat up and unbuckled the belt, undid the zipper, and, with a dexterity only her profession could have endowed, pulled down pants and underwear at once.

He was limp and she gave a quick, derisive giggle. Then she rubbed, tugged, tickled, kissed, licked, sucked, exhorted, entreated, commanded, cursed, and as she was about ready to give up, Antón hardened and his fountain gushed, the spurt arching through the yellow light into a pearly parabola, a plume of sparkle that landed on the prostitute's face and hair. Her nostrils flared and her lips tightened and she spit a flood of insults back at him. He would have collapsed on the bed and slept on that repository of sweat and love fluids but for the voice, Bronx brutal, ordering him to go *chúpale* his mother's pussy, move, get out, which he did, making way for Tico.

Outside it had started snowing. A boy in an oversized sweater came up to them and held out a hand. Tico gave him some change. The women were gone and the liquor store was closed, but some of the men were still standing before it, hunched and gray, snow covering their hair, looking strangely peaceful and harmless. Anything could have happened in that barrenness, and Antón sensed that everything had.

They waited a long time for the train, and when it came, it was empty. The car they entered was from the old BMT line, with wicker seats and leather holding straps. Tico fell asleep as soon as he sat down, but Antón watched the snow through the window, thickening and swirling and purifying the night. For the first time since meeting him, Antón felt close to his cousin, together as they were in the wild wolf's night of the city that devours people as it swallows itself.

A few weeks after the visit to the House of Love Tico moved to Lala's rooming house in Brooklyn. While there, he fell under the influence of activists conspiring to topple the Campión regime on the island. During the few visits he made to the García-Turner household, he talked incessantly about politics. For once, the cousin seemed driven by something other than sex. Tico brought anti-Campión literature for Antón and urged him to join the group he was working with.

Antón was intrigued by Tico's talk, and his heart skipped

when he thought of emulating his great-uncle Antonio. He even attended one of the group's weekly meetings, but was disappointed to find a half dozen men sitting around a table drinking beer while they cursed Campión and vowed to tear him limb from limb as soon as they found him. Antonio would have laughed. He would have gotten up from his seat and walked out, which is what Antón decided to do. Fifteen years would pass before he saw Tico again.

Though Antón's religious fervor declined significantly, Rosa nevertheless remained concerned about the boy's lack of interest in the opposite sex. As a result, she embarked upon an exhaustive scrutiny of her son's life. She searched his closet, leafed through his books, lifted the bed in hopes of finding a girlie magazine, a pornographic book, an unused condom, or any other sign of a healthy masculine libido that might put her fears to rest. Finding nothing but school notes, textbooks, sodality fliers, and pamphlets from the Confraternity of Christian Doctrine that had fallen behind his dresser, she proceeded to keep a daily log listing times when he left and returned and describing his moods before and after. At night she forced a tired Fernando to look over her notations. After three weeks, Fernando lost interest and concluded that while there was no obvious evidence that the boy was heterosexual, there was little in his behavior to the contrary, and if their son was so inclined, there was nothing they could do to keep him from being a *mariquita* or becoming a priest.

Her husband's comments did not satisfy Rosa, and whole weekend nights when Antón was out, she spent awake, gnawed by visions of her son ministering to the poor in some obscure African country, or else making love to other men in the anonymous Turkish baths of the city. How could she know that on those same nights her son was visiting Linda, driven to the House of Love by a force much more immediate than piety and more imperative than lust?

It was hunger, not for sexual release as such, but for entry into the female and the risks involved in that entry—emasculation, mockery, disease, even death—that drove him. Linda was a fallen angel, but she was young enough to be redeemed. Religious fervor could never compare with the excitement of the newfound sacrament.

One night Antón went to Linda's door and noticed that her name had been crossed out. Underneath, the name Terri had been written. When he entered, he saw a bleached blonde with fallen breasts and needle marks down her arms, beyond redemption, even beyond language. The sex was silent and mechanical, and he vowed never to return.

S L A V E   T O

G O O D N E S S

*F*elicia stood at her back door and saw her family being swallowed by the morning dark into a future she was not part of. There was nothing to do but let go, which she did, saving her tears and busying herself with the preparation of as sumptuous a meal as her limited provisions permitted. By mid-morning she was done: red kidney beans with ham hocks, rice, boiled turnips with garlic, and lima beans she had to cook twice because they were tough as leather.

She set the table with the Dutch china and English silverware that had belonged to her parents, poured herself a glass of ice water, and ate, not out of hunger but out of sorrow, as she had never eaten in her life. When she was finished, she went into the kitchen and devoured whatever she found in the refrigerator:

two hard-boiled eggs, three boiled potatoes, half a head of wilting lettuce, one stringy carrot, and a bowl of polenta she had cooked two nights before. Next, she opened a can of sardines, a can of string beans, and a can of creamed corn, mixed them in a bowl, and ate the mixture. All that remained in the kitchen was half an onion already pungent with the smell of decay. She would have eaten that, too, but for the dizziness that swept over her and the stone of lethargy that settled in her stomach. She struggled to the living room, gave a loud belch, and fell into her armchair.

The first thing that Caridad the maid noticed when she returned from her day off was the crocodilian snoring that emanated from the living room. Seeing the good china out, Caridad deduced that her mistress had had visitors, but it was beyond her why anyone would have people for dinner so early in the day. The mistress herself had taught her that only farmers and gluttons ate early.

Caridad called to Felicia, and the lady awoke out of her slumber, instantly composed.

"I am leaving," said the maid.

"Why, my dear?" Felicia asked, trying to lengthen the conversation. She did not know if she could get up.

"I am going to school to be a secretary." She spoke in the empty formal tones she had learned from years of servitude.

Felicia looked at the maid. She was forty-three, a virgin, and could barely write her name.

"If that is your choice."

"I have a cousin who is head of a production crew in my town. He promised me a job. He said I don't have to be anybody's slave anymore."

"Do you think you are a slave?"

"He said anybody who works twelve hours a day six days a week is a slave, or ought to be."

Felicia went into her bedroom and came back with twenty-five pesos and a dress from her youth.

"Here," she said, "last month's wages. And this so you can remember me when you sit at the typewriter."

Caridad took the money and the dress and left the room.

Felicia went to bed and stayed under the covers until the following morning. During that time she suffered one visionary torment after another. She imagined that her family had been captured and were being questioned by the secret police, or that they had been lost at sea and were at that moment being torn to pieces by Caribbean sharks, or that the boat had been blown off course by a storm and shipwrecked on a desolate shore.

Her worst fantasy came just as she entered the darkest pit of night, when despair is the only guide to understanding. She saw her family being so taken with the freedom and wealth of the new land that they forgot about her and left her to grow old alone in this Cracow of the Caribbean that her city had become. She imagined herself having to take to the streets in order to survive, but the only sustenance offered was the bleached bone of ideology.

And then, when all she could feel was the weight of self-pity pressing down on her, the demons appeared, cursing Rosa and Fernando for not staying with her, and cursing her grandson, on whom so much of her energy had been wasted. There was something in his eyes ready to burst forth against her. What good could come of him in that Protestant country to the north, where the only thing people counted was money? The honor and pride and honesty she had taught him would do him no good there.

El Norte was the land of rats, and God showed his face only on Sundays, when it was safe. She wished damnation on the three of them, and one of the demon voices told her Antonio was to blame, too. Was he not the reason she had stayed behind? Antonio the eternal adolescent! He deserved prison and worse. The voice kept saying all this to her, that her family was her downfall and her disease, that without it she would have been happy, without it she would not have had to sacrifice her life; she could have enjoyed herself—danced, drunk, and whored all she wanted, brought men to her bed and quenched the fire that burned in her groin ever since she'd stopped having relations with Luis, that bastard whoreson. He was guilty above all for making her love him so much she'd become a slave to goodness. The voice went on, louder and louder until she could hear nothing else, not even the beating of her heart, and just as she was about to yield to it, she felt a touch at her temple. She turned but found only a pillow next to her head. She felt it again, a soft but persistent rubbing that turned the black ink in her brain to yellow and to white. When she next became aware of her room, it was aglow in light, and she was in need of relieving herself.

It was the morning, coming to save her with its warmth and its demands. She heard a truck grinding its gears in the distance, and she rose suddenly, as she used to in the old days when there was no time for dalliance.

The bathroom tile was cold on her feet, but she did not bother going back for her slippers. She squatted, but did not sit, over the toilet, balancing herself with her arms until she let go of all the poison that had accumulated through the night and the previous day.

In the dining room the leftover food had begun to ferment and two flies were buzzing in sharp angles over the table. She fought the nausea the smells brought to her and cleaned up, then walked outside in her house robe—what did it matter now?—and went to her rosebushes. She had neglected them the last two months, and they were wild and overgrown. If she did not do something soon, the weeds would take over the bed and choke the flowers.

As she lifted a blotched bloom to her face for closer inspection, Julia, Antonio's wife, materialized around the corner and startled her.

"Have you forgotten?" Julia asked with an edge to her voice. "We are visiting Antonio."

She was slimmer now, grayed and ravaged by her husband's imprisonment.

Felicia answered yes and went inside. She smelled her armpits and was satisfied that she would not need a shower, just a quick wash and some makeup. One of her housedresses would do. You did not go to the Rock dressed for a ball. She was ready in ten minutes.

José María Unanue waited in the street with the car running. He and Felicia exchanged knowing looks through the rearview mirror. As they were pulling away, he said something about the fine weather they were having, which she took as a feeble attempt to comfort her.

They arrived at the prison early enough so that the guards could not claim they had missed the visiting hour and deny them the opportunity of seeing Antonio. The two women were led to a room colored institutional gray, the walls peeling and smudged. Either there was only one visiting room or all of them looked identical. They sat at a long steel table with a Formica top across from which hung a framed poster of Nicolás Campión.

An hour later Antonio was brought in, this time without shackles. He was smoking one of the yellow cigarettes the prisoners were given and was clean-shaven. To Felicia, who had seen him only twice since his imprisonment, he seemed wasted but composed. A slovenly-looking guard sat by the door with tired eyes fixed on them. One wrong move, any attempt at affection, as Julia had already found out, and the prisoner would be led away.

"Well, well, well, if it isn't my two old cows." In spite of his light tone, Antonio's eyes were reddening and his jaw was tense.

Felicia smiled.

"How are your lungs?" Julia asked him, wanting nothing but to touch her husband.

"Fine," he said. His breathing was labored and his lips were purple.

"You should stop smoking," Felicia said, lighting one of her own. She could not mention that Fernando, Rosa, and Antón had left the night before last.

"Did you get the package I left last month?" Julia asked.

"Yes, but half of it was missing. Next time double up on everything, especially the canned meat. That way they'll leave me my share."

The guard yawned and swung his leg over the chair arm.

"Five minutes," he announced without looking at his watch.

"Get out of the country," said Antonio with unexpected urgency. "That is what I want from you."

The two women looked at the guard, who made no show of recognition.

"You are prisoners just like me. This whole country has turned into a jail. Don't feel sorry for me, feel sorry for yourselves. At least I have no illusions, I'll die in this rotten place. What will you do?"

"I'll die with you," Julia said.

"Nonsense," Antonio yelled, pointing at Campión's picture. "You will survive me, but you won't survive him. No one will."

Felicia slid two packs of cigarettes to him under the table with her foot.

Antonio openly picked up the packs and gave one to the guard. They sat in silence the remaining few minutes; then Antonio stood up voluntarily and said, "See you in three months," but they all sensed this would be the last time.

Two days later José María Unanue visited Felicia and announced that her family had made it safely to the United States. She overwhelmed him with a dozen questions he could not answer. All he knew was that they had reached Florida; the rest was up to them. If he were Fernando, the driver added, he wouldn't write or phone her for a few months. The secret police never forget, but they do have more important things to worry about than a small-time manager.

"Who?" said Felicia, stung by José María's statement. She meant it more as comment than a real question.

José María answered that there was talk of counterrevolution financed by the CIA.

"Nothing new there," she said.

Now, he continued, there appeared to be substance behind the rumors. There was a group of guerrillas operating around Corrientes, and saboteurs had blown up a ship in the port of San Andrés. The government wanted to keep things quiet, but the jails were bursting. One had to be very careful. The wrong look was enough to get you arrested.

Felicia felt mistrust blossoming in her once again. How did José María know so much? What was he intimating?

"It is clear to me," she said, "that Nicolás Campión is firmly in control. He has nothing to worry about."

It was his business to worry, the Spaniard responded, it was his life to worry. If Campión came to power by hook or by crook, then he could be taken out by hook or by crook. There were a lot of people who would love to see that happen. He asked her where Munda was.

"She's gone back to her hometown. The same morning Fernando and Rosa left. My maid left, too. She said she's going to be a secretary."

José María then said that everything was changing. All of society was being turned around and there was nothing to be done about it. The life she'd been used to was memory.

"I've never had anything long enough to get used to it, José María. Even my family is torn apart, like a sheet of paper. The only really troubling thing about this government is not Nicolás Campión himself but the people who support him . . ." she said, testing him.

She looked at José María, trying to find something in his eyes that would confirm her fears that he was a government agent, but the eyes of the Spaniard were as hard as the rocks of his native land. For once Felicia had met her match.

"They think they are different, that they are better."

José María said that there were historical forces at work.

"Don't tell me about history. I know enough about it to know that it changes people, people don't change it. All this talk about history being like a river is nonsense. History is a storm. You can't change the course of a storm."

Then she believed in fate, he said, but it was more a question than a statement.

"I believe in God."

The conversation went on awhile longer. They talked of food shortages and power blackouts and things that concerned people in those days, but the important things had been said already.

Felicia could not put her doubts to rest. God only knew where José María stood. She had to be careful. Still, she was concerned about him. He shared her allegiance to and affection for her brother. And she pitied his lonely life, which had been so victimized by the whims of others.

She asked him what he was going to do and he said keep going. Life had not given him any choices.

"You could go to el Norte," she said, testing him one last time.

He answered that there was nothing there for him. The truth was, and Felicia knew it well, that there was nothing anywhere for him, not in el Norte, not on the island, not in Spain, which he had left for good reason to begin with. Antonio had once told her that José María knew as much political theory and history as any man, and that it was a pity he'd gotten stuck driving a taxi in the worst possible city for a man with political convictions.

The amazing thing to her was that the Spaniard had maintained his convictions in spite of all. Perhaps the revolution had struck an untouched chord in his spirit, perhaps he'd finally found a purpose that legitimized his misery. Perhaps her doubts about José María Unanue were groundless.

She waited a long time for news from Fernando and spent her days with hands immersed in brown dirt, salvaging her rosebushes from the ravages of tropical plagues and remembering the work she had done in better days, when she first moved into the house by the river. The area around the property was scrubby with nettles, *guao* bushes, and grass as tall as she, a breeding ground for rodents and land crabs. She had called a gardener in, but the man had refused to clear the lot. Too much work, he'd complained, and walked away, waving his arms over his head.

So she had done it herself: cleared the land, planted the lawn that sloped toward the stream, and put in a path that snaked around to the rear, where she had planted bananas, limes, and oranges. Behind the fruit trees she built a chicken coop. The chickens were a mistake. They were messy, and when the wind blew the wrong way, the smell came into the house and impregnated the furniture. Besides, they drew weasels from the empty lot next door which had to be trapped and taken to the river to drown. She could not remember how many she had exterminated in that manner, but they were enough to convince her to make chicken soup until not a single one of her hens was left. The rooster she gave away to León the barber.

Following Lucho's advice, she planted some flowers, easy ones at first—lilies, marigolds—that bloomed well and gave her the impetus she needed to advance to roses, the most difficult flowers to grow because they are the simplest. They had made all the dirt and sweat worthwhile, from the buds of the miniature sweethearts to her favorites, the Madame Delbards with large, perfect blooms. The sweethearts were now gone and the Madame Delbards had almost disappeared, but five other bushes were relatively healthy, among them the white Napoleon that had been Fernando's favorite. She was confident she could save the remaining ones.

A week after José María's visit, two men came to her inquiring about her son's whereabouts, and she did not have to hide the truth. She told them that Fernando and his wife and son had disappeared, gone to el Norte, most probably, and she had not heard from them since. She understood, even as she spoke to the secret police, why Fernando had not written or called. When they asked her for the keys to her son's house, she was able to give them away gladly, eager participant in the conspiracy, and tell the two men that they were doing her a favor. She had enough trouble taking care of her own house. Again she spoke the truth. Without waiting for them to inquire, she handed them the keys to the car as well.

So it was that Felicia simplified her life in the belief that the less she had, the less satisfaction she would allow them in taking it. She eventually gave her possessions away to her neighbors, to passersby on the street, and to her neighborhood nemesis, Mercedes Garcés, to whom she passed on an old pair of shoes and the ugliest dress she owned. For herself she kept the barest minimum: two dresses, three chemises, three sets of underwear, and two pairs of shoes worn enough that they would not have aroused the least amount of envy or suspicion. Her good silver and whatever jewelry she had not given to Rosa to take with her on the boat she buried late on a moonless night behind the chicken coop. She would never allow the vulgar hands of the masses to touch those things that her family had entrusted to her. And so she came to look as ragged as the rest of the populace. Only her demeanor and her posture—those of a true lady—separated her from the weary rabble she saw parading in the streets of the city.

The worst thing that could happen to a country was for a rich boy to take it over in the name of the oppressed. Nicolás Campión had been brought up with everything society had to offer—fancy clothes, fast cars, the best schools—and he had turned on all that like a spoiled child who had never grown up. She wished she had José María Unanue with her so she could tell him. He'd read too much and lost touch with his common sense. What did it matter, anyway? And what pretensions did she have telling the Spaniard what to do or how to think?

Over the next two months, the people closest to her left the island any way they could. The first was Eduardo, with his new wife, followed by Ruperto and his old one; one week after that, Acevedo closed the pharmacy doors for good, stating loudly for all within earshot that he much preferred the old black magic to the new witchcraft. Felicia felt as if strips of skin were being peeled off. Old song, new twist. She did not let out her cynicism, nor did she shed any tears. Her well had been dry a long time.

The last to leave, just before the new Law of Emigration, was Marina. She visited Felicia the night before her departure and gave her a sapphire-and-diamond ring and three gold brooches that had belonged to European nobility.

"If you get desperate, these should bring in a fair amount," Marina told her.

Felicia protested, but her friend insisted. It was too risky trying to sneak them out of the country, and they might as well be put to some use.

"Better you than Campión," Marina added. "May he rot in hell. All I have worked for has been taken from me."

"Yes," Felicia said quietly. Of course her friend had every right to complain, but losing house and jewelry was nothing compared to losing oneself. The one thing that was taken from Marina, for it was the gift she was born with and not something she had bought, was her talent for prophecy, but taken is perhaps the wrong word; better say undermined, derailed, erased by the new system which had mapped out the future of every citizen in the country. The government had no imagination, it had only formulas. If you followed the "Statement for a People's Mandate," you would have no problems and would lead a happy life. Such a dictum left no room for seers and prophets. Only after she had come to this realization did Felicia understand what the pharmacist had said. This was the worst sort of witchcraft. In losing her ability to prophesy, Marina had lost as much as she: the purpose and reason of her life.

"What will you do?" Marina asked her friend.

"I will wait for Antonio."

"Julia can wait for him."

"Her spirit is broken. She is useless. If I leave, there will be no one waiting for him, no reason for him to stay alive."

"You will do him a favor by taking that hope away."

Marina knew well it was the wrong thing to say, and she also knew that her friend would not heed her advice. She was not speaking *ex cathedra* but out of concern. It took no special talent to predict that Antonio would die in prison.

For her part, Felicia wished Marina had left her a sack of potatoes instead of the jewelry. New austerity measures announced by the government had made food even scarcer than before. Rationing became stricter, food lines longer. Residents of the capital replaced their dogs and cats with pigs and chickens from the countryside, which they at first housed in their closets lest the newly created Black Market Police find out. So many people acquired farm animals, however, that it became impossible to keep them out of sight, and the city grew to resemble a huge and raucous barnyard, with cocks crowing in every balcony and pregnant sows snorting up and down the stairwells of apartment buildings.

For the first time in her life, Felicia had to stand on food lines, a chore she would much rather have assigned to Caridad, not because of the waiting itself—her life had trained her well for that—but because it brought her into too close proximity with that part of society she'd long ago passed by, the same group of people that made up the meat and fodder of the revolution. From them Campión would fashion the new society, and they were eagerly falling into his hands. So now everyone was truly equal, everyone knew the awful taste of Paradise.

It was in one of these lines that Felicia overheard a woman describe to her companion how she had made love to her twenty-year-old neighbor the night before, sparing no detail, including the size and girth of the young man's member. Felicia was outraged and embarrassed by turns, but she did not walk away, nor did she make any attempt to drown out the story with a mumbled prayer.

The woman was thirty-five if she was a day, well fed by any standard, and she described positions that defied her age and physiology. Her companion, lighter-skinned and smaller, laughed nervously and waved her hand in front of the big woman's face with each new revelation.

When she was done with her story, the big woman turned around and, flashing an almost complete set of teeth in Felicia's direction, said, "And, lady, I got another date with him tonight."

Caught by surprise, Felicia stiffened and looked straight ahead. She did not know whether to nod and smile pleasantly, to berate her for her vulgarity, or to ignore her. Instead, she surprised herself by yelling *"¡Viva Nicolás Campión!"*

Realizing that any other response, or none at all, would be considered a gaffe in the protocol of the food lines that might cost them their allotment, the two women found themselves, along with about fifty others within earshot, echoing Felicia's words. Their sentiments, however, were focused not on the great leader but on the pound and a half of gristle and bone that passed for their meat ration. It was the people's territory that Felicia had entered, and there was little in it that she liked.

In spite of the untold hours she spent on lines, sometimes a whole morning to receive an ounce of coffee or two ounces of sugar, Felicia suffered from an overabundance of time. She had done all she could to her roses, but lacking the fertilizer and insecticides that used to be available to her, she could not restore the bushes to their former glory. Without her family or anyone else to feed, she had lost the urge to cook, and limited herself to boiling or pan-frying whatever food she was able to get. Worst of all, she did not have Antón to care for and educate. Where previously she had spent hours teaching him the proper mode of conduct for a boy of his station and showing him the ways open to him in the future, now the afternoons stretched ahead like empty avenues blazing into the evenings, when she prepared her meager suppers—toast and warm milk, if it was available, or else leftovers from lunch. She had few visitors now, and those who came, such as Filomena Brull, her old canasta partner, preferred the daylight hours. Marina's simple question "What will you do?" began to haunt her.

When at last she received a letter from Fernando, she had just returned from standing in line, happy that she'd been able to get an extra pound of chicken, and had not expected the mail so early. It was the only piece delivered, and it wasn't the regular mailman who handed it to her. She studied the envelope awhile: the red-and-blue chevrons around the edges, the airmail stamp with a picture of an American airplane on it, and the address in Fernando's quick, jagged handwriting. She turned it around and saw that it had already been opened, but she was too excited to be disturbed by the violation of privacy.

The letter described, in the cold dry tone she should have expected from her son, their life in the new country. It told about their stay with Lucho and Jill in Miami, and how they'd moved to New York after he had found a job with a Brazilian leather importer. Antón was attending school and Rosa was doing well.

Her parents had decided to stay in Jacksonville with their cousins the Abibs. He ended the letter, *Your son who loves you, F.*

It was a page-and-a-half telegram. Of course they were doing fine. She would have heard otherwise sooner. She reread the letter several times, hoping to find a sign, no matter how small, that might indicate that Fernando was capable of human emotion. But no, there was only the reluctance of someone who guards his psyche with the armor of propriety. Her son would never change and she was the fool for having wanted more than he could give.

This did not keep her from hoping that better letters might come, if not from Fernando, then from Rosa or her grandson, in whom she'd seen, even at a very early age, a talent for deep emotion. She wrote back, addressing the letter to the three of them, making her wish known without bitterness and without any indication of the disappointment she experienced at Fernando's attempt.

In any case, her epistle, for that is what she decided to call it, extended over twenty almost transparently thin onionskin pages, of the sort she favored. In it she detailed, without emotional coloring of any sort or value judgments for which she might be taken to task by the authorities, the course of her life since their departure, from the police's first visit to the two hours she had spent in the meat line that very morning. Anyone inspecting the letter for signs of counterrevolution would have a very trying time. Never mind that the letter was as dry as her son's.

The writing, which flowed as naturally as her breathing and which she found difficult to stop, even to light a cigarette, soothed her and brought to her mind Antón's biography, written years ago when she'd had the breathing troubles and he was still an infant. Had it not been for that exercise, she would not have survived her tribulations. The letter seemed equally as therapeutic, glossing over the excess of time so that it passed without her notice and keeping the despair that stalked her everywhere at bay.

After sealing and addressing the envelope, she decided on a whim that she would retrieve the biography from the back of the closet, where it had lain all these years.

The day you were born [it began] *was the most glorious day for our family. Everyone—your uncle, your great-uncles and their wives, and, of course, your parents and I—loved you and hoped for the best for you. At no point in your early years did you disappoint us, nor did we diminish our illusions on your account. A boy like you, we all knew, was given to a family only once every three generations.*

Felicia was astounded. Could she, even in the depths of her guilt and expiation, ever have written such drivel? She read on:

Your name is a derivation of Antonio, the name of your great-uncle, who is a fine man. He is the center of every party and always makes me chuckle with his jokes, but he is serious-minded at bottom and has a great heart, as well as a great intellect. He is a good one for adventure, and even now that he is gray and worn around the edges, women find him irresistible.

She put the papers down and pulled her half-knotted handkerchief out of the pocket of her housedress. If she was going to continue with the biography, there was no way she could keep on with nonsense.

Then she felt something at her temple, almost like a finger

rubbing. She turned and thought, for a moment, that she had heard Antonio's voice in her room, but it was nothing more than the breeze entering through the venetian blinds.

She had to write the way Antón's life really was, or could be. Nothing less would do. She understood that there was a lot she would not know about, given not only the nature of boys at the age when they discover the meaning of secrecy but also the fact that the most important things about someone's life can never be recorded. Her motives for writing the biography years ago had been to dispel any shadow of her rejection that might linger into her grandson's later life, and to affirm that the creation, human beings included, was awash in goodness. But why insist on a lie? At present, her primary impetus for writing was to occupy her days. She would give herself the freedom to speculate in order to cover the blank spots. It was, but she did not yet know it, the biography of a shade she was about to embark upon.

BIOGRAPHY

*A*s far as Felicia was concerned, Antonio's dying began the day he was incarcerated. Its culmination, announced in the monotone of José María Unanue's voice one warm autumn morning, was the source not of additional sorrow but of an uncontrollable, cathartic wave of relief. She thanked José María for letting her know and waited for him to leave before giving free rein to her thoughts.

That José María had links to the new regime was clear now. How else would he have known that her brother was dead the same morning it happened, well before the official notification reached Julia?

Decorum had been thrown out along with the bathwater of the past and Felicia decided there was no need to dress in black or keep to the house for the prescribed seven days. The island held nothing for her. It had the awful smell of a revolution that had stopped revolving and had started rotting. If there was any mourning to be done, it was to be for her country and for the revolution that had promised so much and given so little.

Next morning she took the bus to the Ministry of the Interior and filled out the necessary papers for an exit permit. She had given José María's name as a reference and a woman had pulled her aside and asked her a number of seemingly innocuous questions about him: how she had met him and how often he came to her house, and the last, which seemed to come out of nowhere, if she thought he was a true revolutionary. Felicia answered yes, keeping her doubts about him to herself, but she couldn't help thinking that she had been used to obtain information about him, as perhaps he had been used at some point to obtain information about her brother. The one thing she would not have imagined about herself was that she was an informant, but on the bus ride home the thought hung over her, darkening her mood.

She could not stay on the island any longer. That same afternoon she told José María about her plans and even enlisted his help in moving her papers through the bureaucracy. In one year she was in New York.

The city was already descending into winter. Barren, stunted saplings passed for trees and dirty slate-blue pigeons for birds. The day she arrived a cold drizzle was falling which continued for a week and kept her inside nursing her joints and wondering if she would ever see the sun again. When the clouds finally broke and she could walk outside, bundled against the cold like a tropical Eskimo, it was language, that English which turned to mush in the mouth, that pushed her back in. *Casa* was house, *pájaro* was bird, *árbol* was tree, and *calle* was street. The world in English was not a world to her at all.

She had tried to have Antón teach her a few English phrases, but the times they sat together he seemed diffident and distrustful and none too eager to help her unravel the knots of language in her ears. The lessons lasted all of one week.

When she brought out the canasta deck and invited him to play, things improved somewhat, and over the cards he told her about school and sports and other matters of interest to him. Still, he began to think of her inquiries as ploys to divert his attention from the game, and when he spoke, he did so guardedly and, more often than not, monosyllabically. Only when Antonio came up in the conversation did Antón grow animated and ask all manner of questions about his great-uncle, such as how many policemen he had killed during his student days or why he had never become a politician.

After two weeks, grandmother and grandson were playing three games a day, which she invariably won and which actually whetted, rather than calmed, Antón's desire for victory. One afternoon, during a particularly long game, she asked him about his religious life, and he shot back at her to be quiet and not distract him. She realized then that she had become her grandson's adversary, and she did not want her concern to be misconstrued as intrusion. It was then she concluded that she could not stay in their home, despite the entreaties of her son and daughter-in-law. The only way out was for her to move.

She gave Fernando all the right reasons: the weather, the language, her arthritis. The five thousand dollars he owed her would make a good down payment on a house in Miami, where many of her friends had settled.

Miami in those days was a bleached bone stretching west and south from Biscayne Bay, as if it wanted nothing to do with the sea. Its topography, or lack of it, its square, dull houses, and the grid layout of its streets were perfectly suited for exiles who did not want to be distracted from the past and from the delectable contemplation of their memories. They made sure that whatever life they had in the new land was a mere shadow of what they had left behind. They bought used cars and fixed them superficially so that they were constantly breaking down. If it wasn't the carburetor, it was the alternator; if it wasn't the alternator, it was the valves. "The Studebakers and Packards of the island," they would reminisce. "Those were real cars." Their houses, too, were weak, unstable things. Any strong wind would call their permanence into question. "Nothing," they would say surveying the ruins after a hurricane, "can compare to the buildings of our land. They were built to last. Even the trees here topple over as if they had no roots."

The truth was that nothing and no one in Miami had any roots. The city was built on water, or more accurately, the water had been drained from the land so that the city could exist. Left to its own devices, the water would seep back in and the land would revert to swamp and mangrove. Exiles were the perfect denizens of such a place, and they were making Miami, with the ocean on one side and the Everglades on the other, a fervent, distorted image of the larger, more permanent island they had left behind.

Felicia went about settling in Miami with the clarity of someone who has more past to her life than future remaining. With Jill and Lucho's help, she searched for furniture in secondhand stores and cloth for the curtains in fabric outlets all over the city. She put an oak-and-wicker rocker by the living-room window, and next to it a pressed-wood table where she could set her cigarettes and handkerchief. The television, a white console model with gold trimming, she angled against the far corner, and on it she displayed a green glass rooster Ruperto had sent her as a house-warming present. Across from the television and up against the wall, she placed the canary-yellow couch she paid fifteen dollars for, the one piece that was like nothing she had ever possessed.

Despite the couch, the interior became a mirror image of her house on the island, and her visitors marveled that, when they closed their eyes, they heard canaries singing, felt the tropical breeze soothing their foreheads, and smelled the flower of nostalgia tantalizing their nostrils. Marina said she sensed the presence of the old spirits and gave the house the name of Déjà Vu.

With the furniture in place, Felicia fell into a routine she would follow until the day of her death, identical to the one she had observed in her homeland. In the morning after prayers, she took her shower, had breakfast, and cleaned. At eight she sat down to read and write. At eleven-thirty, she started cooking, and she ate at one, alone or with company, followed by a nap and a few hands of solitaire. The highlight of her day came at mid-afternoon, when visitors called—Father González, still the atheist, who inexplicably brought her prayer booklets and postcards of the saints; Acevedo the pharmacist, with his theories and declamations; Dr. Figueras, unlicensed now, but eager to cure a lady of the highest order as long as the shades were drawn and no one saw him practicing his art; and Marina, always Marina, who filled the empty places of Felicia's life with warmth and friendship, and with a prophecy or two.

In a year's time, a steady stream of weekly visitors was passing through her house because to be in her presence was to be taken back to what they used to be, what they used to know, and how they used to live. Outside was a present that did not belong to them, but inside Felicia's house the past lived, immutable and eternal. It glowed in her eyes, it rang in her voice, and it was entwined in the tresses of her hair.

On the rare afternoons when no one visited, Felicia became anxious and all she could do was smoke and knot her handkerchief, or else empty out the refrigerator or clean one of her closets. And it was on one of those afternoons, when the rain had kept away her callers, that she brought out Antón's biography. It was still wrapped in brown paper and tied with a shoestring. She opened it at random and started reading.

José María once told me that the United States was created out of a refusal to pay taxes. He also said that in those days there was no sense of nation or oppression in the colonies—that came later—and that people were content to work the land and not be bothered. A man's home was his kingdom and he made his own laws and lived in balance with nature. He knew what he could take from the ground and what he had to give back —ultimately his own flesh. José María said that in the old days the dead up there were buried in their back yard or on church grounds to remind people of this. He said that without this understanding, which is not the kind you can put into books or discuss in classrooms but which you gather from the earth like you gather crops, there can be no progressive society.

He claimed that we would not have that understanding in our country because it was too small, and whatever good land there was had been taken by the rich long ago and the only thing for the rest of us to become was merchants. The merchant has no tie to anything but to money and to the sea or the road, or whatever means he has to transport his goods. The merchant feels no fellowship to anything else that lives. He does not care where his food comes from as long as it appears before him on the table. He does not respect the land. Only the man who loves his land like he loves himself can be good. That is why there was a revolution, and we are paying the consequences.

The United States is the grandest country on this earth and, according to José María Unanue, the only one that still harbors hope within it, and so the only one that is truly free. He calls hope freedom and vice versa, and it has nothing to do with laws or with the right to vote, but it works in spite of all those things.

He says he has no hope, and I believe him. That does not mean that I trust him. The more I know him, the less I trust him, because what he is saying is true. He has had a very sad life, sad and bitter. The only things that seem to matter to him are his theories, and theories, as he himself knows but will never admit openly to me, are useless in order to live a productive and happy life.

You ask why he does not go to the land of hope, to el Norte, where you are. I will tell you why. In el Norte there is no difference between appearance and reality, no one is special, or marked, and though there is hope, there can be no illusion. If José María Unanue were to go to el Norte, he would have to abandon once and for all the past on which he has built his life. It is a miserable life, you say, and you are right. But it is his life and he is too old to put it aside and take on a new one. If he had a family, it would be different; then he would have what is called posterity, and the struggle to remake his life would be worthwhile, but by himself as he is and as he has ever been, about the only freedom he would have would be the choice of where to be buried, and maybe not even that.

That is why I find it hard to trust him, because he is forever trying to justify his hopelessness. If he is not free, it does not make sense for others to be. The only thing I can count on is his allegiance to your great-uncle Antonio. As long as that holds, no harm will come to me.

Her reading was interrupted by the doorbell. It was Father González, the parish priest now retired in exile. His umbrella had been turned inside out by the wind and the rain had drenched him from head to toe, making his decrepitude more pathetic than ever. His collar was yellowed and smudged with fingerprints and the sleeves of his cassock were frayed. She could tell that he had tried to shave before coming but had left splotches of gray growth on his jowls that gave his face a mangy look.

She offered coffee, which made his eyebrows quiver, ever so slightly, with anticipation. When she gave him the demitasse, his hands shook so badly that he had to put the cup and saucer on the table before him, bend over with great difficulty, and sip until he was done.

He asked about her spiritual health, then went on about the moral strength he gained from visiting old parishioners, Felicia especially, for being in her house transported him to the old parish and he felt rejuvenated. He inquired about Antón, whom he remembered fondly from the School of the Most Holy Sisters of the Resurrection as a wonderful child with a special gift for holiness. Felicia listened to the Spaniard and concluded that he was speaking from the textbook of habit. What did the old atheist care about holiness?

She answered something about the boy doing quite well in Jesuit school.

Father González raised his eyes from the empty demitasse. He was far away, in a place in his mind no Jesuit had ever touched.

For a moment, Felicia thought the priest had gone into a trance.

"He'll be either a saint or a maniac," he said finally. "The rain has stopped. I must be on my way."

Felicia walked Father González to the outside gate. As she closed it, she felt a wisp of breath at her temple. She rubbed the place with her right hand and returned to the biography.

She flipped a few more pages to a section on Captain Turner, their English ancestor who had brought the Turner surname to the island in the eighteenth century.

Forget what anyone, including I, might have told you about him. Samuel Turner was a buccaneer fleeing from Francis Drake, who wanted to flay him alive for some offense the family knows nothing about. Turner was eager to become a respectable citizen, and so he bought a piece of land in Corral Falso and tried to raise sheep, but the results of the enterprise were catastrophic. The climate around Corral Falso is, as you well know, the most miserable on the island, and the sheep's fleece soon turned green from mold and fell off in large, useless clumps.

Captain Turner lost the considerable fortune he had made in plunder, but ever the optimist—his only redeeming quality that I am aware of—he embarked upon another, no less ridiculous venture. On what we must surmise was nothing more than a hunch, he decided he could recover his fortune by selling men's silk undergarments door-to-door among people who had discovered underwear only three years before, and that through the intercession of the Dandy Pirate himself, as Samuel Turner became known among the townspeople.

My grandmother once told me that Samuel Turner suffered from the inability to speak Spanish for more than ten minutes at a time, after which he would unconsciously fall into English, this in spite of the fact that when he could, he spoke beautifully literate Castilian learned through twenty years of pillage, rape, and murder along the Spanish Main. This handicap caused him a lot of embarrassment and difficulty in Corral Falso. People laughed at him behind his back and considered him to be not much better than the Chinese coolies who lived around the slaughterhouse.

Samuel Turner was well on his way to the poorhouse when one of his underwear orders was switched and he received instead a shipment of umbrellas from his supplier. It was then, through this unmerited stroke of fortune—God is infinite in His mercy—that the Dandy Pirate struck an untapped vein in the town.

Before this time, people stayed home when it rained in order to avoid being drenched. The streets emptied, the stores closed, even the church shut its doors. The advent of the umbrella allowed the people of Corral Falso to continue their activities without the interruptions of the downpours that bathed the town on a daily basis during the rainy season. The second and much more significant consequence was that Samuel Turner became a hero and the umbrella a symbol of status and distinction among the respectable families of Corral Falso.

Even during the dry season, when it rained at best once a month—and that an anemic drizzle—the townspeople draped umbrellas on their arms as they strolled around the central plaza in the late afternoon. Soon everyone in Corral Falso owned one of the contraptions and Turner could barely keep up with de-mand. There were small ones for children, pink-and-white ones with frilly edges for the ladies, and large somber ones with handsomely carved hardwood handles for the men.

Turner made enough money to buy the town's sawmill and

general store and to gain the respect and admiration that Corral Falso had denied him for ten years. Men started imitating his curious manner of communicating, shifting from Spanish to English even though they had no idea what they were saying, and adopted his style of dress—woolen pants and stockings, a waistcoat and long-sleeved cotton shirt—in spite of its impracticality in the horrendous climate of the area.

One day Samuel Turner disappeared, leaving behind his wife and seven children, and all his wealth. Some claimed that he had gone to Brazil, where he had become a rubber baron; others maintained that he went back to England and was hanged in London for crimes against the crown. Whatever the case may have been, men soon dropped the use of woolen clothes and went back to their linen guayaberas and white pants, but the Turner linguistic affectations extended well past his disappearance, and even today one may hear expressions and twists of phrase in Corral Falso, such as Good wedding to you in the shadows, madam, *and* Send me the bill in the potato market, *that are heard nowhere else on the island.*

Felicia could not remember why she had included the Samuel Turner story in the biography. There was little moral value to it, and considering how many other tales of family struggle she could have drawn upon, it seemed an indulgence, done merely for the sake of telling a tale. Perhaps she meant to forewarn her grandson about the language problems that persisted in the clan, and had at one point all but destroyed her, but elsewhere in her writing she had already made a brief reference to her aunt Olga, who started babbling like an idiot after having her fifth child, Arístides, but who regained her lucidity a few moments before her death to curse her son and all the sorrow he had caused her.

She made a mental note to excise the Turner episode and went on reading.

She had plenty of reason to write the next part. It was a result of a letter Rosa wrote to her while Felicia was still on the island, in which her daughter-in-law related how, ever since learning of his great-uncle's death, Antón had become obsessed with Antonio. The boy was asking all manner of questions to which they could provide only half-answers. Most alarming was Antón's growing admiration for Felicia's brother, and for his eccentricities and adventures, an attitude that had been imparted, to a great degree, Rosa pointed out, by Felicia's conversations with Antón. Both she and Fernando had tried on a number of occasions to address the boy's mistaken views about his great-uncle, but Antón insisted on seeing him as a hero endowed with fortitude and courage. Rosa concluded her letter by requesting that Felicia write her grandson with the truth about Antonio.

Had circumstances been different, Felicia would have struck back with her legendary acerbity and put her daughter-in-law where she belonged. Distance, however, leads to temperance and temperance to reason. She did not write her grandson a letter as Rosa had requested; instead, she had included the rectification in the biography. The reading of it now was as difficult as the writing of it then.

Your great-uncle was neither a saint nor a devil but essentially an average man, blessed with some wit and intelligence, at times too easy a prey to his temptations, at others subject to an indifference that rankled even the people closest to him. In the end, I think he was a man who searched out adventure to ward off those things of which he was most afraid—old age and death. To this day, I do not know why they put him in jail. Some people are born with physical deformities, others are born evil, still others are born unlucky. Antonio was one of the last. He died in hell without a loved one to bring dignity to his last moment. Though the authorities brought misery to him, they never broke him. Your great-uncle was an average man, but that does not detract from his greatness; rather, it adds to it. On the other hand, Nicolás Campión is the biggest son-of-a-bitch who ever lived and I cannot ever forgive what he did to my brother, and to the rest of us, for that matter.

Life here has been turned upside down. People have lost their manners and abandoned any concern for the rights of others. The more vulgar one is, the higher her status in the new society. Two months ago, after I applied for my visa out of the country, two members of the neighborhood committee came and officially confiscated the house in the name of the state and of the people. They were merciful and let me have the maid's room, because, as one of them said, the state never puts anyone out on the street. They pulled my rosebushes out and cemented over the back yard. Last week six scholarship students arrived from the countryside and moved into the bedrooms. Studying, though, is the last thing I have seen them do. Mostly they speak in obscenities and argue with each other.

Our country once glowed with life and the heart of its people. Once there was joy in spite of darkness and warmth in spite of fear. What is there now? It used to be that one could grow anything on this soil, it is so fertile, but they are paving it over so that nothing can be planted, so that there is no hope. Antonio claimed that consciousness was a hoax perpetrated by an uncaring God on an unsuspecting species. Given our sad history, I am tempted to believe him. If we had no memory, there would be no history, and without history there would be no guilt or regret.

Life would be a series of disconnected situations to be dealt with as one could. We would not know that we had seen better days, and the present would be the exclusive concern of our minds. But we have consciousness and history and regret, and the only way to cope with them is to place one's faith in God, trust that He is merciful and caring and not a tyrant like Nicolás Campión.

In the meantime, we have to deal with Campión. What has happened to my rosebeds is nothing compared to what has befallen the island. Where once there were cane fields, Campión has built factories. He has razed orange groves to plant rice and he has drained rice fields to plant oranges. He has dynamited mountains to make lakes and filled in rivers to make highways, and everything is a failure. The oranges rot, the rice wilts, the lakes leak, and the highways sink.

Only the sun is the same as when you left. It changes mood every hour. In the morning it is friendly and playful, with no intention but to bring forth life and shake off the cobwebs of night. As the morning grows, however, the sun's smile turns to a grimace, and by noon, especially in summer, though it can happen any time of year, it is a fierce animal ready to take you by the nape and drop you exhausted in the shade. By two in the afternoon, it has turned into a force no one can withstand. You never knew anything could have so much power. If you are very still and give yourself totally to the heat, you will hear the music of the sun, constant and regular. You can hear the plants grow, the sky expand and deepen, the earth suck sustenance out of the air, and you can feel on your skin, if your head is clear enough, a moist glow, as if an angel were breathing on you. If it does not rain, the sun will soften at five, exhausted as it is and eager to replenish itself. That is why night drops so suddenly.

When it rains, the waters come heavy and full in the late afternoon and cool everything down. The plants are grateful. You have never seen such humility as that of a rose when it receives the waters of heaven, and one has to be grateful, too, that the sun's power has been deflected for a few hours. If you live in the tropics, you know it will return, relentless as ever.

The sky is blue mostly, but sometimes the clouds billow up like cotton smoke, and other times will gather and turn very black and lightning will rain down. God pity whoever stands under a palm tree. I imagine that you would find that midday dark to your liking, considering your poetic nature, but it displeases me, especially when I am by the ocean. The sea is blue, too, and I don't think you will find as many shades of that color anywhere else on earth. I prefer it when it is close to green and calm, although I was once out on a boat where the ocean deepens, and it was very dark, almost black, and I thought I was looking into the eye of God.

Felicia could read no more. She looked at the late-afternoon sun angling through the window and realized that if she could fool others, she could not fool herself. This was not her house and Miami was not her land. The sun shone differently here, the birds sang unfamiliar songs. Everything had a flatness to it, everything was too clean and fit. Whether she lived in Florida one year or twenty, she could never reproduce what she had left behind.

The following summer Fernando had finally taken a vacation and come with Rosa and Antón. Her son was enchanted and called her new house home. He was reluctant to leave and extended their stay an extra week so that he could revel in the illusion she had created and revert to his ways on the island before politics put an end to them. Rosa liked it, too, for by using Felicia's house as a base she was able to reestablish contact with her socialite friends and brag about her husband's successes in New York.

Antón was doubtful, but his skepticism was bred out of disinterest. Neither the past nor the family held anything for him. As in New York, he was uncomfortable around his grandmother. He complained that he was bored and mocked the visitors that came to glory in Felicia's presence. Only when the canasta deck appeared on the table did Antón's behavior change, and then he insisted upon playing for hours. The more her grandson lost, the more determined he became that they should play on. Felicia sensed the danger of the daily confrontations, but it was her home they were playing in, and she was certain she could teach him a lesson, though she was unsure what.

On the day before they were due to leave, she decided to let him win. He was about to enter the university in a few weeks, and he came to the table full of himself, as only a young man can be who has discovered his capacity for knowledge but is yet ignorant of the shape of his mind. With fierceness and arrogance as his weapons, he was ready to battle the person he believed to be his most formidable opponent.

Antón said a muffled good morning, had the coffee and toast she had set out for him, and waited for her to deal the cards.

She won two quick rounds before lighting her first cigarette. As she dealt the third she asked him if he had a girlfriend. Antón shook his head and watched the bony, veined hand flick the cards with amazing dexterity.

"Why not?"

"I haven't found the right girl yet," he answered, not quite sure what else to say.

"There is no such thing. You keep waiting for the right girl and you'll wind up like José María Unanue."

"Who's that?"

"The man who helped you out of the island, remember?"

"Vaguely."

Antón picked up the cards. He had a great hand—two jacks, two deuces, three aces, two jokers, a red trey, and a seven. If the dead hand was half as good, he could win with his eyes closed.

"He was an old friend of your great-uncle Antonio. Very faithful and decent. Every time I asked him if he had a fiancée yet, he answered that the day he found a woman like his mother, he would marry. Of course he never did. A man's mother is his mother."

"I am too young to marry," said Antón.

"You are never too young to think about the kind of woman you should marry."

Felicia eyed her cards with a deadpan expression. She had taken a drag of her cigarette and, instead of inhaling, was holding the smoke in her mouth, elongating her face and keeping any emotion from appearing there. Antón discarded and she took a card.

"He lived in a rented room off Piedra Street," she continued, "and took his meals in a café frequented by thugs and over-the-hill *pelotaris*. Antonio loved to go there with him. Your great-uncle was a great one for the low life. Poor José María. I doubted his honesty many times the last years. He was the loneliest person I have ever known. He lived to do your uncle favors and never asked anything in return."

"What happened to him?"

Antón felt his attention being drawn away from the game, a ploy his grandmother used whenever the hand was not going her way. This time he was aware of the trick and compensated by cleaving his concentration in two.

"When I left he was still driving the taxi. My last letter to him last year went unanswered. Not that he was a great letter writer, but he usually acknowledged mine with a line or two. Julia claims he is in jail, but it is just a supposition on her part. No one knows for sure, God bless him."

He put down two aces and a joker to make the ninety-point meld and picked up the dead hand. It had fives and sixes mostly, cards Felicia had been discarding. He had her. If he was patient and waited for the pile to fatten, he might make canasta of canastas and win the game with this one hand. He leaned back and worked to suppress a self-satisfied smile. It was his turn to make believe he was more interested in the story than in the game.

"Doesn't he have any family?"

"Not on the island. He left Spain as an apprentice cook in a cargo ship. He was fifteen at the time. He sometimes spoke of a sister in Bilbao, but that was years ago."

She interrupted herself by producing an exact meld—two aces and a joker, two queens and two deuces—and picked up her dead hand.

Antón stiffened and made a face between surprise and disgust. He had not expected her to get the 150 points yet. He would have to change his game plan, freeze the pot, discard his wild cards and aces if necessary, and wait for her to run out of black treys and sevens. Stingy as she was in giving up the pile, she would eventually have to discard a five or a six; then he'd take it, not as fat as he had hoped, but good enough.

Felicia riffled through the dead hand deftly and discarded a black trey.

"Maybe his mother was a saint, but who wants to marry a saint? Don't make the same mistake, or you'll wind up doing your own laundry."

"Don't worry, Fifi."

Felicia heard the nickname he had not used since he was twelve and her throat tightened. He was using her ploy against her, she realized, and lit another cigarette.

He picked up a card and discarded a deuce.

Felicia studied her hand carefully, then took a card and discarded a five, her last.

He was tempted to take the pot. He counted that he could make five canastas, including a canasta of wild cards, and he had the foreboding that she was planning something devious; on the other hand, a few more rounds and he would have the game. He controlled himself and took a card from the pot. He put down a joker this time and glanced at her face, looking for the merest sign that she was bluffing.

She threw down a deuce and blew smoke to the side.

"You must treat a woman firmly," she said without moving her eyes from her cards. "But not harshly. And you must show love, but not too much. Adulation will only delude her into thinking she is better than you. And you must be proud, but never arrogant. That will make her contemptuous, and nothing will harm a man more than contempt. A man's ego is a fragile thing, and a bitter woman can shatter it in an instant."

"What do you mean?"

"Men are strong when dealing with each other, out on the street. And they hurt each other in predictable places. But there are certain spots they cannot reach. They don't know how. A woman knows that behind the façade a man puts on every morning is a creature weaker and more vulnerable than herself. That is why men and women, no matter what their relationship, are always at odds with one another."

Antón presumed to listen, but his attention was focused on her hand and on her face. The discard pile was full now and there were few cards left in the pot. If they reached the last card without the pile being taken, the hand would end in a stalemate. It was close to noon and the heat was intensifying. He felt a drop of sweat trickle down the edge of his jaw.

"Above all, don't let a woman lose her trust in you. If that happens, you'll be lost. She will question your every move, she will hate your friends and your family, and she will isolate you from them. Then she will ruin you. When a woman doesn't trust a man, she will eat his wallet. That's the only thing left she can take from him. It doesn't matter how rich you might be, she will make you crawl in the gutter."

"How do you know all this?" he asked her.

"I am a woman."

Then it happened. She gave him not the six he was expecting but an ace, not a bad card considering four were showing. He had two in his hand and she probably had the eighth.

"I got it!" he almost screamed, showing her his aces and picking up the pile.

"It was just a matter of time. Don't bother counting, you win."

"Yes, I do. Finally."

"Finally," she echoed, not without discomfort. "You were lucky."

"And I played an excellent game."

"That you did. The best ever. You were lucky. We'll play again tomorrow. Don't expect any kindness from me."

"I won!" Antón insisted, surprised rather than boastful.

"What have you won, a game?"

"But you always win. You have been playing for thirty years. You are the Queen."

Felicia laughed derisively.

"I did not have a chance at anything else," she said. "Besides, I cheat."

"You what?"

"When I can, that is. In order to cheat and not get caught, you must be a very good player. Antonio knew, and he announced it every time he lost, but no one paid any attention."

"Did you cheat this morning?"

"Of course," she lied. Then she leaned forward on the table and planted her feet firmly on the floor. "Don't waste your life. You have all the freedom in the world. Do something with it."

Antón did not want to listen. Whatever fierceness he had felt at beating her had left him. He fought the urge to drop the subject.

"How did you cheat? Tell me how," he pleaded.

Felicia straightened her back very slowly as if she were uncoiling her pride. Smoke curled out of her nostrils and her eyelids were half closed.

"That is the secret within the secret," she said indomitably.

PART

THREE

*F*ifteen years later, in a small town in New Jersey, the name of which is insignificant, Antón turned over his vegetable plot in early spring. He had been gardening ever since his wife, Alice, suggested he take to the hoe and spade four years before. He had done so, skeptically at first, but the first year's results had astonished him: big tomatoes bursting with the blood of the earth, magical carrots that improved vision just by looking at them, and onions so pungent the neighbors wept when he cut them. The second year was good, too, but the third year's harvest had been meager at best. He had picked only ten green peppers, all but two of them covered with blotches of black rot, and five tomatoes with strange yellow growths on them. The lettuce had been devastated by slugs, creatures he detested beyond reason and which he attacked with every chemical weapon he could legally buy. This spring he was hoeing because it was the only thing he could do. Two days before, he had quit his job, and so far he had avoided telling Alice.

He worked carefully, driving the hoe half a foot deep and pulling it up and around, making sure that every inch of the black topsoil was exposed. He was heartened to see a few worms wiggling out of the clumps that broke on the surface, and he dug with special care to keep from harming them. It was early in the year and there were few weeds. Those that he found he pulled out mercilessly. He did not want any green in his garden, not yet, and weeding now would make planting and harvesting a lot easier.

He could do this forever, he thought. He could do this forever through success and through failure and never have to look beyond the flat rectangular world of his plantings for any of the things he had been told he needed. In the garden he did not have to answer to others; he did not have to look busy, productive, or involved. When the harvest was bountiful, it was his glory; if it failed, he could blame it on the weather, the insects, the poor soil, finally on fate. Here he could be himself, not somebody else's image of himself. Language and style were irrelevant, and his relationship to plants was purely functional: plant and water them and they would bear him fruit. In the garden was the true anonymity and total safety of the self.

In the seven years following his college graduation, Antón had wafted through sixteen jobs, but none had to do with the earth. He had worked as a truck driver, a journalist, a security guard. He had driven cars cross-country, sold encyclopedias to Marine recruits and worthless building lots in the Everglades to retirees. He had enrolled in school to become a commercial pilot, but had to give up the flying lessons because they engendered a recurring dream from which he woke instants before crashing into the ocean. There were also stints in graduate school that eventually led to a degree in ancient literature. At some point he had started writing, merely to distract himself at first, gradually taking it more seriously, to the point of beginning a novel about a character dimly like his grandmother.

Then came Alice and his job at a college, teaching composition, and he thought for sure his wanderlust was over. The college job, however, had been the worst. Where he expected to find the energy of youth, he came upon a Sargasso of indifference, and where he anticipated torrents of intellectual exchange, he found the stagnant waters of academe. Every night he came home with his heart weighed down and his head ringing with the bickerings of two demons: the demon of self-doubt, low and obese-sounding, and the demon of mortification, shrill and implacable. When the two spoke in unison, he felt his birthmark burn like a prairie fire.

He had met Alice Winslow at a reception in a bookstore. He didn't have much to say to her then, but he looked through the guest book afterward and took down her phone number. He tried to remember what it was about her that had first attracted him: her hair the color of honey exposed to the sun, her well-set Anglo-Saxon jaw, the smell of honeysuckle and oranges she ex-uded as she passed. Perhaps, rather, it was her restraint and her impenetrability.

He called and they went out a few times. Sometimes Alice was warm and friendly, sometimes cold and stern, but she was always in control, even after they made love the first time, when she turned away coldly and asked him to leave so she could sleep, then phoned him the next morning full of cheer and good humor.

Thrown off-balance, Antón pursued her, thinking he had found the answer to his questions. In so doing, he had ignored the basic arithmetical axiom that if there are many questions, there must correspondingly be at least as many answers. Back then, however, he still believed that *amor vincit omnia*, even death, the source of all questions. He saw Alice, with her ordered life and her pragmatism, as the Answer. He forgot himself and fell in love with the concept behind her, rather than with her person. Now he knew better: Virgil was a charlatan. The truth was that death, not love, conquers all.

Nevertheless, the pursuit of Alice charged his life and gave it the direction it had lacked. He called her daily and insisted on seeing her several times a week. He brought her books and wrote her love poems, which she did not understand but accepted anyway, on the off chance that Antón might become a famous writer someday.

Five years older than Antón, Alice had been married before and she felt that her possibilities, personal as well as professional, were diminishing. He was kind and bright and full of promise. With the right person next to him, he might make something of himself. While she kept her emotions in control, she encouraged Antón just enough to keep him in the thrall of his illusions.

In six months they were married. The ceremony was an agnostic affair, officiated by a female Unitarian minister who yawned twice during the exchange of vows and who left the reception as soon as she was paid. Fernando, Rosa, and Felicia had attended—they had little choice in the matter—but they could not disguise the skepticism which kept their words guarded and their affections measured. Felicia, especially, saw something like ice in Alice's eyes—something only a grandmother could detect.

Alice's family treated the wedding as if this were her first marriage. Her younger sister kept bobbing in and out with her camera, recording the event for an uncertain posterity. The stepfather, a corset salesman, was the life of the reception, with his sideshow humor. Her mother, profile rigid and impeccable, made sure everything was in order and kept the caterers moving to her clipped commands.

The first year together was a glorious one for the newlyweds. All was put aside for the liberation of the bird of lust. Initially, it was all a fumbling and a stumbling, not knowing what to say, where to touch, how to kiss. He liked to watch her disrobe until her pubis flamed before him; then he pulled her to bed and devoured her fire while she deepened like a bowl only the sea could fill. On weekends when the weather warmed, they spent long hours in the garden, she planting her flowers, he sitting on the porch steps watching her work and listening to her sing the Protestant hymns she was so fond of, over and over, until he knew by heart the landscape of the Puritan spirit that was her legacy and her birthright: " 'Tis a gift to be simple, 'tis a gift to be free . . ."

And confusing desire with possibility, he convinced himself that he belonged here with Alice, way up in el Norte—" 'Tis a gift to come down where you ought to be . . ."—in order to transform himself into a suburban creature blessed by love and delight, till by turning and turning, he'd come out right.

He spread mulch on the soil and over that, five bags of fertilizer. He mixed everything well and evened it out, then hosed it down until the mixture glittered black and rich and pungent. By midmonth he would be able to plant radishes and onions. This harvest would be better than his first, he thought, and a sudden giddiness overtook him. He smiled inwardly and said aloud, "There is no

God but green," and liking the statement very much, he repeated it, hoping to remember his discovery, but then he questioned the accuracy of his metaphor. If green was God, it followed that weeds were God, too. He made a note of the proposition, leaned on the hoe, and stretched his free arm upward. The giddiness had left him, but not the possibility that gardening was as admirable a human pursuit as he had known.

Full of purpose and the courage that the earth had given him, he put away the tools and went inside to tell Alice the news he had been keeping from her for two days. He found her in the bathroom, holding a wad of hair she had collected from the shower drain. Before he could speak, she said she had a sewer committee meeting and would not have time for dinner. She dropped the hair into the wastebasket and slipped past Antón down the stairs and out of the house.

That's when the itch started again. First, there was a burning sensation in the center of his birthmark, followed by random pricks that multiplied and spread to the edges, until the whole of the brown surface was alive. He had tried scratching before, but that had only drawn blood and made the discomfort last through the night. The friction excited the itch and made him reach heights of pure but unbearable misery. Only a cataplasm of hot mustard and whiskey he had concocted one especially desperate evening brought any relief.

He prepared the mixture in the kitchen, fixing himself a healthy drink of whiskey as he worked. Brown mustard was best, but there was none left in the refrigerator. He had once tried Chinese mustard, but it had been so strong that, for days after, he felt a burning afterglow over his kidneys. Today, it was yellow American.

Antón returned to the living room and stood with his back to Alice's antique mirror. He undid his pants and pulled his shirt up. The birthmark appeared as healthy as ever. Roughly the shape of Iceland in the concave sea of his back, it was tipped fifteen degrees toward the cleave of his buttocks and transversed on its northeastern quadrant by the tropic of his waist. As he applied the paste, he felt a yellow solace spread over his lower back. His eyes teared, a sure sign that the cure was working, and he lay facedown on the couch.

He had first felt the itch the night his parents had received Felicia's letter announcing the death of Antonio. Dinner had tasted of decay and the dust of the grave, and he had gone to bed early. As he lay in his room waiting for sleep, he tried to imagine Antonio's last moments in a damp cell with no company other than the cockroaches scurrying along the floor. He thought of his uncle heaving for breath, trying to huddle against the stone wall for warmth and, failing, realizing where he was and where he was heading. Antonio must have brushed it all away, smiled through his cough and fever, and fallen into the siesta of eternity.

At that moment Antón felt an unmistakable pressure, as if a thousand pins were pushing against but not puncturing his birthmark, followed by a burning itch, the pins coming alive and jabbing through the skin repeatedly. The itch grew in intensity until it seemed his kidney would catch on fire, then ebbed as quickly as it had come, leaving behind a glow like that of embers just before they die.

His back was quiet now. He raised himself off the couch, reached for the drink on the coffee table, and took a long swallow. As darkness crept into the house, he thought that of all the people he had known, it was Antonio he had most admired and wanted to be like, undaunted as he was by duty or the appearance of duty and using the world, including his family, as the fountain where he slaked his multiple thirsts.

As such, Antonio was the antithesis of Felicia, who had drummed into her grandson that his family was his destiny and his responsibility. Much as Antón fought it, her attitude prevailed, even after he left the island. Everything he did in New York, from playing baseball to going to a dance to taking an exam to ogling a woman on the street, seemed governed by her strictures. Her voice, soft and loving but inscrutable, had become imprinted in his mind. The more he tried to drown it out, the more his birthmark itched. It became his obsession to eliminate Spanish from his consciousness and make English the language of his thoughts and dreams. He whittled away at his accent and toned down his mannerisms so that they were controlled and Anglicized. If he became another person, surely her voice would disappear.

Then Felicia came to live with them in New York, and she was no longer just a voice inside him but a real, live island grandmother, clumsy and underdeveloped, whom he had to take to the doctor, the grocery store, the beautician. "I have no senses in English," she would say to him as they left the house. Antón would feel a dark mood spreading over him, and he would hunch his shoulders and lower his head as he walked next to her. Out there for the world to see, Felicia was the mark of his foreignness.

"It hurts here," she said, grabbing Antón's hand and moving it up and down along her ribs as the stupefied doctor watched.

"She wants a body wave and be sure not to burn her hair," Antón, red as a beet, would have to tell the hairdresser, who stared invitingly at him.

Her stay was mercifully brief, made tolerable only by the canasta games they played every afternoon. As soon as she left, Antón breathed a sigh of relief. At last he could stop being a dutiful grandson and continue with his metamorphosis. By the time he entered college two years later, he was signing his name as A. G. Turner, speaking accentless English, and behaving as if he had never heard of the island, let alone been born on it. In so doing, he ignored Antonio's first lesson, "Never diminish yourself," as well as his seventh, "The Lesson of Quixote," which stated that you should never let a disguise dominate you.

It was during his college years that Felicia reappeared in his life, in the shape of Ester Oliva. Antón first noticed Ester in a political science class. The lecturer had delivered a lengthy defense of Nicolás Càmpión as one of the great liberators of the century when a woman dressed in black sitting by the large French windows had stood up and challenged him. The woman spoke with such conviction and authority that the professor closed the discussion and continued with his lecture.

Antón was stunned. This was a woman of passion. He would have stood up against the professor, too, but he was carrying a C in the course and his statements would have lacked the force of hers. And so he had gone against Lesson 17, "The Lesson of Moses": "Whenever the option is presented, never take the petty road. Always go for the grand gesture."

After class Antón approached her. Ester Oliva immediately looked through his disguise and recognized him as a compatriot. When Antón asked her how she knew, she answered that only someone who was not American could be so American.

She was on her way to her next class, and they talked only briefly. She was a government major and was convinced of her mission to fight the Campión regime in every possible arena until it was toppled. Before leaving, she invited him to a meeting of her campus organization that night.

Antón remembered the gathering of the Student Alliance for Democracy as a blur of boredom and pomposity. Only Ester Oliva, who happened to be the president, stood out. Once again she was wearing dark clothes. Her hair was tied back in a bun, exposing a strong, heroic neck, and on that neck two blue veins bulged slightly and forked away from her right jaw when she spoke. Her rhetoric was restrained but convincing, and she had learned to use the first person plural *we* in a natural, magnanimous way. Though she was not a mesmerizing orator, of the sort favored among islanders, she nevertheless held the group's attention, if not their hearts, with her brilliant command of facts and her scalpel-sharp analyses.

Later, while he and Ester were walking home, Antón made a disparaging comment about the membership of SAD and Ester surprised him with her candor. She said that for most of them this was their entertainment. She said they would leave school and go on with their lives and be embarrassed that they ever joined a political organization, especially one led by a woman.

"Only Fico Brull is serious," she had said. "And he's dangerous."

Antón asked her what she was interested in and she said, without hesitation, "My country." When she asked him the same question, he felt jealous that he could not answer as simply as she—my country—as if the island were still a reality and not a dream.

He could have said, but didn't, that he had turned away from his country because you cannot retrieve a fantasy and you cannot reconstruct the past. He had surged into a present that could be his only in proportion to how fully he erased his old self. Marina used to call the United States the land of answers, and she was right. Answers lead to the world of the Vibra Bed but never the world of dreams. In the new land there could be no "my country," because that was an illusion, not an answer. In the new land "my country" became "my self." He did not say any of this because it was too complicated to know it simply and clearly in the same way that Ester knew and could formulate her response.

What was he interested in? The night, the city, the sunset, poetry, art, music, he said, sounding like a personal ad. He stopped.

She was smiling at him strangely. "You and the rest of the people on this campus. What moves you, truly?" she asked.

He wanted to say that she moved him, but that would have been melodramatic. Instead, he said he did not care about the island or democracy or liberation or Nicolás Campión. Antón told her where politics had landed his great-uncle Antonio, despite his instincts and his intelligence. He said that the only political act worth anything came out of survival in the Darwinian sense, not from dogma. As such it had biological origins and had to be spontaneous and unplanned. The rest was Machiavellian manipulation and only the Fico Brulls of this world would succeed at it.

They kept walking in silence, and Antón worried that he had said too much, but when they reached her door, she asked if he would come to the next meeting.

Antón attended the next meeting of the Student Alliance for Democracy and every one that followed it. In their walks home, he wore his skepticism like an armor and lambasted every political organization that laid claim to the island. Ester defended political commitment and sacrifice and said that without it the island might as well sink into the ocean. He countered by saying that islanders had an overblown sense of their own importance. The island was a third-rate nation with third-rate problems. Maybe it deserved to sink. This upset Ester and he had to apologize and then said, half meaning it, half not, that if he could feel about the island the way he felt about her, he would be in the front lines fighting for the liberation.

"But I am the island," Ester said. "And so are you."

Antón grabbed Ester by the forearm and turned her to face him. He kissed her on the lips, which quivered at first, then softened and opened fully.

They held each other and kissed every week after that, and would have become lovers, Antón now thought, had her graduation not gotten in the way. At the time, however, he could not shake the feeling that her involvement with him was, first and foremost, a political act. In two months she went off to fulfill her destiny. He stayed behind with two more years to go and a hole in his heart that he eventually learned to cover up but could never fill. It was thus that he came to understand his great-uncle's Lesson 23, "The Lesson of Marilyn Monroe": "Stigmata never heal."

Antón remained a member of the Student Alliance for Democracy even after Ester Oliva graduated from the university and Fico Brull succeeded her as president. She had been right about him: Fico was dangerous. In him were all the elements of a dictator but one, intelligence. He always walked a step ahead of whoever was with him, leaning forward as if he were about to burst through a door, and he carried a revolver at all times, a fact that impressed and cowed the other members of the Alliance. Here was a leader of the old school, fearless and ready to do battle at a moment's notice with anyone who stood in his way.

The problem for Fico Brull was that there was no one to battle. As a result, much of the organization's energy was spent trying to find enemies for him, mostly unwitting professors and students who, eager to ally themselves to a third-world cause, had expressed their solidarity with the Campión regime. The organization attacked its enemies, real or imagined, in every form possible, from sending anonymous letters to the school newspaper describing a particular professor's sexual practices, to making catcalls during his lectures, to phoning his home and yelling obscenities at his wife and children. Caught by surprise and unprepared for such virulence, Fico Brull's opponents invariably cracked, lowered their heads, and went back to their books. In a matter of months, he had vanquished all his antagonists within the university and was hungry for larger game.

And so the insatiable Fico Brull organized a trip to the United Nations to participate in a demonstration against the Campión government. Antón agreed to go, not out of allegiance to the cause—by this point he was aware that the only cause SAD was pursuing was Fico Brull's aggrandizement—but because he knew there would be representatives from every major political group in exile, and he secretly hoped to run into Ester Oliva.

By the time they arrived at the United Nations, upward of one thousand people had gathered across the street. The demonstrators huddled in small clusters, and the SAD contingent joined one of the more vocal of these. For some time they stayed in place, but as the group grew, the people in the back pushed the front edge against the barricades. The ones in front pushed back, and the resulting motion gave the crowd a fluid, pulsating appearance.

Antón was distracted, searching for Ester, and he found himself next to Fico Brull. Fico was in his glory, waving a placard over his head and exhorting his compatriots always to attack, never to surrender, when the crowd surged forward and pushed the two of them within arm's reach of a mounted policeman posted behind a barricade. Fico dropped his placard, pulled out a machete from underneath his raincoat, and tried to hack off the police horse's head. Due to the weapon's dullness or Fico's lack of strength, the machete bounced off the horse's neck and Fico swung again. This time the horse reared backward and Fico missed completely, falling to the ground underneath the animal. Almost immediately a patrolman materialized out of the crowd and started beating him around the head with a nightstick until red started flowing and Fico's blood sprayed on the curb. Before Antón had a chance to react, he had a billy club across the back of his neck and his face was being pushed against the pavement.

It took Fernando the better part of a day to get his son out of police custody and all of that night to extract from him the promise never to get involved in such silliness again. "Why waste your time dreaming, when this land is like a lake of opportunity ready to be grabbed?" Fernando told his son, mixing his metaphors.

Antón did not tell his father that what he saw before him was not the waters of opportunity but an ocean of longing, and the more he grabbed, the less he could hold. That was twelve years ago, before deception and dissatisfaction, before marriage, before he had "a life."

As he basked in the memory of Ester Oliva, he heard the back door opening and smelled the dank air of New Jersey wafting through the house. The cure had worked. His birthmark had settled down. He was trying to button his pants when the light went on and Alice materialized in the doorway to the kitchen.

"What's going on here?"

Her voice was clipped and measured. Antón was defenseless.

"My cure," he answered.

"It smells terrible."

She let go of the switch and went upstairs.

He fell back on the sofa. It had started raining outside, a soft suburban drizzle that brushed against the window behind him and eased his way into sleep.

Alice's short-lived first marriage had taught her to place her independence above her emotional entanglements. She insisted that she and Antón have separate bank accounts, separate closets, and separate bookshelves. Alice chose the cars they drove and the house they lived in, and how often to make love: twice a month, she had determined, for she had read, and had decided to believe, that too frequent sex with an uncircumcised man was unhealthy for a woman. Sometimes they would skip a month altogether, for from their wedding night on, Alice was riddled with a host of female ailments that kept them sleeping with their pajamas on for extended periods of time.

When she was free of cystitis or yeast infections and in between her periods, which were spontaneous and unpredictable as tropical storms, her indifference got in the way. Had Antón bothered to count, he would have discovered that, in their years of marriage, they had made love forty-five times, and on at least five of those occasions, she had drunk enough wine not just to lower her inhibitions, which were as much a part of her as the bacteria that ravaged her womb and the flash flood of her menses, but also to make her barely conscious, so that he might as well have been violating a corpse.

In truth, Alice had never loved Antón, much as she tried to convince herself otherwise, and so it was easy for her to assume a commanding role and to treat her husband as an adjunct to her decisions. Her sense of fair play, instilled in her by well-meaning liberal parents, and a vestigial kindness, which bubbled to the surface in spite of her better instincts, had kept her in the marriage beyond any hope of its salvation. In the meantime, there were affairs with other men: a Polish official, a Russian student, an Iranian geologist, and a few others, all circumcised, with whom she had brief encounters. She chose her lovers carefully to avoid any long-term entanglements and to confirm further her sense that she was in complete control of her world.

Then the Argentinian came into her life. His name was Manuel Flores and Alice met him when she taught English to adult foreign students. She could not help but notice the handsome man with the brown hair whose eyes fixed on her all through the period. Before long they were meeting after class for brief chats. He was an arms merchant by profession and he brought her exotic gifts from distant places, which she hid from her husband in the attic of their house. Manuel Flores's manners, formal but never condescending, were irresistible, and soon Alice was charmed into love by this man, the likes of whom she had only read about in the stories of American women expatriates. When she found out he was married, there was a momentary twinge of jealousy, but subsequently she was glad, for it would further guarantee the temporary nature of the relationship.

They became lovers, meeting in hotel rooms or in her house while Antón was at the college, and they would make love the afternoon long. Manuel Flores was unquenchable and more than eager to satisfy every one of the fantasies Alice had been reluctant to reveal to her husband. He tied her up and sprayed whipped cream on her; he taunted her with juicy pears and rubbed her with ripe bananas, which they ate together in ecstasy; and when she asked, he slapped her buns until they turned red, then fed her vanilla ice cream from a dripping cone, just as her father had done when she was a girl.

The day came when she recognized that she would do anything for this Argentinian stuck to her by sweat, passion, and fructose: leave her job, abandon her husband, fly to Patagonia if he asked. That was the day Manuel made a dozen promises to her and that was the day that she told Antón she was leaving.

Antón had reacted unexpectedly. Instead of wrath, there had been indifference. He simply heard what she had to say and returned to his work in the garden. The thought that his wife was having an affair intrigued and excited him. For a few moments later that morning he entertained the possibility of allowing Alice to do as she pleased, and he fantasized about making love with her after she had been with her lover, but it was only a fantasy and not anything real or good.

His musings were interrupted by a phone call from his father telling him that his great-uncle Ruperto had died unexpectedly in Miami. Under different circumstances, Antón might have felt real sorrow at his great-uncle's death. As it was, he was glad for the opportunity to leave, and took a plane south that same night.

By the time he returned ten days later, Alice had moved into an apartment with lively, vibrant furniture she thought her lover would like and fresh flowers—zinnias and daisies—his favorites. She waited three months for Manuel to come. Then she received a letter in which he reneged on all his promises, declaring in his broken, euphemistic English that he could not throw his wife to the garbage, not now, not ever. Alice did not cry, nor did she allow herself the luxury of despair; instead, she burned the letter, threw away all the gifts Manuel had given her, and renewed the oath her mother had lived by: "The only man worth trusting has the shadow of a gravestone over him."

Alice returned to Antón, not contrite but disappointed. By then the marriage had begun to taste like one of his jobs. His birthmark flared as never before and his sweat acquired an acrid, nefarious smell. He forced himself to feel outrage. He wept, threw books at the wall, dishes at the floor, and cursed at her, calling her *cabrona*, that Spanish word bearing all the venom that the English "bitch" lacked. He left for three weeks, visiting friends, his parents, even his grandmother in Miami briefly. He would have stayed away for good had not a force he did not understand, perhaps a dim sense of hope commingled with inertia, interfered. The fact is that he had no way of knowing for certain that the marriage was over. Not having a cause or a lover to escape to, he did the only thing he could. He went back to New Jersey to face the truth: Alice, the pink-lipped, bottom-blue Unitarian maiden, had betrayed him.

The rain had intensified throughout the night and Antón was awakened in the morning by the tinny drip of water on the gutter pipe. Outside the window, a male cardinal hopped from branch to branch on the lilac bush. Beyond the back yard, the Sourland Mountains sloped away into the eastern flatlands of the state. To the right, the wooden skeletons of new, expensive houses marked the edges of the farmland that had recently been sold to developers. In a few months, fifty sewer lines would be running into town, but for him this was not an important realization.

He rose from the couch, finally, compelled by the weight of a full bladder on his urinary tract, and went upstairs to the bathroom. The door was locked. The fullness had turned to pain, and standing only intensified it. He knocked several times and was shifting his weight from foot to foot when Alice opened the door.

She was naked, skin blushed from the shower and thighs

smooth as a baby's. Without her clothes, she was as clean and white as a frozen continent, and every curve of her, from the arches of her feet to her full calves, to her lithe back and straight neck, seemed to lead with natural logic to her dusk-colored hair. She was the measure of his success and the mirror of his failure. She was the ice field, the blasting wind; she was el Norte.

His bladder was calling. He went to the toilet and lifted the cover. It was sanity returning.

"What's with you?" she asked, holding the hair curler in her right hand like a weapon.

"I had to go," he answered.

She resumed fixing her hair with the nonchalance of someone who knows the power of her station. It was her house they were living in, her town, her land, and her authority that dominated the household. It was, in short, her marriage, while he was a mere appendage, dangling in the breeze of her certainties. He hesitated a moment before flushing—she hated when the toilet was not flushed—then went downstairs to make coffee.

Antón fully expected Alice to ask him why he was not getting ready for work that morning. Instead, she passed him in the kitchen on her way out and mentioned that she had another sewer committee meeting that night and would not be home for dinner. Antón watched her as she walked down the flagstone path by the lilac bush and into the garage. It struck him as strange that there should be a committee to deal with something as lowly as sewers. Even shit deserves to be managed, he thought, and he knew no one better qualified to do that than his wife. When he heard the car back into the alley and drive away, he poured himself a cup of coffee and sat down to think what to do next.

At the time of Antón's marriage to Alice, the Campión opposition in exile had reached its zenith and split into three groups, B–10, G–7, and O–15, all named, for some clandestine but no doubt politically expedient reason, after bingo numbers. The membership of these organizations included anyone with a strong enough aversion to Nicolás Campión, from former members of Sotelo's secret police acting out of retribution, to disillusioned ideologues, to pangful students who had left the island in their infancy and now were compelled to redeem their roots, to wily businessmen who saw the fatherland as a virgin and lucrative market, to would-be adventurers tired of desk work and family life. The bingo groups, as they became known in the exile community, had made a number of celebrated, though minor, amphibious assaults on the island that did little other than give Campión the excuse he needed to tighten his grip on the people and cement his tyranny. Greedy for the publicity and covert CIA funds that were periodically parceled out among all of them, the groups soon turned their attention away from fighting the Campión regime to waging open battles with each other in the streets of Miami, in full view not only of their exiled compatriots, who accepted this sort of gangsterism as part of their heritage, but also of the native population, who were outraged that their city had been overrun by trigger-happy anarchists and whose protestations eventually reached federal ears. It was then that CIA support had dried up and that the number of new recruits had slowed to a trickle.

Fico Brull, Antón's old college mate, had joined B–10, the most extreme of the groups, and had been arrested twenty-two times for conspiracies, felonies, and misdemeanors so obscure they baffled the most competent of his lawyers. Presently, he was serving ten years in prison for manslaughter, after he had tried to blow up the World Bank with a bazooka and had accidentally killed the secretary to the representative from the Republic of Mauritius.

Hidden away in suburban New Jersey, Antón found it easy to stay out of exile politics. Teaching, planting, and writing were his only interests. If anyone in town or at the college asked him about the island or Nicolás Campión, he answered whatever he thought they wanted to hear, then changed the conversation to a local topic. The few important developments in Miami or New York came to him by phone from his parents or in the occasional letters his grandmother sent him. That's how he had learned about Fico Brull, and that's how Antón found out that Tico, his lost cousin, wanted to talk to him.

After two tours of duty in the navy, Tico had joined G–7, the largest of the exile groups, during a period of intense terrorist activity. He was saved from an ill-fated sortie to the island from which none of the expeditionaries returned by a case of gonorrhea that he had picked up while in Central America on an arms-buying trip. Tico was reassigned to recruitment and warned to stay away from prostitutes.

Tico's phone call came as Antón sipped the last of his morning coffee. He had not expected the call. Nevertheless, despite the years, he instantly recognized his cousin's voice.

Tico kept the pleasantries to a minimum. His tone was serious, and his voice lacked the verve it used to have. It wasn't a different man who was speaking but a charged one. He asked Antón to join G–7. Antón refused, lying that he was happy with his life the way it was. The cousin insisted. He said that there were great plans in the works. "The hour has come," he said twice.

Antón was doubtful. The G–7 leadership had always been comprised of men with clear ties to the Sotelo regime, and the organization's policy statements were fiery with fascism.

"But we have changed," Tico said. There was a ring of conviction in his voice. "We have new leaders committed to democracy."

"They're all committed to democracy until they gain power," Antón said.

The cousin ran through a list of names that meant nothing to Antón. Then he mentioned Ester Oliva.

Antón felt as if all his breath were being sucked out of him, and his knees buckled. Tico added that he and Ester were having lunch in New York that day and why didn't he join them.

As Antón hung up the phone, a surge of energy coursed through him. It began in his birthmark, moved to his chest, and settled in his throat, where it grew until he thought it would spurt out of his mouth. He rushed out the door to his vegetable plot. The black surface lay ready for growth and he sensed a kinship to it. He, too, had been waiting all these years and now something was about to sprout in him. Before leaving, he wrote Alice a note about quitting the college and left it on her dresser, where she could not miss it.

Antón had agreed to meet his cousin and Ester Oliva at a café on East Seventeenth Street, near Union Square. It was a good day, sunny and cool, and he decided to walk from the train station. He took Seventh Avenue down, and by the time he reached Eighteenth Street, he felt awake and restored. The island was far away in time and distance. New Jersey was a long shadow. Miami was a specter floating over the Florida flatness.

If there was any place he might call home, it was New York. He had traveled the whole length of Manhattan, from the Battery to Spuyten Duyvil. He'd gone east to Rockaway and Throgs Neck, south to Great Kills. He had played baseball in Van Cortlandt Park and swum in the Hudson, skirting condoms and dead rats. He had seen the sun come up over Coney Island, the sun set from Washington Heights, the snow bury Fifth Avenue, and the summer heat beat down on the Grand Concourse till it melted. He'd watched as sex spread open before him like a red beach in the Bronx and the empty faces of the damned darkened the bars and coffee shops off Times Square. He had fallen in love in Fordham, gotten arrested in front of the United Nations, and been struck by a shaft of sunlight on Sixth Avenue so bright his eyes went blank and he stumbled into a parking meter. He had been propositioned by boys in Greenwich Village and whores on Eighth Avenue. He'd come face to face with art and music and filth and hate and greed. He'd walked past a woman sitting on the curb holding her dead rabbit on her lap as if it were the Son of God and a lady in a fur coat choking on a hot dog in Central Park while her husband fed the squirrels. New York was the city of everything, the first and the last and the in between.

Here he was again, walking the streets he had walked every day of his life in el Norte, surrounded by cars, taxis, trucks, bicycles, horns honking, tires squealing, brakes screeching, radios blaring, and it was all comforting and familiar. It didn't matter if he was handsome or ugly, native or foreign, Felicia Turner's grandson or the King of Persia. No one around him cared if he joined the resistance or not, if he was happy or miserable or alive or dead. It was among the anonymous masses, finally, where he could let all his masks fall away. If New York wasn't home, nothing was.

Elated at being nobody, Antón looked in a store window and saw a face, not unlike a rodent's, that was at once pleasing and ridiculous. For a moment he thought there was someone looking out inside the store, and then he realized it was his own reflection, between two mannequins, that was staring back at him. He saw himself almost smile and his eyebrows lighten and arch upward. Not bad, he thought, this transparency!

He arrived early at the café and ordered a coffee. Fifteen minutes later Tico entered, followed by a woman with the somber look of a chosen one. Ester was heavier now and had streaks of gray in her hair. She was wearing a dark blue suit with a plain white blouse buttoned to the neck. She had no makeup on, not even lipstick, and her face was round and muted. Under her lower lip was a thin scar a half inch in length. Something about her reminded Antón of Miriam Marrero, his mother's friend, and of Mirta the Beautiful, though there was no frivolity or shyness in Ester's behavior; rather, an intoxicating seriousness and purity of purpose.

They greeted each other. She ordered a sandwich and iced tea and spoke first, leaving no room for reminiscence. She said that it was a mistake on his part to assume that G–7 was a homogeneous organization. She explained that there were a number of people like her committed to democracy and social justice and she emphasized the need for unity around a common goal— toppling Nicolás Campión and establishing a legitimate government.

"Ester, tell him what's been happening," Tico said.

"We have money and support coming in from the highest circles," she said.

Antón would much rather have spoken about the days at the university, but he realized the only thing in Ester's mind was the liberation of the island. She had not changed.

"How high?" he asked.

"The highest," she said.

"The White House?"

She did not reply but continued about weaknesses and rifts within the island power structure. The people were tired of privation, and the intellectuals, the same ones who had supported the revolution until very recently, had come out publicly in favor of changing the system. The time was ripe for one major thrust that would crack open the Campión government. G–7 had learned from intelligence sources that the army did not have enough gasoline for its tanks and that the air force had over 60 percent of its planes grounded for lack of parts.

"And what do you have?" Antón asked her. "Men like him?" He pointed at Tico, trying to make light of the matter.

"Men like me," Tico said, dead serious as Antón had never heard him before. "And men like you."

Ester continued. She explained that the attack was being co-ordinated with insurgency groups inside the island, that a number of high-ranking Campión men had vowed passive support, that the G–7 training camp was about to start operating.

"Join us," she implored finally. "This is your chance to do something that will have real meaning."

Antón felt an upswell of his old feelings for Ester, but he squelched it and said he would think about it. As they were leaving the restaurant, the cousin said he should not think too much. He and Ester were returning to Norfolk, Virginia, that afternoon. The training camp in the Everglades was due to open in three days.

Antón spent the rest of the afternoon walking the streets of New York. The elation he had felt in the morning had left him, and a fear, not of death, but of action, had taken its place. More precisely, it was the possibility of fighting and dying for the wrong cause that fed his skepticism. The soldier, the revolutionary, he thought as he walked, must blind himself to the intricacies of ideology, that is, he must be impervious to doubt; otherwise, he cannot follow orders and he cannot fight. Then he remembered something he had heard Antonio say in one of his lessons: that only those who realize that their enemy is behind them as well as in front will live; only the wary survive. If Antón joined the expeditionary force and came out alive, he would stand redeemed, not just before Felicia and his family, but before himself. He would also, in no small way, be the man he had always wanted to be—Antonio's nephew, the true revolutionary tugging at death's ear. Not to go was to remain forever in a loveless relationship and in a hopeless place, subject to the tyranny of regret.

By the time he got home that night, Alice's car was already in the driveway. He got out of his Buick and noticed the moon. Its light settled on the soft suburban landscape like a fluorescent coating made of his will. He shook himself and entered the house.

Alice was cleaning the kitchen floor as she did every Thursday night.

"Don't I deserve an explanation?" she asked.

It surprised Antón that she knew about his meeting with Tico and Ester. He did not remember the note he had left her.

"I was just having lunch," he said defensively.

"At nine o'clock? You are always just having lunch, you are always just quitting your job."

Her statements rode the squeaks of the mop on the linoleum, pitching upward at the end of each stroke and adding a tone of superiority that was as disdainful as her diligence.

He said nothing in response, aware that his voice could never carry the power of his eyes. He merely stared at her.

"Grow up!" she said. "If you are going to be silent, be silent. If you are going to write, write. Right now you are a nobody doing nothing. No job, no purpose. Make up your mind."

"And if my mind does not include you?"

Pausing to rinse the sponge, she glared at him with cold gray-green eyes—the eyes of el Norte—and said by way of closure that he was making excuses for his failure as a man.

"This house, this place is my Corral Falso," he yelled back, not quite knowing what he meant.

He walked across the wet kitchen floor, and as he opened the back door, he accidentally tipped over the wash bucket. He turned the corner just in time to avoid the wrathful mop that whooshed past his head and landed in the flower bed by the fence.

Outside, the houses and their yards glowed with an odd green light. He got in his Buick and drove over the greening Sourland Mountains, north first, then toward the river; he turned south on the road parallel to the water and completed the rectangle by heading east a few miles down. He drove the same circuit for two hours, until he found himself in the driveway of his house, unable to break free of the force that held him like an electron in a reluctant orbit around Alice, the same force that had made him return once before when he thought he had left for good. He turned the car off and entered through the kitchen.

The house was dark and silent but for the faint murmur of Alice's snoring floating down from the second floor. Upstairs, the snoring was louder, more powerful, like the grumblings of a drunken stevedore. Something was not right. He went into the study and stood in the darkness, his mind foggy from the driving. When he switched the light on, he saw his desk, swaddled in red paint. His typewriter was flooded, his manuscripts were sopping and illegible. Once, in a fit of indulgence after one of their arguments, he had said to Alice that writing was like bleeding oneself. Now she had turned the cliché into a bitter joke, and the sum total of his work—of non-work, she would have corrected—lay in red ruins before him. He should have burst with anger; he should have attacked the set of English bone china Alice inherited from her grandmother or hacked away at the ponderous oak dining-room furniture she had spent countless hours restoring, and thus paid back the wrong in kind. But there was no wrong. All these years he had been languishing as a writer who has had many more dreams than publications, and Alice had, in a few moments of self-righteousness, freed him with a gallon of red paint. He was not angry or pained; in a way he was grateful.

He gathered what clothes he could wrestle out of the closet without waking her and a few books from the shelves downstairs and walked out. In the car he felt his throat relax and a warmth like honey spread down his gullet. He was going to Norfolk.

He drove south on 95 past Philadelphia and into Delaware. Close to the Maryland border, exhaustion dropped its blanket on him and the hallucinations came: first a tractor-trailer barreling head-on toward him, followed by a large white wall rising up from the road. He rolled down the window, turned the radio volume up as high as it would go, and pinched his earlobe until the pain made him gasp. If he drove through the rest of the night, he could reach Norfolk by late morning.

He took the next exit and stopped at an all-night diner for some coffee. Back on the interstate, the hum of rubber on concrete settled him and he surged ahead, reaching Washington, D.C., as the eastern sky brightened with dawn. One hour south of the city, the traffic slowed to a crawl, then stopped altogether. Ahead there was smoke rising over the highway, and off in the distance sirens were wailing. Antón pulled onto the shoulder and turned the motor off. He left the car and started walking with a group of other drivers in the direction of the smoke. He smelled a barnyard, diesel, something cooking, and heard a chorus of squeals, not unlike the sirens but less portentous, more pathetic. One hundred yards ahead, cars had stopped sideways on the road; others were resting on the median, where the force of their braking had taken them. Before them all, blocking the road, were two trucks mangled together. The cab of one, a Mayflower moving van, lay embedded in the other's trailer, and both were on fire. Around the wreck were dark mounds, hogs everywhere, some still alive, trying to get up. The worst of the squeals came from inside the trailer, where many of the pigs were trapped.

The sun was well up on the horizon and the surrounding fields had turned the color of fire and blood. A man on the roof of a car aimed a shotgun into the trailer, trying to kill the burning animals one by one. One trucker sat by himself, knees to his chest, on the left shoulder. He was bleeding from the forehead and looked strangely peaceful and innocent. The other driver was still inside his cab, roasting with the hogs, beyond the heroics of several men who were trying to open the door.

Antón watched, shaken not by the horror but by the beauty and order of the scene—the black smoke curling against the indigo-blue sky, the yellow ship on the side of the moving van sailing into the porcine inferno. A few minutes later the police cars, fire trucks, and ambulances arrived, the composition fell apart, and chaos, human chaos, reigned.

As Antón walked back, a man sitting on the embankment directly across from the Buick called to him. He asked what was up and Antón answered, "An accident."

"Bad?" he asked again. He was thin and leathery and spoke with a twang softened by a wad of chewing tobacco.

"Pretty much," Antón answered, trying to be casual. He'd be exposed to a great deal more carnage in war.

The man said he would wait until the road was cleared. He pointed to his truck on the left shoulder and said he had been driving twenty years.

"Been everywhere. Seen everything. Where you headed, buddy?" he asked Antón.

"Norfolk."

"What's that?"

"I'm going to see somebody in Norfolk." He was so tired that language was like smoke in his mouth.

"A girl? You got a girl in Norfolk?"

"No. A guy I know who just got out of the navy."

"You gotta watch out for those girls in navy towns. They'll fuck anything in uniform. They'll marry you and have a dozen kids and you don't know if they're yours."

"That so?" How easy it was to talk like a man.

The man spit and a brown wad of saliva flew in an arc and landed close to Antón's feet. Then he mumbled, "Man, what do you know? You don't know nothing."

"I know I'm driving to Norfolk."

The man stretched his neck and laughed, wiping the side of his face with the back of his hand.

"You can't know too much. I'm just going to wait here until they clear the road as if nothing ever happened. If you got a place to get to, why look at something that makes you doubt you ever will? Watch those navy girls."

Antón got in his car and sat until the traffic started moving again. He drove past the smoldering ruins of the pig truck and the moving van as soon as a lane was cleared. His time for waiting was over.

He reached Tico's apartment in the early afternoon and had to ring three times before someone came to the door. The man who answered had not shaved in several days and was holding half a sandwich in his right hand. When Antón said that he was looking for Tico Alouf, the man mumbled his name, Fred Union, and waved Antón in. Tico was out but would be back soon.

Fred Union said he had served with Tico in the submarine and their tours were up at the same time. He said also that he was from Mississippi, one of seven children born to a sharecropper, but he would not be caught dead going back there.

He offered Antón a beer and went on about his navy career and how he had joined at nineteen in order to avoid the draft. He said he had never regretted the decision, except for the time his father died while he was out at sea and he had arrived home too late for the funeral. He'd been married once, but the woman was bad, a first-degree whore. According to Fred Union, the best women in the world were Filipinos.

"They give whatever you want," he said. "And sexually they're the most liberated."

After three beers on an empty stomach, Antón wanted nothing but sleep, but Fred was determined to illustrate his last statement by describing his sexual adventures in the Philippines.

Midway through his antics with three girls in a Manila bordello, Tico showed up. The cousin greeted Antón with an embrace.

"So you decided to join us," Tico said.

"Yes," replied Antón, disappointed not to see Ester.

Fred Union disappeared into one of the back rooms and left the two cousins alone.

"What about your wife?" Tico asked.

"I didn't tell her. She wouldn't understand. The marriage is over."

"Since when is understanding a requirement of marriage?" Tico asked.

"It was like trying to use a metric wrench on an English nut. We came together but kept slipping, damaging each other."

"So you and Alice didn't fit. That shouldn't surprise you."

"She always claimed she knew where she was going and I didn't."

"She had a point, until now."

Tico brought a whiskey bottle over to the coffee table and poured two drinks. He raised his glass and offered a toast to the good old days. Antón felt obliged to smile.

"Where is Ester?" he asked the cousin.

"Gone back to Washington. She's in the political arm. We're military."

In the silence that followed Antón became uncomfortable. He told the cousin that maybe he should be in the political arm as well. He hadn't had any experience in the military. The cousin tried to calm him by saying that that was the purpose of the training camp. He was no different from most other recruits.

"What is Fred's role in this?" Antón asked. "I don't trust him."

"CIA," Tico replied.

"You can't be serious," said Antón.

"One of the best. You believed his story, didn't you? Look," the cousin said. "Don't worry so much. The fact that the CIA is involved is to our benefit."

Antón then asked Tico what had made him volunteer.

"I had to do something. I had enough of the submarine service. If it works, we'll be heroes."

"And if it doesn't?"

"We'll be martyrs. You still have time to turn around and go home, Antón. Your life will continue along on its doggy way, dull and dead. I, for one, would rather be dead from a bullet than dead of the doldrums. Just think, we'll be making history, liberating our country, honoring our family."

Rather than captivating, Tico's grandiloquence had the effect of disappointing Antón. Had the cousin been more perceptive, he would have realized Antón was clearing the way for a decision he had already made.

The next day, Antón phoned his parents, who were away, and his grandmother, who was not convinced by his lie about going on a hunting trip.

"You are acting like your great-uncle Antonio," Felicia said to him before hanging up. He took it as a compliment.

The last person he called was Alice. He offered a greeting, was rebuffed, made inquiries after her welfare, was answered monosyllabically, and, with little other option, took his leave and hung up. Something in him died and he felt his stomach harden. In the distance between them, all that he would have of her was a figure in a corner of a tapestry, a woman in a garden gardening, on her tongue the lyrics of a Shaker tune.

They left the next morning in Tico's car, a white BMW that had seen better days but could reach 100 mph with hardly a purr.

As they entered the interstate, Antón asked the cousin who was the head of G–7's military arm. Tico answered Valdés de Cuna, the real-estate baron who had served in Sotelo's cabinet and left the island with a reputedly substantial portion of the national treasury.

"Nice man," Antón said sarcastically.

"But he is," Tico insisted. "In the old days, he and I used to play dominos in the back room while the others gave their speeches. He used to say that we islanders liked to eat a lot of shit."

"What are his ambitions?"

"He wants to be President. He is as rich as he is ever going to get. At least he won't be corrupted by money. He is a man on a mission."

Tico lit a cigarette and waited for Antón to ask what it was.

"To kick Campión in the ass and get the country back on its feet in five years."

"He'll have to sell the island off to the Americans to do that," Antón countered.

"Campión sold it to the Russians. A small country like ours is like a whore—always having to sell itself in order to survive. If I'm going to get fucked, I'd rather get it from the guy with the fattest wallet."

Tico's theory of international relations was hardly new, but Antón insisted that Davids had to confront Goliaths, if only to sustain their self-respect.

"You're naïve," Tico countered. He maintained that weaker beings always live at the mercy of the stronger ones, and the same could be said of nations. Anytime it wanted, the United States could curl one of its tentacles around the island and choke it. He could have added, but did not, thinking it would weaken Antón's resolve, that the invasion would succeed as long as the United States upheld its promise of support. The moment there was a change of mind at the White House, the moment a dissenting voice was taken seriously or a crisis in another part of the world diverted the President's attention, that would be the end of the expedition, of G–7, of the two of them.

They drove through the day and into the night, stopping only for food and gas, and reached the outskirts of Belle Glade shortly before midnight. From there Tico insisted Antón climb into the back seat and put on a blindfold, standard operating procedure, he called it, using his navy voice.

By the time Tico let his cousin take off the blindfold, the sky was gaining light and the shadowy outlines of scrub pine were visible on either side of the road. Ahead to the left were barracks; on the right, there was a larger official-looking building with the lights on. They drove up to it and parked.

An armed guard approached the car and asked Tico to identify himself. The cousin mumbled a code word and gave the man some papers he unfolded from his shirt pocket. The guard led them inside the large building, where another man dressed in military fatigues sat behind a gray metal desk puffing on a cigar. Behind him were color-coded maps of the island. A single bare light bulb hanging from the ceiling illuminated the room. The man was Valdés de Cuna.

After greeting him, Tico explained why they were there. Valdés de Cuna congratulated them both on their decision and extended his hand to Antón. He remembered the Turners from the old days, especially Felicia and Antonio, with whom he had had dealings.

Valdés de Cuna called out the name Griego, and almost immediately, as if he'd been standing guard in the back room, a thin, frail-looking man came in. He was dressed in brown polyester pants and an untucked madras shirt that was too small for him. He stood at attention and saluted, and as he did so, he exposed the right side of his belly, hard and tanned, with a thick blue vein running down below the belt.

"*A sus órdenes,*" he said. El Griego's eyes were devoid of emotion, like a reptile's, and his voice sounded as if it came from a larynx made of galvanized steel.

Valdés de Cuna ordered him to take the boys over to the barracks and get them some breakfast. Before they left, he poured three shots of rum. His head was clear over the other three men and his body blocked out half the window. There was none of the excess fat on it Antón had learned to expect on the well-to-do. His face was smooth and free of wrinkles, though he was well into his fifties. His neck was as thick as an athlete's, making his head seem too small for the rest of his body. His hair, dyed black and receding from the forehead, was perfectly cut and combed back. His vanity seemed an anomaly in the camp, but it was not an observation that Antón lingered over. The leader offered them one drink each and raised the third in a toast.

"Now we're really going to get the bastard," he said, and drank.

Antón hesitated.

"Drink," Valdés de Cuna commanded him. "You won't be seeing liquor for a while. Might as well enjoy it. Drink, Captain Nemo, drink!"

*R*uperto's death had been a surprise to everyone but Felicia. He had moved in with her after leaving his wife in Puerto Rico and the accursed life of a beautician behind forever. "No matter how hard I tried," he would tell whoever was within earshot, "ugly women remained ugly." For one full month Felicia had noticed her brother's normally erect posture sag in the rocking chair where he rested after dinner and his electric eyes flatten in long stares through the afternoon. Dr. Figueras, the same one who used to make incognito visits to the house years before, had declared Ruperto to be in excellent health. But Felicia knew that her brother was dying.

The night before it happened, Ruperto called the funeral parlor where he had worked ever since settling in Miami and said that he was not feeling well; but there were three wakes scheduled and the director urged him to come in. When Ruperto returned in the morning, he had lost his shadow and his eye sockets had deepened to the point where no light came out of them. He sat in the rocker and asked for his coffee, and when Felicia brought it, she saw him, chin to chest, hands clenched on his lap. Without touching him or checking his pulse, she knew that his moment of truth had arrived. She called the doctor and her son Eduardo; she called Ruperto's wife, Areli, in Puerto Rico, who responded with tinny whimpers but refused to come to Miami to claim the body. It was the last time Felicia would speak to her.

He was buried in a less than dignified manner. While the legal complications as to who was responsible for the body were straightened out, the corpse lay in a morgue freezer for eight days. As a result, his few remaining friends and the family members who stayed in Miami waiting for Ruperto to be released into the hands of the embalmers grew weary of keeping their mourning in check and turned what should have been a somber week into a festival of cardplaying, drinking, and jokes.

The wake was a ramshackle affair, lasting only an afternoon. The hall in which he was laid out had already been assigned for the evening, and the funeral home director was unwilling to move the later wake into another room, no matter that Ruperto had been his faithful evening coordinator for over a year. It was enough, he told Fernando, that he was giving the family the usual employee discount. The burial was quick and efficient without a priest to lengthen the proceedings with a homily. Even unto death, Felicia felt bound to accommodate the prejudices of those close to her.

After the symbolic shovelfuls of dirt were thrown on the casket and the small group dispersed to their cars, Felicia saw Antón as he stood over the open grave, a question furrowing his brow, his pale cheeks drawn against bone. To her he was still the child she had seen walk away from her on the dark morning seventeen years before.

Back in the house, while the mourners feasted and drank, Felicia pulled Antón aside and admonished him that if he kept going the way he was, he would wind up like Simeon Stylites.

"St. Simeon, you know. He lived atop a pillar. As the years passed he had it heightened. The day came when he was so high off the ground the faithful could barely hear him preach. His only company was his own feces. He was too good for his own good."

Waving her finger before his nose, she added, "You won't know what you have until you lose it."

Alone the following morning she realized she could have told everyone in the family the same thing. Her brother's death had crystallized the possibility she had fought against since the death of her husband that the family, her hope and her support, was splintering. Her two sons were busy making their way in the new world, and the other grandchildren were too young still to be anything other than pesky distractions. The process of elimination led to Antón, in whom she saw the faint seed of posterity, or imagined such.

Felicia trusted her instincts more than her intellect, more than her sentimentality, and certainly more than her guilt. Life went on and she received her guests—fewer now that her brother was gone—as she had in the past, with a pot of beans or stew and freshly perked coffee. She spent more and more time in funeral homes paying her respects to friends and relatives she had known from her youth. Some months she went to as many as six wakes, but her average was two, enough to have her generation decimated in a few years. It was at Arístides Berza's funeral, as she looked at his waxen face before the casket was closed for the last time, that a voice at her ear, a voice that sounded as if it came out of an ancient mist, told her she had six months to settle her affairs. That same night she called her old friend Marina for advice on the matter.

Nothing, not even the blindness that had come upon her as a result of advanced diabetes, kept the old seer from coming to her friend's aid. Marina was married again, not to the wealthy Presbyterian she had mused about before leaving the island, but to a butcher twenty years her junior, who doted on her and brought her elephantine roasts and red, juicy sirloins fresh from the block. Marina had taken to wearing dark glasses to cover her sugar-bleared eyes; her skin, once tight against layers of fat, now hung loosely around her neck and down her arms. Her hair was still dyed red, and her presence, preceded by the jingle of her jewelry, was as mesmerizing as it had been on the island when her career was at its height.

She offered Felicia the name and phone number of her cemetery's agent. There was a nice plot left next to hers, shaded by a royal poinciana not far from the service road. Felicia was not convinced. She preferred cremation. Marina thought that was all right, too, as long as the ashes were not entrusted to any relative to keep. "Better the wind," she said, "than a box on someone's mantel."

They spent the rest of the visit comparing funerals they had attended and exchanging the bland gossip of the old, which limits itself to the diseases, conditions, and operations to which friends in common are prey. Toward the end, Felicia brought up her grandson's aimlessness.

"This is the land of waking," Marina told her. "Ours was the land of dreaming. Here people matter in relation to their objects; there we mattered in relation to the people who dreamed with us. Our objects died when our dreams did. That is why we need inner light to illuminate our path; here everything is lit, everything is clarified, and morning never ends."

"He had so much promise as a child. He might have been somebody," Felicia mused.

"Today he is nobody. Tomorrow he will be a different man, and the day after that a different one still, and none of these men will have anything to do with you. We will be dead soon. Nothing will matter after that."

"He is lost."

"He is not. There are no accidents in this life. He is teaching himself a lesson."

"What?"

"That he can only be fulfilled in blood, that past and future are one in the present, that he's already been marked to do what he has to do no matter how far he roams. He will learn to trust the inner light, but that is irrelevant to you right now. You have very little time left."

The lady took to her preparations with a zeal that, while unsettling the younger family members, nevertheless made her age gracefully in their eyes and kept from them the sense of dread that burdens families when one of them teeters at the edge of darkness. Much needed straightening; words had to be said, hurts healed, friendships concluded, angers explained, secrets unveiled, illness borne honorably in silence, and her memory assured.

Death became the purpose of her life. She pulled out from under the mattress the money she had been saving for five years and placed it in an envelope in her top dresser drawer, where it would be easily accessible. It was her belief that her children should not be burdened with the cost of the funeral she had planned for herself. She wanted a lavish affair that would last the full two days and not a moment less, replete with food and liquor for the guests and gifts for the children. In a note she included with the money she wrote that white was to be the color of her death, white the limousines and white the funeral dress; that none of her relatives should work that day; that the children should in no way be reprimanded and should be allowed to do as they pleased. And there should be no rain, but the sun should shine, the sky blue as the love of the angels and the earth smooth as a baby's thigh.

Fifty-seven years of smoking began to manifest themselves. Her voice grew rough and gravelly, and she became afflicted with a short dry cough that never went away. Her sons urged her to give up tobacco, and the doctor issued the usual ultimatums, but she saw no reason to stop. Cigarettes were her companions and allowed her mind to drift upward with the smoke; besides, other, more immediate ailments occupied her—a weakened stomach, rotting teeth, and a rheumatism that stiffened her joints and kept her awake nights with a pulsating, fluid pain in her extremities like the motions of the sea that she took as persistent messages from the other world. The casing of her life was wearing out. To forgo smoking at this point would only forestall the process.

When not accommodating herself to the unavoidable and thereby helping others do so as well, she sat in the rocker with her cigarettes and her handkerchief, looking back not with nostalgia or regret but rather as one rereading a favorite book, in full knowledge of the basic plot, and thus better able to appreciate the nuances of the author's style.

Once, after a particularly virulent attack of rheumatism that made the joints of her hand feel as if they had been dipped in molten lead, she remembered the last time she had seen her mother. Her eyes were fixed on the flickering oil lamp at the foot of her sickbed and her mouth was frozen in a soundless scream. Her cheeks, injected with the yellow venom of death, had repelled the daughter and made her gag when she kissed them. Felicia vowed then, at the age of thirteen, never to let death tyrannize her like that.

She remembered, too, the *verbenas* at the lyceum in Corral Falso and how all the town would attend and the music wouldn't stop until the sun came up the next morning. At one of these dances she had met Napoleón Silva, the famous general who had mutinied against the dictatorship of Inocencio Fuentes. Napoleón was then a young lieutenant visiting his family on leave. Resplendent in his gala uniform, he was the center of attention of all the girls, who hoped to get at least one dance for their efforts. But he had ignored them and danced only with Felicia. They saw each other daily after that, until it was time for him to return to the regiment; then he turned from her and went to his ambitions like a man possessed. When he came back to town a year later, Felicia heard that he was engaged to the daughter of an oligarch from the capital.

Her disappointment lasted until the next *verbena*. By then she had already met Luis García, one of several eager young men who hovered around her at the parties. He was a serious, formal fellow with soft amber eyes and a nervous way about him. He was still in his father's shadow, and everyone expected him to carry on the family export business. At the time she had no way of knowing of the worms that would invade his personality years into their marriage and lead him to bankruptcy, drink, and the beds of countless women.

Sometimes images came to her: the flash of light through a

milk-streaked glass; or the smell of leather and horse sweat in the old farm's tack room; or the feel of the sun on her skin and the sound of early-morning waves outside the window of the hotel, the first time she made love. She remembered how her fear increased to a giddy terror all through her wedding day, and longing swirled in her like a wind becoming storm, the two emotions growing together until they became one white-hot ball. And when the time had come, after the celebrations and the dancing and the guests, she waited in bed for her husband, who slipped under the covers naked. They kissed and his hands groped all about her body, going places none had before. She felt his manhood, hard like no flesh, slithering up her thighs, then his entry into her and the jabbing thrusts. She remembered as if it were yesterday, and she still loved him—Luis, Luisito—who had given her so much pleasure and so much pain.

The last time Felicia saw her grandson, he showed up unannounced at her front door, three months after Ruperto's death. His troubles with Alice had only gotten worse and he looked awful. His hair was tousled and prematurely gray; his forehead was blemished and swollen over the eyebrows; the nose loomed over his thin lips and overwhelmed his diminutive chin; his cheeks, colorless and glassy, lay flat against the bone and his ears protruded outward as if they'd been cut and reattached without concern for balance or design. To his grandmother he seemed once again the ratlike creature that had so disturbed her over thirty years ago. Still, her immediate reaction was to embrace him, and as she did so, she could feel through the damp jacket and unironed shirt, not the meat life ought to put on a man, but the jags and heavy matter of bone.

It was a Saturday and the living room was crowded with guests. Marina la Ciega was there with her ruddy husband, Bill. Lucho was there as well, smiling like a man about to enter Paradise, and Eduardo and his wife, Lidiana, with their children.

Antón sat in Felicia's rocker. Eduardo handed him a drink and Lidiana brought him a plate of food, which he ate, not voraciously as he would have in better days, but judiciously, as if each forkful carried the whole weight of existence. As he finished the food and started on his second glass of Scotch, he noticed the figure of a girl wearing a towel flash out of the bathroom and enter one of the rear bedrooms. It was María Antonieta, Eduardo's twenty-one-year-old daughter.

Her appearance in the living room a few minutes later jarred Antón's leaden mood. From her spread the sweet scent of flowers and holiness. She kissed everyone present but only shook hands with Antón.

"What a waste!" said Eduardo.

Surprised, Antón looked at his uncle, and Eduardo repeated his exclamation.

"Stop it!" said Lidiana, materializing out of the kitchen. "The girl has made up her mind. If she wants to be a nun, then so be it."

"María Antonieta will make a very good nun." Marina spoke up in her sibylline voice. "She will be blessed by God and all the saints, but she is destined for secular greatness."

María Antonieta did not take her father's complaint seriously, nor did she acknowledge the seer's prophecy. A few minutes later a car drove onto the gravel shoulder in front of the house and she was gone.

"What a thing," said Eduardo. "She's going out on a date."

"To a prayer meeting!" Lidiana broke in, working to aggravate her husband.

"Nevertheless, if she's going into the monastery . . ."

"Seminary," Lidiana corrected him.

"Convent," Marina corrected her.

"Monastery, convent, seminary," Eduardo protested. "If you people were not so intent on showing me up, I'd be able to finish a sentence."

"If you weren't so drunk, there wouldn't be any need to correct you," said his wife, ignoring that she herself had been corrected.

"*¡Carajo!*" yelled Eduardo. "I know better than anyone when I'm drunk. And let me tell you something else."

He was wiggling his finger at his wife, but he meant it for everyone.

He did not get to continue. Felicia, aware that the gathering was about to deteriorate and eager to send her visitors away on a positive note, addressed the one person who had been silent throughout.

"What do you think, Antón?"

The whiskey had taken effect. She saw him focusing his concentration on the muscles of his mouth. Finally he spoke.

"Ma-ri-an-to-nie-ta."

Felicia stared at him through a plume of cigarette smoke. She knew how difficult language could be when it turned solid in the mouth.

"Is-a-luf-ly-air. A lughly gull."

"Yes. She is lovely."

"And . . . viv-a-shusss."

Later, after the guests had left and Antón had moved to the yellow couch, he raised his head and asked Felicia clearly, as if his drunkenness had temporarily lifted, if María Antonieta was happy because she was young or because she was certain of what she wanted. Or was it that she was simpleminded?

"At twenty-one it is easy to be full of cheer," Felicia said.

For once there had been no tension between them. Antón had come to her seeking help, and she responded. She had been waiting for this moment ever since arriving in exile.

He mentioned the troubles he had had with Alice, and Felicia advised him to wait.

"Don't say the final word," she told him. "That is the one you will have to live with."

As soon as she said it, Antón slumped sideways on the couch with his eyes closed and his jaw opened. Out of his mouth came a pestilential odor that made her bowels harden. How many times had she smelled the same combination of masticated food and liquor belching out of her husband, Luis? She arranged cushions around her grandson as best she could and spread a bedsheet over him so that he might not catch the evening chill.

She sat at the dining-room table to wait for her niece and dealt herself a hand of solitaire. It was another one of her many habits, acquired as a young wife to allay the anxieties brought on by her husband's increasingly late arrivals. She was too old for anxieties now, but the habit had stayed with her and become one more companion for her solitude. María Antonieta would be home soon.

Felicia was nearing the end of her hand when she heard her brother Antonio's greeting, *Vaca vieja*, from the distant past. She stopped, looked around, wondered if she was asleep or awake, alive or dead, or whether someone was playing tricks through the window. He had been dead eighteen years.

¡Vaca vieja!

It was not coming from outside but from the seat directly across from her. She felt a shiver down her arms and her chest tightened with held breath.

Red jack to black queen.

She turned toward the living room and saw Antón lying sideways on the couch, his back to her. Behind her the kitchen was dark and empty.

Red jack to black queen.

She uncovered a red jack and placed it under the queen of spades in the sixth position.

Ace of diamonds.

She flipped the next three cards and the last was the ace of diamonds. She moved it to the top and waited for Antonio to speak again.

"Antonio," she whispered after a long silence. "Antonio, where are you?"

I am dead. Muertecito. Deader than you could ever think the dead could be. And if you ask the dead what the dead are like, they'll point to me and say "Like him, like him." Antonio is the deadest dead of all the dead who are truly dead.

"I don't see you."

Then you can see the dead. All the dead are one and all around you like a soup of nothing.

"Why have you come?"

Red jack to black queen.

The lock on the front door moved and car lights shot across the room, followed by the crunch of wheels on stone. María Antonieta flew into the living room the same way she had left, bringing with her the gusts of reality. She smiled at her aunt, who felt strange and troubled, but more than relieved at her niece's appearance.

"Do you feel all right, *Tía?*"

"Yes, yes," answered Felicia, unblinking. "I'm gathering the cards. Would you like some milk?"

The girl declined and went to the bedroom.

That night Felicia spent trying to call back her brother and, when that failed, remembering him as a young man coming home in the middle of the night weary and morose, reeking of bordellos, or else nervous and jumpy and smelling of gunpowder after one of his battles with the police.

Dawn was the usual blessing. It came in grayness, not brilliant as she would have preferred, but cloud light was better than none. She sat up and looked at her toes, mangled from rheumatism, nails brittle and cracked. It was the first time since she had given up vanity on her fiftieth birthday that she realized how far from birth she was: eighty-two. Long life indeed, and not a day had she been bored, not a day had she doubted that everything was not as it should be. She thought of this as she wiggled her toes, pleased this morning that there was no pain and she would be limber enough to wash the kitchen floor, trim the lawn, transplant a rosebush.

Felicia kept Antonio's apparition to herself until María Antonieta left for the convent and Antón went back home. Then, when quiet returned to the house and the long afternoon hours were hers to prove to herself and to God that she deserved whatever it was He had prepared for her, she resorted to the one person whose authority in matters supernatural was beyond reproach.

Marina la Ciega had honed her gift to such sharpness and accuracy that she no longer needed her husband to help her walk, for she could sense when the sidewalk ended and stairs began, or when a gate blocked her way. Her divination had become her eyesight. She knew, well in advance of Felicia's call, what Antonio's apparition meant.

"He is calling you," Marina told her friend. "He will come two more times, and on the last you will have to go. You must not tell anyone else, unless you want to die sooner than your appointed hour.

"Above all, keep your ears open to him. And you must clear your heart of earthly hopes. Disentangle yourself from the tendrils that bind you, and when you are called, dive into the murky waters. Bring nothing with you. It will be hard at first and you will be tempted to hold on to your comb and your eyeglasses, but your eyes will soon become useless and you will be guided by a deeper sense. Don't be afraid to reach bottom. That is best. Underneath the mud are the bones of your parents and brothers, and of all the dead. If you can slip through the bones—few can on the first attempt and some try for the eternity of time—then you will reach the rose of all existence."

Felicia waited thirty days for her brother's reappearance. She was at the stove preparing the bland food the doctor had ordered to keep her blood pressure in check—boiled potatoes and turnips, broiled fish without sauce, a cup of tea, and, in defiance of the diet (for what was a diet if it was not violated?), French toast with plenty of syrup—when she heard Antonio's peripatetic voice greeting her—*Vaca vieja, vaca vieja*—like a metallic ghost speaking through a fan. For the first time since her exile she broke into a sweat, no matter that it was winter and the day was cool.

Enjoy, gorge yourself.

"Did you come to Ruperto?" she asked, beside herself.

Every day for four years.

"Marina said three times."

Every day for four years.

He said nothing more, and just as Felicia reached for the cigarettes on the counter next to the stove, she heard, *Stop smoking*, this time from outside fading away. She looked through the window and thought she saw an angel disappearing into the Florida sky.

Stop she did, and in a short time she gained weight and her cheeks acquired a youthful hue that few people alive had had the fortune of beholding. Her voice, too, changed, losing the smoker's rasp and turning soft and mellifluous. All who saw her maintained that she looked not a day over seventy, although, she liked to point out, at her age that was hardly a significant consolation. The last thing she wanted at this stage, after all her preparations had been dutifully accomplished, was to grow younger and retard death.

Antonio's third and final visit came on the eve of her birthday, just as she was sitting in the living room to have her breakfast orange.

Today, he said.

She wanted to argue that it should not happen on a Sunday, that she was being taken to lunch by her children, but she found herself speaking to a wall.

They found her in the bathtub with the shower spurting water on her chest and new-rounded belly. Her face was drained of expression and her lids drooped halfway down her eyeballs. Small sounds, between moans and whimpers, bubbled softly out of her mouth. It was an aneurysm, a ripe berry birth had planted on the crown of her frontal lobe, that burst and hemorrhaged. The blood streamed down the sides of her brain, taking what paths the gray mass allowed, like a spider grasping its fat prey with long, graceful, coagulating legs. Felicia's brain was being strangled by the slim fingers of fluid that contained her past and her hope, what she was and what she could be. In an hour her pupils were the size of pinheads; in another the doctor was advising the family that the hemorrhage was massive, that there was nothing to be done, that it was just a matter of time.

Felicia Turner, widow of Luis García Yanés, daughter of Gabriel Turner and Rosaura Fontana, granddaughter of Wellington Turner and Magaly Noriega, passionate lover and eager wife, dutiful mother, indomitable grandmother, faithful friend, pillar of the family, fountain of patience, interlocutor between generations, planter and reaper of roses, scourge of despair; Felicia, boss of all bosses, patron of posterity, Queen of Canasta, lay silent and supple in a hospital room attached to machines measuring the progress of her egress from time and into memory. Nothing needed to be done. Her sons announced the circumstance to those who had known her well and those who had known her little and those who had not known her at all: Felicia Turner Fontana de García had been stung by the spider of death.

W I L L

$\mathcal{T}$he two cousins were handed fatigues and led to an enclosed holding area along with forty-seven other recruits, some already in their uniforms, others wearing civilian clothes. They looked lost and slightly mystified, as if they had been awakened too early and had found themselves in a place totally foreign to their dreams. Coffee and doughnuts were passed around, but no one spoke. Antón made an act of faith, of the sort he practiced during his religious fervor, on the sincerity and genius of Ester Oliva, and took two doughnuts and a cup of coffee, which tasted surprisingly good.

After ten minutes a short barrel-chested man in olive drabs came out of the office door. Under his left arm he held a clipboard and in his right hand he had a plastic ballpoint pen that he used for gesticulation. He introduced himself as Sergeant Smith and explained that over the next four weeks he was going to shape them into a unified fighting machine, that others would soon be joining them, and that under no circumstances would they be allowed to contact anyone on the outside. He spoke in a flat, mechanical tone, making his deep Southern drawl more pronounced. In the same tone he added that they should be proud to be liberating their country from the grip of a ruthless dictator and equally as proud to be training on American soil under the banners of freedom and democracy.

As if on cue, the screen door swung open and Fred Union came out. He planted himself behind the sergeant, who introduced him as specialist in charge of weapons training and operational and intelligence briefing. Fred took a step forward and gave a quick salute. His face was clean-shaven now and set straight ahead, without the affability Antón had witnessed in Norfolk. The sergeant next introduced el Griego as the drill and exercise leader. El Griego materialized from beside the building wearing fatigue pants and jungle boots and the same shirt he had had on earlier that morning. Without a word, he got on the ground and did fifty quick pushups, then said in a voice full of metal shavings that they were going on a five-mile run and that whoever beat him would be the new drill instructor.

The run, which only el Griego and two others were able to finish, was followed by an hour of calisthenics, two hours of weapons instruction, lunch, intelligence training, target practice, drill instruction, more calisthenics and physical exercise, dinner, and something called political awareness, a course purposely scheduled last so that the exhausted volunteers were more than willing to agree to any proposition placed before them.

By the end of the first day two men, an overweight history

teacher and a lanky bookkeeper with frayed nerves, had requested to be discharged; the rest lay in their bunks without moving, too tired for sleep. One of them said that he did not understand what running and exercising had to do with fighting, and a few others spoke up, before Tico, safe in the anonymous dark, raised his voice and warned that if they wanted to do things their way they could go to another camp. There were enough of them in the Everglades to satisfy everyone, faggots included. The original voice screamed hoarsely that he would cut the *cojones* off whoever said that and Tico yelled out *Maricón*, in a high falsetto. Soon he was joined by other voices, until the lights came on and el Griego entered as calmly as if he had just returned from an evening stroll. He was holding a length of hose in his right hand and had a burning cigarette in the fingers of his left. He uttered one sound, a shush, but it was more like a snake hissing or a boiler valve letting off steam.

The next day, during the lunch period that was extended to accommodate the arrival of sixty more volunteers, Antón asked his cousin if he thought these men could be trusted in battle.

"No," Tico answered. "Not yet. They haven't been broken. Just like I wouldn't trust you."

"I don't waste my time acting like an adolescent," Antón shot back.

"Maybe it would be better if you did."

"I don't know about any of this," Antón said, relying on an old habit.

"The only person you need to trust is yourself. Four days ago you decided of your own free will that you wanted to join the force. You had your reasons. We all do, but you can't go through life changing your mind every other day."

Later that afternoon, after weapons instruction, Sergeant Smith called Antón over and asked him about his flying. Antón confirmed what his papers indicated: he had taken thirty hours of lessons. In that case, Smith said, Valdés de Cuna wanted to see him right away.

The leader, who was just finishing his lunch when Antón entered, stood up and received him effusively, repeating that he knew Antón's family and that he was proud to have a Turner on board. Valdés pulled up a chair for Antón and explained that they had five B-26 bombers arriving soon and three small craft in their possession, but so far only two pilots. Valdés said to Antón that he was very fortunate; pilots received preferential treatment and did not have to go through basic training. Antón tried to explain that he had only taken lessons, that he did not even have a license to fly any kind of plane, let alone a bomber. Valdés reassured him that he would teach Antón everything he needed to know, and before the end of the training period, he would be flying B-26's as if they were Piper Cubs. And so it was that, in the space of forty-five minutes, Antón left the infantry as a buck private and entered the air force as a second lieutenant, absolved from all duties and responsibilities except that of learning to fly.

Within a week, he was soloing in a Champion Scout over the heads of his comrades as they sweated through yet another day of training. He would often tip his wings at them in greeting as he passed, but they took it the wrong way and soon began to shun him. Even Tico, who had stood by him all this time, showed signs of resentment. When Antón brought this to the attention of Valdés de Cuna, the leader told him not to worry about the others, they would do all right.

"You are one of the elite. You will be flying right into the enemy's mouth."

"We will be flying up against advanced fighters. They'll tear us out of the sky in no time."

"The Americans have promised us air cover. Campión's MIGs don't stand a chance against U.S. Navy planes."

Antón felt a strong surge of attraction to Valdés and his cavalier bravery. Had Antón been a few years younger, he would have followed the man anywhere.

"What makes you so sure the Americans will deliver?" he countered, fighting back the need to surrender himself.

"They have given us everything we have asked for so far."

"Valdés, we don't have live ammunition to practice with."

"There has been a delay. American politicians keep getting in the way. In the meantime, don't fret so much. Enjoy your flying. This will be the easiest thing you will do in your life. And when it is all over, I will bring you with me to rebuild our country. Have a drink."

He poured two shots of rum and offered one to Antón, who considered refusing it but thought better of it and downed the liquor quickly.

Indeed, Valdés de Cuna was right. Two days later at dawn, twenty-five truckfuls of ordnance arrived from the U.S. Army. Still, the leader's nonchalance worried Antón. He also could not help noticing that, of late, the training had slackened and the men were spending much of their time playing cards, telling stories, and arguing with each other.

When Antón learned from Valdés that the invasion had been delayed by three months, a cloud settled over his head that he found impossible to disperse. His faith in Ester Oliva began to falter. Summer would arrive soon, and with it the rains, and with the rains mud and mosquitoes. It occurred to him that the enterprise was a huge mistake, that regardless of American support they would not stand a chance unless the populace on the island revolted, something even God would find impossible to guarantee. And if they were successful in deposing Campión, what would happen afterward? Valdés de Cuna was a good man, as good as you could expect, but there were other backers with vast and shadowy ambitions. Rumor had it around the camp that el Griego had been planted among them by one of Sotelo's intimates in order to assassinate Valdés as soon as it became expedient. No, Antón was not convinced that this Democratic Liberation Force would succeed at anything except being manipulated by one band or another.

The flying kept his doubts at bay. Busy with political matters, Valdés de Cuna left him to his own devices, and Antón took to the skies at will. He learned to fly the other two planes at his disposal besides the Champion, a Cessna 172 and Valdés's own Beechcraft Bonanza. Sometimes he went up three times a day, trying out maneuvers in the different planes and thinking, especially when he flew at high altitudes, that he could spend the rest of his life doing this. At five thousand feet there were no imperatives other than staying aloft, free from himself and from the demands of others. But planes will not stay up forever. They run out of fuel, they become victims of gravity. The horizontal state is always calling. Thus, Antón's sense of freedom was temporary at best, and illusory. In the last analysis, he was subject to the supply of a refined liquid that kept the motor running and kept him hopelessly entangled in the camp, in society, in government, in the petroleum and aeronautics industry, in decayed organic matter, in carbon molecules, in the myriad chemical processes, past and present, that led directly to him, now, approaching the airfield in order to land before he ran out of fuel and crashed.

As the plane's wheels touched the earth and returned him to

his entanglements, he understood that the call to action implicit in Tico and Ester's attitude and, further back, in Felicia's as well, had nothing to do with the heroics of war and liberation, for these, too, come to an end, and winner and loser both must return to daily living. The question "What have you done?" really meant "What have you practiced?"

It was the fourth Sunday he had spent at the camp, and that night his birthmark acted up. He felt the burn and itch spread across his back, race up his spinal cord, and flare like a Bunsen burner at the base of the skull, where it produced a vision of disturbing power and clarity. In this vision, he was a character in a book. Every time he tried to break free, every time he tried to do something on his own, he was pulled back by a rope stretching into a hole in his back. It was an extravagant vision filled with colors and the voices of many women. One voice, very much like Felicia's, announced that she had to go.

Antón fell fast asleep and was awakened some time later by Valdés de Cuna, who ordered him to get dressed. Outside the door, he told Antón that his grandmother had become quite ill and was in the hospital in a coma. He said he was bending the rules and letting Antón go to Miami to see her.

"Your uncle Antonio was a good man and I owed him more than one favor."

When Antón asked, Valdés de Cuna explained that Ester Oliva had phoned him with the news. He gave Antón the keys to his Lincoln Continental and warned him not to breathe a word to anyone about the camp.

"You have seventy-two hours," Valdés de Cuna said, and shook Antón's hand.

Antón was on the interstate by the time the sky grew light. His head began to throb, his ears to ring as if someone were pressing the doorbell to his cranium, and his eyes to sting with tears he hadn't remembered shedding. He left the highway and stopped at a convenience store for breakfast.

As he sat on the curb to have his coffee and Danish, a group of teenagers pulled up in a fast red car with two surfboards strapped on top. The driver, happy and hyper, moved with the fleetness of a star athlete. The girl with him was pretty and tanned. Two other nondescript boys scrambled out of the rear. They would be graduating from high school soon, if they did not kill themselves first. Antón imagined them wrapped around a telephone pole, all that blond athletic prowess, all that confident future, turned into a mass of flesh and cracked bone. He mourned for them and he mourned for Tico and his comrades at the camp, slogging through the monotony of training. He mourned for Alice, too, slim beautiful Alice of the gardener's hands and the tender nape. One day she glowed with adventure, one day she jumped like a hot mare when he touched her. One day she became ice and turned away.

But all that seemed superfluous now. Of the people he knew, Felicia was the only one whose devotion to him was unconditional and undiminished by his own indifference or antagonism. Above all, she was the source of a love that transcended generations and preceded all other kinds of love—of country, of mate, of God. Primitive and ancient beyond any individual to claim or any moment to contain, it was the allegiance to his origins that compelled him to reach Miami ahead of death.

As he finished his breakfast in the middle of the Florida nowhere, he watched the teenagers slide back into their vehicle. The driver gunned the motor till the car shook, then exploded onto the sizzling road. The Lincoln started gently, defying the raw power of the teenagers' car with an understated purr. Antón resumed his trip during the hottest part of the day. He had wasted enough time in his life. He drove with the sudden certitude of a man who knows that at the end of everything is death.

He reached Felicia's hospital room too late for final words. She was lying on her side, illumined by the dim light that slipped through the blinds. Her lips fluttered with each breath, and her hands, hard and veiny but still beautiful, rested as they never had before, one stretched out by her side on the mattress, the other curled on the downward slope of her belly. In a semicircle around the bed were Rosa, Felicia's cousin Florencia, and María Antonieta, dressed in the gray habit of her order. There was nothing to be done.

After ten minutes, he joined his father and uncle Eduardo and a dozen visitors in the waiting room. Someone had brought sandwiches and beer, and when they were done with that, they passed around a whiskey bottle wrapped in a brown paper bag. More visitors arrived, and the room, designed to serve the whole wing, was invaded by twenty-five of Felicia's friends and relatives waiting, not in dread or sorrow but in drunkenness and laughter, for the old lady to breathe her last. Already the noise was such that it could be heard in the nurses' station. Lucho, blessed and happy, danced in her honor, while Eduardo beat out a rhythm on a pile of dog-eared magazines, and Fernando, accompanied by Florencia's husband on spoons, sang Felicia's favorite tunes. Well before the clock struck nine and visiting hours ended, the party was in full swing. The crowd spilled into the hallway and the din could be heard two floors down.

It was more than the head nurse could tolerate. Tall, with portly airs, she walked to the door of the waiting room and stood before it, her large eyes frozen in blue fire, her jaw locked tight. Everyone grew silent and looked at the bulky female form in white. The nurse was unimpressed with the numbers. This was her territory and there was no question as to her authority. She brought her gaze down on Antón, who stood squarely in the center of the room, and asked—but it was more demand than request—that the music stop, that all smoking materials be extinguished, bottles capped, food wrappers placed in the trash container, loud conversation and irreverent laughter silenced, and the group moved downstairs to the lobby, where the disturbance would be minimal. This was the terminal ward, after all, and the relatives of other patients were complaining about the jovial atmosphere.

The crowd abandoned the floor, and only three people remained in Felicia's room. Antón defied the nurse by staying in the waiting room, even as the hall lights were turned off and the cleaning lady swept the floor under his feet and the graveyard shift entered; nurses busy with medicines and charts, efficient and kind, who did not bother him, who, in fact, turned off the lights in the room and arranged the cushion behind him after his eyes had closed from all that heat and all that travel and all that sorrow. Felicia was dying.

Later, much later, María Antonieta came in.

"I needed a break," she said.

Antón saw her pale, tired face and thought that Eduardo had been right. María Antonieta's beauty was being wasted.

"The convent agrees with you," he said, clearing his head of the half-dream that curled in it like a plume of smoke from one of Felicia's cigarettes.

"Yes. And you? What are you up to?"

He was tempted to disclose that he was training for the invasion, but he answered instead that he had left Alice and had been traveling for a few months. He admitted his concern that Felicia's death meant the end of the family as well.

"Two months ago she told me that she wanted her ashes to be taken to the island and thrown to the wind."

"I didn't know my grandmother was that much of a romantic," Antón responded, though by romantic he meant fool.

"She was the ultimate romantic."

He said it was an impossible idea. The authorities on the island would never approve the request.

"I think she wanted you to take care of it."

She smiled, not a beaming smile, but a slow parting of the lips, softened by hours of no sleep, and then she had to go. Lidiana and Florencia believed their prayers were not as holy without her leading them.

"How old are you?" Antón asked her at the last moment.

"Twenty-two."

God is very lucky, he thought. He tried to make himself as comfortable as the hard foam cushions would allow and fell back asleep.

He dreamed he was on a beach and he was king, teaching his subjects how to surf on the large waves that began breaking half a mile offshore. The sand was red and the beach was dirty with piles of refuse. The sea was black and very deep, except where the waves broke and turned into mountains of foam that he rode gloriously in to the feet of his people. Behind them, surrounding the beach, was a town of adobe buildings with red tile roofs. He saw a woman walking bare-breasted on the sidewalk and he thought he should forbid public nudity, but they were beautiful breasts, deserving of exposure, and when he finally looked at the face, he recognized María Antonieta. She was—of this he had no doubt—the most beautiful woman of the kingdom, and he understood that a king's role is not to repress but to show people the measures of tolerance, not to control but to embrace. He rode a few more waves for the crowd, which included Alice, his parents, and a dozen of his children, but it was María Antonieta's visage that kept recurring, classic and beautiful.

When Antón next opened his eyes, he was face to face with María Antonieta, who was bending over him explaining that it had happened, that Felicia was finally gone.

By mid-morning the family had gathered at Felicia's house waiting for the funeral home to open and the wake to proceed. All had been arranged beforehand, and the only thing to do was read the stale, faded letters she had left behind.

Antón was given his biography, wrapped in brown paper and tied with a shoestring. He went out back to the rosebushes his grandmother had planted when she moved into the house. There he unwrapped the package and read the brittle loose-leaf sheets. They contained his life, to the merest detail, from the instant of his birth to the moment of his reading. They spoke of all things and of nothing, of the family, of his power, of the need to accept his reality—Felicia the philosopher—and ended with her confession—Felicia the flagellant—that she had tried to control and manipulate his life to suit herself. *I have nothing to leave you*, she concluded, *but my love and my blessing. The rest is up to you.*

The wake lasted twelve hours less than the forty-eight Felicia had requested, and in all that time Antón avoided approaching the casket. Instead, he observed the people who had gathered to pay their respects: from Marina la Ciega and three others of Felicia's surviving classmates, to a man named Casimiro—fingers gleaming with rings—who claimed, but never bothered to explain how, that Felicia had saved his life; to Remi of Roma, the world-renowned hairdresser to the stars; to the ex-boxer Kid Candela, who lost twenty-three consecutive fights before deciding—at Felicia's urging—to retire; to a contingent of nuns from the convent of the Most Holy Sisters of the Resurrection in Exile; to representatives from G–7 and two other terrorist organizations. Ester Oliva came as well, and Antón spoke to her briefly before she disappeared through a back door, still shining with the special kind of beauty of a woman marked by destiny. Some he had never seen before; others had never seen him. All, however, recognized his stature as firstborn grandson and alluded to events in a history he had no memory of. He returned their kisses and embraces and joined in their laughter. It was all he could do to keep Felicia's spirit alive.

Hundreds of people came to the wake, and floral arrangements crowded every inch of space around the casket, along the walls, and in the hallway outside. When the wake was over and only the family was left in the viewing hall, Antón approached his grandmother's corpse and knelt and tried to pray. It was then that he noticed the smell, sweet and pungent and organic, coming from all around him and settling over Felicia. It was a scent he had smelled before thought, before language, before he knew what it was to live or to die, to suffer and to dream, before he had a name, before the world was the world.

Felicia's cremation did not take place until late the following day. While they waited, the family discussed how best to fulfill her wish that her remains be spread on the island. Fernando thought that they should go through government channels and have the ashes sent by airline. Eduardo mocked the idea, claiming that it was a sure guarantee of having their mother flushed down a toilet. He suggested contacting Arturo, the fisherman who had smuggled the three of them out, and pay him to do what was necessary. Antón said little, other than to volunteer to pick up the ashes the next day.

The urn containing Felicia was a heavy pewter monstrosity, garlanded with Grecian wreaths that looped into handles, the kind of thing she would have hidden away in a dark closet or given to someone she did not like. Antón signed the release papers and took the urn to the car. As he opened the passenger door, a small plane flew overhead. He looked up at it, no bigger than a sparrow, passing a cluster of clouds to the south and filling the air with its purr. It made him long to fly and reminded him that he had to get back to the camp. Then, in a flash of insight—the kind that occurs spontaneously and changes the course of one's life irrevocably—it occurred to him that he could fly to the island with Felicia's remains and spread them over the capital. Never mind that the island had the best air defense system south of the Tropic of Cancer. Never mind that the odds were against him getting there, let alone getting back. All concern drained out of him, and he stood happily by the Lincoln in the parking lot of the funeral home, the late-afternoon sun blasting down and the heat from the pavement rising to meet his face. Under the circumstances, it was not necessary to convince himself of a safe return. He had surrendered not to patriotic ardor or ideological imperative but to familial love, Felicia's ultimate legacy.

Antón opened the car and placed his grandmother on the passenger seat next to him; together they headed back to the camp. He did not phone his family. To explain to them what he was about to do would have broken his resolve.

Rosa and Fernando did not start worrying until two hours after Antón was supposed to return. Fernando maintained that he knew something was suspicious all along when he saw his son driving the borrowed Lincoln. "Who but a drug dealer or a show-off would drive such a car?" he had asked rhetorically. Rosa called the funeral home and was informed that her son had picked up Felicia's remains some time before. She phoned Eduardo, whom she thought Antón might have visited on the way home, but Eduardo had not seen his nephew since early that morning. Rosa and Fernando tried to calm themselves by telling each other that their son was under a lot of pressure, that he was probably taking a ride somewhere to clear his mind.

But a parent's role is to worry, not to understand. Little did they realize that Antón was, indeed, himself, or put another way, that he had finally allowed those elements that formed him at birth to manifest themselves in one definitive act. To an observer, flying to the island might have looked desperate or insane, but that in no way detracted from its validity; quite the contrary, his temerity showed that his ancestry was bursting forth out of him, not in madness, no, but in folly.

As the hours passed, they called dozens of people, the last Alice, who had not heard from Antón in over three months and expressed little concern about his disappearance. In their desperation they visited Marina la Ciega and implored her to invoke her special powers on their behalf. Marina received them reluctantly. She was still bearing the weight of her grief over the death of her old friend. Her face, fixed impassively ahead and twisted in a permanent frown, was deeply etched by many struggles with truth.

"Put aside your worry," she grumbled at them, waving her arm over her head in a dramatic gesture left over from her years as prophetess.

"Is he all right?" Rosa asked, close to snapping. Her anxiety had turned her into a stretched sinew. Every car passing by, every ring of the phone, every knock at the door could be her son.

"Woman, if he weren't, you would feel it in your womb. For now he is. He is fulfilling himself in blood. He is doing what he must. He is facing his truth, the one truth we all face," and in saying this she smiled a smile not of merriment but of understanding. Without allowing Rosa and Fernando to ask which truth she was referring to, as if there ever were more than one, she walked back into her room to let the dark waters of mourning wash over her.

While his parents worried, Antón drove northward. In the back seat of the car he sensed a force like a spirit dog that was keeping him from wavering. The creature had eyes like the dead of his family—Antonio, Ruperto, Felicia—fixed on the back of his head. He could not betray what had entered him.

He parked outside the dirt access road leading to the camp and waited until four in the morning. Then he drove in with the lights off and his foot barely on the accelerator, letting the car glide behind the barracks. From there he walked the five hundred yards to the airstrip, crawled under the barbed wire, and crept up to the shed by the gate where the keys to the planes were stored. There usually was a guard stationed by the door, but of late, most men slept through their duty.

When he peeked around the side of the shed, Antón saw that the lawn chair where the guard usually sat was empty. His relief was greater than his surprise and he entered. He placed his grandmother on the table by the window and felt along the wall where he knew the three keys were hanging. He found the one to the Cessna, square and longer than the others, on a plain metal ring. He picked up the urn and put the key in his pocket, smiling to himself at how easy it seemed. Then, as he turned to leave, he heard a click, and a light flashed in his eyes, blinding him.

"*¿Qué te pica a tí?*" he heard behind the light. It was the gravelly, metallic voice of el Griego.

Antón wanted to answer that nothing itched him, but he did not speak or breathe or blink. He waited a second or two, then he swung the arm holding the urn as hard as he could where he thought the man's head was.

He heard the muffled clunk of the pewter hitting bone. The flashlight bounced on the wooden floor and the body fell, solid as timber. Before leaving, he pointed the light at el Griego's face and saw that his eyes were still open and there was blood dribbling on the floorboards from behind his ear.

Had he stopped to think, he would have realized that he had quite possibly killed a man, but there was no time for thinking. He ran to the Cessna, unhitched it, and climbed inside, strapping Felicia to the seat next to him. Knowing that he would not have much time to warm the engine before Valdés de Cuna and the rest of the men heard the motor and came to investigate, he taxied to the opposite end of the strip, long as it was to accommodate the still absent B-26's, and gave himself a few extra minutes. Though he could not see them, he knew the men were coming toward the plane and would do anything to stop him. With that last thought, he pulled on the throttle. The Cessna waddled forward, gained speed, and lifted. As he rose, he thought he saw figures on the ground pointing guns at him and he might have even heard the whiz of bullets past the cabin, though the noise of the engine made that an unlikely possibility.

Once over the trees at the edge of the field, he banked away from the camp and headed straight east, in the direction of Palm Beach and the ocean. He would follow the coast down until it curved away; then he could lower his altitude and fly under radar straight to the island.

Half a dozen people, up early in the capital that day, reported something incredible: a small American plane flying ten feet off the ocean swooped up over the breakwater and dropped what appeared to be a rain of ashes over the Boulevard of Fallen Heroes. The authorities, afraid that the world would find out how easily the island's air defenses had been breached, apprehended the group and sent them to the psychiatric hospital in Corrientes. One other man, who ran through the streets yelling that the Angel of Freedom was passing over, was quickly arrested and whisked away. The plane circled back out to sea in the direction of el Norte. It was the last time anyone saw or heard of Antón García-Turner.